Hannah Dennison was born and raised in Hampshire but spent more than two decades living in California. She has been an obituary reporter, antique dealer, private jet flight attendant and Hollywood story analyst. For many years, Hannah taught mystery writing workshops at the UCLA Extension Writers' Program in Los Angeles, California.

Hannah writes the Honeychurch Hall Mystery series and Vicky Hill Mystery series, both of which are set in the wilds of the Devonshire countryside where she now lives with her two crazy Hungarian Vizslas.

www.hannahdennison.com
www.twitter.com/HannahLDennison

Murder in Miniature at Honeychurch Hall

Hannah Dennison

CONSTABLE

CONSTABLE

First published in Great Britain in 2021 by Constable

Copyright © Hannah Dennison, 2021

1 3 5 7 9 10 8 6 4 2

A CIP catalogue record for this book
is available from the British Library.

ISBN: 978-1-47213-380-9

Typeset in Janson Text LT Std by SX Composing DTP, Rayleigh, Essex
Printed and bound in Great Britain by Clays Ltd, Elcograf S.p.A.

Papers used by Constable are from well-managed forests
and other responsible sources.

Constable
An imprint of
Little, Brown Book Group
Carmelite House
50 Victoria Embankment
London EC4Y 0DZ

An Hachette UK Company
www.hachette.co.uk

www.littlebrown.co.uk

To Stefanija Winkler
Always a friendly smile in the sky

Chapter One

'Well, I can honestly say that Violet Green won't have anything worth buying unless you are into teapots.' Mum pushed her empty plate away and delicately dabbed her mouth with a floral linen napkin.

It was a Sunday on a boiling hot September day and, as was our usual habit, we were sitting eating lunch in her kitchen in the Carriage House. In a mad rush of domestic fervour, I'd even made banana bread.

'That smoked cheese was excellent,' she said. 'How many calories do you think?'

'It's Godminster cheese from Somerset,' I said and cut myself another slice. 'And since when have you been counting calories?'

'I'll have to walk them off.' My mother lifted her wrist and pointed to a black plastic watch. 'I bought a Fitbit. Delia has one. She tells me she walks fifteen thousand steps a day and she's lost ten pounds.'

'But you sit down all day and Delia is on her feet rushing all over the Hall cleaning *and* she walks or cycles everywhere because she doesn't have a car.'

Mum whipped out her iPhone and with painstaking slowness tapped on the keyboard. She scowled. 'I knew it! To walk off that cheese will take me a whole hour! Who has a whole hour to walk off some cheese?'

'Certainly not me,' I said. Perhaps I needed to get a Fitbit. The waistband of my cotton skirt was definitely feeling tight. 'And to answer your original question, no. I am not going to look at Violet's teapot collection. Her sister used to do a lot of car boot sales. Violet is finally clearing out Lavender's bedroom and has given me first refusal.'

'Car *boot* sales?' Mum said with scorn. 'Well, don't get guilted into buying anything. You know what she can be like.'

Violet lived at Rose Cottage in Little Dipperton where she also ran the tearoom. It was one of the many cottages that still belonged to the Honeychurch Hall estate. It was common knowledge that the sisters were financially strapped, but I often felt Violet milked it with her ever-so-humble attitude that would put Uriah Heep to shame.

'You'll end up buying her junk out of pity and donating it to charity shops . . .' Mum grumbled on.

'Give me some credit,' I retorted.

Mum stood up and headed for the counter and flipped the switch on the kettle. 'Tea? I recommend you have tea here. I was there last week and Violet's version of tea is heating up the dishwater from the washing-up bowl.'

Although Violet's tea was awful – she was notorious for reusing her tea bags at least four times – I regarded my mother with surprise. I knew she wasn't a fan of the elderly lady but she wasn't usually this unkind. Mum was in a bad mood and often this meant that her writing wasn't going well.

'How's the new book coming along?' I asked.

'Slowly,' Mum said. 'I'm stuck on the black sheep. My editor wants a bad boy with a heart.'

'What's the title of this *Star-Crossed Lovers* novel?'

'*Exposed*,' Mum said.

'Well, I hope that's not a sign of things to come,' I remarked drily.

My mother's secret life as international bestselling romance writer Krystalle Storm was becoming harder for her to manage and it worried me. Her books were now sold in the village but no one knew it was Iris Stanford who penned them. But it wasn't just that. Mum hadn't paid any income tax on her royalties since time began and much as I wanted her to come clean, I felt it was too late. She would almost certainly face a jail sentence.

'Monty has asked me to marry him,' Mum blurted out. 'He proposed last night at the Jockey Club Summer Ball after the firework display.'

I was speechless. I thought of the odious Sir Monty Stubbs-Thomas who I knew all too well on the auction circuit and who I'd unfortunately come to know a little better these past few months since he had been ardently pursuing my mother.

Mum drifted over to the oak dresser to pick out two porcelain mugs from her collection of Royal commemoration
plates and china that lined the shelves. A framed photograph
of HRH Prince Philip, Duke of Edinburgh stood centre
place. Mum touched the frame. 'A wonderful man. I had
such a crush on him, especially when he wore his uniform.'

Finally, I found my voice. 'You can't be serious. I bet Sir
Monty is after your money.'

'That's not a very nice thing to say,' Mum replied.
'Although I think you're right. He's asked if he can help me
with my investments.'

'You don't have any investments,' I said.

'Yes I do. They're in the attic—'

'That cash should be in a bank,' I said firmly.

'I have lots of cash in the bank,' Mum said mildly. 'It's in
Jersey.'

'No, *all* your cash,' I said. 'I don't like it being here.
You don't have a burglar alarm. Anyone could find it.'

'No one is going into the attic except for me,' Mum said.
'But why can't Monty be captivated by my sparkling wit
and personality?'

'I didn't mean he wasn't,' I said. 'I just . . . don't like
him.'

'He's harmless.' Mum scanned the shelves for our mugs
and selected the one emblazoned with an image of Queen
Elizabeth I. 'In case you wondered.'

'Wondered what?' I asked.

'The Virgin Queen for me today,' Mum said. 'You'll be
relieved to know that I have been restraining myself.

Monty and I have not taken our relationship to the next level. Yet.'

'*Yet?* Ugh.' I gave an involuntary shudder. At least my mother's last flame was relatively acceptable.

She took down a second mug. It was the beautiful Duchess of Cambridge. 'For you, darling. Because, like Kate Middleton, you are still waiting for your Prince to come to his senses.'

'I don't want to talk about Shawn,' I muttered. 'Anyway, I thought you didn't want to get married again.'

'I don't,' said Mum. 'But Monty won't have it. He keeps calling me Lady Iris. I suppose if I did marry him I *would* become Lady Iris.'

I studied my mother's face and saw mischief in her eyes. 'You had me worried for a minute! I thought you were seriously considering it.'

Mum gave a dismissive wave. 'I don't want a husband. I had one for almost fifty years. I like my freedom. And to be honest, I don't find him *that* attractive. He has this annoying habit of cleaning his front teeth with his cotton handkerchief at the dinner table.'

'Well, his front teeth are rather . . . large.'

'Like a beaver's,' Mum sniggered. 'Or perhaps a hippopotamus.'

I laughed, too. 'Now you're being catty.'

'I know,' Mum said but didn't look remotely sorry. 'I've never been so spoiled. He showers me with presents – take this new perfume.' Mum thrust an arm under my nose.

'Gosh. That's pungently floral.'

'It's called Reine de Nuit—'

'Queen of the Night—?'

'And cost two hundred and thirty-five pounds. I looked on the Internet.'

'So?' I said.

'And I've never been driven around in a Rolls-Royce before or taken to the members' enclosure at Newton Abbot Racecourse. We even sat at the *top* table last night!' But then Mum's smile faded. 'Indulge me, Kat. Allow me to have a bit of fun. I loved your dad but he wasn't what you call a live wire. Monty is . . . well, different. And besides, it's making Delia pea green with envy.'

A fly landed on the banana bread. Mum snatched the plastic green fly swat and delivered a killer blow.

'Oh, Mum!' I wailed. 'I was going to eat that.'

Mum gawked. 'Did you make it?'

'You saw me bring it into the kitchen,' I protested. 'I'm determined to learn to cook.'

'I know what you're up to,' Mum declared. 'Trying to become a domestic goddess for Shawn.'

My stomach gave a little lurch. At the beginning of the school holidays, Detective Inspector Shawn Cropper had transferred to London of all places, along with his twins and his mother-in-law, to start a new job. We had agreed to see 'how things went'. His words, not mine.

Shawn's departure had left me feeling very confused. Our relationship had always been off and on – and, if I was to be honest, more off than on. Shawn had not been back since but he was taking some time off and coming down to Devon in just a few days' time.

Since the twins would be staying in London with their grandmother, I'd invited Shawn to stay with me and had been hurt when he said that since his own home hadn't been rented out yet, he would rather stay there. It did not bode well for our relationship.

Mum returned to the table with our tea and a loaf knife for the banana bread. 'I do think it odd that Shawn's not coming down with the twins,' she mused. 'It's the beating of the bounds and the village treasure hunt this coming Saturday. I would have thought his boys would have loved that. Eric has been working on the clues for weeks.'

I had thought the same thing.

'Well, Delia is determined to do it,' Mum went on, oblivious to my misery.

'Do what?'

'Beat the bounds! Walk the boundary,' Mum said. 'That's why she's been getting fit.'

'How far is it?' I said.

'Twenty miles,' Mum declared. 'I just might join her. You should too.'

'No, thanks,' I said firmly. 'It's too hot for that sort of thing.'

'You really need to support the community,' Mum scolded.

My mother made a good point. Although we had both been living on the Honeychurch Hall estate for almost two years now it was only recently that we had finally been accepted into the fold.

As DFL's – or those 'Down From London' – Mum and I were outsiders. But after some false starts, the warm acceptance by the Dowager Countess, Lady Edith Honeychurch, had gone a long way towards garnering favour with the villagers. Mum had inadvertently become the Honeychurch family historian and I – thanks to Edith's generosity – had leased not just Jane's Cottage where I lived, but also the gatehouses where I ran Kat's Collectibles & Mobile Valuation Services.

Initially, I had had terrible reservations about moving from London to the wilds of the Devonshire countryside, but I was very happy here now. I had made friends. My antique business was booming. The only blot on the horizon was my relationship with Shawn. I only hoped he would soon tire of the city and want to come back. There was no question of me moving there. Besides, I had made a promise to my dad before he died that I would always keep an eye on my mother. Unfortunately, his fears had not proved groundless since my mother always seemed to be getting into trouble.

'Get the *Dipperton Deal*,' Mum said suddenly. 'You'll find the flyer and a map are inside.'

I spied the local newspaper on the kitchen counter and did as I was told. The front page carried a colour photograph of a hard-looking woman in her sixties with a honey-coloured bob. She was dressed in a cream tailored suit and was standing next to the shoulder of a liver chestnut horse adorned with award ribbons. The jockey leaned down into the frame, beaming from ear to ear. The tagline said, 'Pearl Clayton with Oyster Girl'.

'What a beautiful horse,' I said.

'I met Pearl Clayton last night,' Mum bragged. 'She's just bought The Priory near Modbury. Apparently she wants to run for Mayor, so she's got fingers in all sorts of pies.'

I picked up a green flyer and read:

The Beating of the Bounds and Treasure Hunt
By kind invitation of
Dowager Countess Lady Edith Honeychurch
Assemble: St Mary's churchyard at 8.30 sharp
Picnic Lunch: Gibbet Cross
Maps & Refreshments sponsored by Pearl Clayton
Donations in aid of the church roof

'I see what you mean by fingers in pies.' I was impressed. 'She's done a good job with the map.'

The boundary was highlighted in green. It was beautifully illustrated and showed great attention to detail that included the numerous footpaths, bridleways and green lanes that covered the Honeychurch Hall estate and outlying parish. Even all the cottages in Little Dipperton were labelled and the churchyard of St Mary's had a smattering of headstones.

On the northern boundary stood Gibbet Cross and beyond that was Dartmoor where the artist had added granite tors – Moreleigh Mount being just one – and several abandoned tin mines.

'Beating the bounds takes place every seven years and is a custom that goes back centuries,' said Mum. 'In the days before maps, it was a way for villagers to know where their parish ended by literally walking the boundary line and swatting landmarks or distinctive stones – often called boundstones – with sticks.'

Three small symbols of what looked like the letter A with a horizontal line on top were spaced around the boundary line. 'What are those supposed to be?' I asked.

'Picnic tables,' Mum declared. 'And that one' – she jabbed a finger at a miniscule green triangle – 'is where lunch will be provided at Gibbet Cross.'

I was surprised. 'But . . . isn't a gibbet another name for gallows?'

'Oh yes. The upright beam is still standing there,' said Mum. 'I'm told the view is spectacular.'

'Spectacular?' I exclaimed. 'I wouldn't think that would have been any consolation to a condemned man.'

'And a man condemned by one of the Honeychurch ancestors no less,' Mum said with relish. 'The sixth Earl of Grenville was Justice of the Peace and regularly sent poachers up to Gibbet Cross to be hanged.'

I thought of the numerous signs – 'Trespassers will be Prosecuted', 'Poachers will be Shot' – dotted around the estate. 'Fortunately, poachers only get shot these days,' I said.

'I think Pugsley has a twelve-bore.' Mum pulled a face. 'If anyone is poaching, it'll be him. No! Wait. Eric doesn't need the twelve-bore. One look at those eyebrows would give any rabbit a heart attack.'

'Mum!' I protested.

'And I bet he doesn't have a licence either,' Mum ran on. 'I've a good mind to report him to the authorities.'

I rolled my eyes. 'I thought you were getting on better with your friendly neighbour.'

Mum shrugged. 'Define the word "better"? If you mean, am I happy that he decides to burn old tyres at his' – she made air quotes – '"end-of-life" scrapyard when I have my washing out on the line, then yes, we're the best of friends.'

'Well, on that happy note, I'm off to see Violet.'

But no sooner had I stood up, there was a cacophony of barking and the sound of heavy footsteps. The kitchen door burst open and Mr Chips, Edith's Jack Russell, tore inside leaving the man in question frozen in the doorway, shovel in hand.

Eric Pugsley looked as if he'd seen a ghost.

My heart skipped a beat. 'What's the matter? What's happened?'

His heavy beetle brows went into overdrive as he tried to speak.

'Oh, for heaven's sake,' Mum muttered. 'Spit it out!'

'There's been a murder,' he croaked.

And with that, Eric dropped his shovel, pitched forward and passed out.

Chapter Two

Somehow we managed to get Eric and his 'bulk', as Mum rudely put it, into a sitting position despite Mr Chips continuously barking and getting in the way. Finally, I had to usher the little Jack Russell out of the back door and into Cromwell Meadows. I knew he'd find his way back to the Hall.

'Another roundhead then.' Mum stood over Eric, arms akimbo. 'I would have thought you'd be used to digging them up by now.'

I had to admit that Mum had a point. During the Civil War one of many battles had taken place on Honeychurch land, specifically in Cromwell Meadows behind the Carriage House. There had been heavy casualties on both sides for King and for Parliament. It wasn't the first time that Mr Chips had dug up a skeleton and I doubted if it would be the last.

'Not a roundhead. It was . . .' Eric made a peculiar strangled noise. 'It was my mate Charlie Green and it's all my fault.'

Mum's eyes widened. 'You knew him? And you say he's dead and it was all your fault?'

'Charlie had moved to Dublin,' Eric whispered. 'Everyone knew he'd done a runner.'

'Well, obviously he must have come back,' said Mum.

'Where did you find him?' I said gently. Eric was clearly upset.

Eric pointed in the direction of the pine forest behind the Carriage House. 'In a shallow grave in them woods. I was hiding the clues for the treasure hunt and Mr Chips went digging.'

Mum frowned. 'Charlie Green? Charlie Green. No. The name doesn't ring a bell.' She thought for a moment. 'When was the last time that you saw your friend?'

'Seven years, almost to the day,' Eric said. 'It was the night before the beating of the bounds. I can't believe it. I mean I *can* believe it. But I can't believe it.'

'You call the police, Mum,' I said. 'I'll make Eric some tea.'

'I'd rather have brandy,' Eric said tentatively.

Mum brightened. 'I think we should all have one.'

Eric tried to stand but swayed on his feet. I darted forwards to help him into a chair at the kitchen table as Mum opened and closed the kitchen cupboards before returning with a plastic picnic beaker and a bottle of cooking brandy. She poured out a couple of fingers before picking up her iPhone.

'I'll go and get *our* brandy and call the police out in the hall.' She mouthed, '*He did it! He killed him,*' then added a cheerful, 'Be right back.'

Eric downed the cheap brandy in one go and reached for the bottle to pour another. 'I thought she was starting up again.'

'Who is she?' I prompted.

'Her and him,' said Eric.

'Her and him?' I prompted again.

'Charlie and my Vera.' Eric pulled off his knitted beanie and raked his fingers through his thick dark hair. 'Vera told me he was in trouble and I didn't believe her.'

'Vera?' I frowned. 'You mean your *wife* Vera?'

'They'd been having a fling but she swore it was over.' Eric nodded miserably. 'You never met my Vera. She was a beauty. Kindest woman ever walked God's earth. Gentle as a lamb. Died in her prime, she did.'

Eric had a very short memory. Not only had I met the extremely volatile Vera Pugsley, I had found her body in the grotto. Even though it had been a horrific experience, Vera had been a handful, and that was putting it mildly.

Eric took a swig of brandy.

I had a sudden thought. After seven years, surely there wouldn't be much left of Charlie Green. 'Are you positive it's your friend?'

'Recognised his leather biker jacket right away,' said Eric. 'Red and gold eagle on the back – he was lying face down. Oh – and his Doc Martens.'

Mum came back with two cut crystal balloons and a bottle of Courvoisier. She set them down and poured us a generous slug each. Eric topped his beaker up with the cheap stuff.

He didn't seem to notice the intentional slight or perhaps he didn't care.

'The police are on their way,' she said.

Eric sat bolt upright. 'The *police*? No police!'

'Don't be ridiculous. Of course we have to call the police,' Mum declared. 'What did I miss?'

'Charlie Green also knew Eric's wife Vera,' I said. 'They were friends.'

'*Friends*. Oh, I see what you mean.' Mum gave a knowing nod. 'And was Charlie a local man? Should he be added to our below stairs family tree?'

Eric shook his head. 'Charlie wasn't from around here. Well, he *was*. But he wasn't.'

'I'm sure the police are going to find that very helpful,' Mum muttered.

'He lived in the village?' I suggested.

Eric frowned. 'No. Why?'

I knew that Eric was in shock, but trying to get information was like pulling teeth with a spoon.

'But you knew he moved to Dublin,' I said. 'How?'

'Because he sent the old biddies postcards,' Eric went on. 'And every time he sent one, Lavender Green would brag about it. But all along—'

'Lavender *Green*?' I said sharply. 'Violet's sister? Why would Charlie be sending her postcards from Dublin?'

Eric looked at me as if I was stupid. 'Because she's his aunt. Well, they both are.'

'Well I never,' said Mum.

'It would have killed old Lavender if she'd not died

before I dug Charlie up,' Eric went on. 'Charlie could do no wrong in her eyes, but Violet . . .' Eric shook his head. 'Now, she couldn't stand him.'

Mum leaned in. 'And why was that?'

'Because he blew right through the family fortune with his horse gambling and messing about,' said Eric.

Violet and Lavender Green had a fortune to blow through? This was news to me and given Mum's surprised expression, it was news to her too.

'A fortune in what?' Mum ventured. 'Teapots?'

'The Greens were loaded,' Eric declared. 'Lived over Moreleigh way. Charlie's great-grandfolks owned mines all over Dartmoor at one time. Charlie inherited the lot when his dad died.'

I felt a wave of shame. Mum and I were always making fun of poor Violet and her frugal ways and now it turns out that she and her sister had been made into paupers by their reckless nephew.

'We went to school together,' said Eric. 'Him, me, Shawn, too. Shawn didn't like him much either. Charlie used to do the clues for the treasure hunt. He was good at riddles was our Charlie, but yeah, he was a bit of a black sheep.'

'A black sheep?' Mum perked up. 'A black sheep you say?' She whipped out her ever-handy stack of Post-it notes and a pen from the dresser drawer behind her. 'What did he look like?'

Eric thought for a moment. 'Like a ferret. Long nose, pointed chin. Skin and bones—'

'Yes. Bones now, I'm sure,' Mum said. 'Was he tall? What colour were his eyes? His hair? Did he have a moustache?'

'Mum!' I protested again. 'We're not playing a game of Guess Who!'

'How old was he?' Mum went on.

Eric frowned. 'He was my age.'

'And what age is that – forty-five? Fifty?'

'I'd rather not say, thank you very much,' Eric snapped. 'And I never looked into his eyes so I don't know, but he had red hair. We used to call him coppernob.'

'Lovely. Thank you so much.' Mum ripped off a Post-it and stuffed it into her pocket and shot me a satisfied look.

'You mentioned he gambled on horses,' I said.

'Oh, he had a good eye for a winner.' Eric nodded. 'You ask his lordship.'

Mum gave a little gasp. 'Lord Rupert and Charlie Green were friends?'

'Yeah. That's right. Until they had a falling-out.' Eric picked up the empty bottle of cooking brandy and then spied the Courvoisier. Mum promptly got up and moved it out of his reach.

'Well, this has been very informative,' said my mother somewhat smugly. 'And I'm sure the police will have lots of questions, especially since you mentioned it was your fault.'

'Eh?' Eric's eyebrows vanished under his hairline.

'That's what you said when you arrived,' Mum said. 'Kat and I both heard you. And that's what I told the new police officer who should be arriving any minute.'

'You stupid woman!' Eric exploded. 'We need Shawn on this. We don't want a stranger. Her ladyship will be very upset!'

Mum's eyes flashed with indignation. 'How dare you call me stupid! Shawn isn't here. A murder has been committed outside my house. The killer could still be at large . . . unless *you* did it.'

'Don't be bloody stupid!' Eric shouted again. 'Of course I didn't.'

'But you obviously know who did!' Mum fumed. 'Oh, good grief. Are you *covering* for someone— Oh God, no!' She gasped. 'Are you covering for his . . . *lordship*?'

Eric put his head in his hands and didn't answer.

Was Mum right? Was it connected to the Honeychurch family – a family that Eric had said on more than one occasion that he'd 'lay down his life' for?

But before we could question him any further, there was a smart rap on the kitchen door and a male voice cried, 'Police! Open up!'

Chapter Three

The door opened and there, along with Detective Sergeant Clive Banks – a dead ringer for Captain Pugwash – stood Shawn's replacement, one of the tallest men I had ever seen.

As the stranger stepped forward and into the kitchen, there was a nauseating crack and yelp of pain followed by a torrent of muttered expletives.

'Steady on, guv,' said Clive with a smirk. 'Don't forget to duck.'

'Gosh,' I said. 'Are you all right?'

'Fine, fine,' he croaked.

I suspected this wasn't the first time it had happened. I noticed that the newcomer's high forehead sported several purplish and yellow bruises.

He flashed his ID card, holding it long enough for me to take a good look. I read 'Detective Inspector Gregory Mallory'.

The inspector had to be at least six foot three. He positively dwarfed Clive, who just reached his shoulder. He was devastatingly handsome with a strong square jaw, cropped dark hair and grey-green eyes – a fact that did not go unnoticed by my mother who just stared. It was almost as if she was imagining him on the front cover of her latest tome.

Whereas Clive looked hot and sweaty in his summer police uniform of crisp white, short-sleeved shirt, the inspector wore a pressed light-grey suit and pale-blue tie. His shoes were polished to within an inch of their life. Despite the heat he looked cool as a cucumber and he exuded professional efficiency.

Clive made the introductions, emphasising that Detective Inspector Gregory Mallory preferred to be addressed as 'Inspector' or 'Mallory' and made sure to point out he was Shawn's 'temporary replacement'.

Clive added that Mallory hailed from the big bad city of Plymouth and, since Clive was standing out of Mallory's line of sight, added a mocking eye roll that made his feelings about his new boss clear.

Mallory pulled a notebook and pencil out of his top pocket.

Eric straightened up in his chair and put his beanie back on. He seemed worried.

Clive clapped a hand on Eric's shoulder. 'You okay, mate? Bit of a shock, yeah?'

'Tea?' Mum said brightly.

'I could do with a cuppa, Iris,' said Clive. 'Although . . . is that brandy?'

'Banks!' Mallory, said sharply. 'No, thank you, Mrs Stanford.'

'Another roundhead, eh?' said Clive cheerfully.

'Not a roundhead,' Eric said. 'Old Charlie Green. He's copped it.'

Clive's jaw dropped. 'Well, I'll be blowed. He was no great loss if you ask me. Always wanting money. I lent him a hundred quid once and never got it back— Wait. Didn't your missus and him have a fling once?'

'Yeah.' Eric scowled. 'Bastard.'

'He was,' Clive agreed. 'A right bastard.'

'Banks!' Mallory exclaimed. 'We are investigating a potential homicide here—'

'There's nothing potential about it,' Eric declared, clearly fortified by Clive's presence. 'Why else would Charlie be lying face down with his skull smashed in?'

Mallory's expression darkened. 'I trust you didn't tamper with the evidence in Honeywell Wood.'

'Eh? Where?' Eric looked confused.

'Apparently that's the proper name for the pine forest out the back,' said Clive. 'The guv meant did you touch him.'

'Didn't need to,' said Eric. 'He was wearing that leather biker jacket—'

'The one with the red and gold eagle?' Clive ventured. 'I remember that jacket. Was his Harley there too?'

'No,' said Eric rather too quickly. 'Why would you say that?'

'Stands to reason,' Clive went on. 'He must have got to

the forest – sorry, *Honeywell* Wood – somehow and he was always riding that motorbike.'

'Enough!' Mallory exclaimed again. His eyes met mine. I gave a sympathetic smile that he did not return.

'Lighten up, guv,' Clive said. 'We're all friends.'

'Clearly not,' said Mallory, 'otherwise the deceased would not be lying in a shallow grave with his skull smashed in!'

Eric raised a hand. 'I think it was me who smashed the skull by accident.'

Mallory struggled to stay calm. 'But perhaps the skull had already been smashed in, hence the cause of death.'

'Yeah, maybe,' Clive mused. 'But where exactly was he killed? Everyone knows his lordship didn't like him, which begs the question . . . What was Charlie Green doing at Honeychurch Hall?'

'Banks! Enough!' Mallory snarled. 'Get the crime scene kit from the car and go outside and wait for the ambulance.'

Clive frowned. 'Oh, you mean the barrier tape and booties and stuff like that?'

'Yes, Banks, stuff like that.' A tick was developing in Mallory's right eye. 'We need to establish a C-A-P.'

'A what?'

'A common approach path!' Mallory struggled to keep his temper. 'We need to *identify*, *secure* and *protect* the area; *sketch* the crime scene, mark out and *protect* the perimeter! How did the deceased get there? How did the killer escape? Use your head, man.'

'I thought that was what we were doing.' Clive seemed

unfazed. 'Okay. But I think I'm more useful here, Greg, sorry, I meant, guv.'

'*Go!*' Mallory snapped.

Clive shrugged and, casting a final look of disdain at his new boss, stomped out of the kitchen.

Mallory took a moment to compose himself. He turned to a fresh page in his police notebook and looked up with a thin smile.

'Are you sure you don't want a cup of tea, Inspector?' asked Mum.

Mallory ignored her and turned back to Eric. 'Let's start again. Your name, sir.'

Eric's eyebrows shot up. 'Me?'

'Yes, you,' said Mallory. 'Please spell your full name.'

'My full name,' Eric echoed.

I had a feeling we might be here for a long time.

'Oh, for heaven's sake!' Mum exclaimed. 'It's Eric, E-R-I-C Pugsley. P-U-G-S-L-E-Y.'

'Is that correct, sir?' Mallory asked.

Eric nodded.

'And it was you who found the remains, sir?'

'Well, *I* didn't,' said Eric. 'The dog did. He was digging.'

'And the shovel?' Mallory enquired. 'The one in the hall? Is that yours?'

Eric nodded again.

'When did you realise that the dog had disturbed a body?' asked Mallory.

'I saw the Doc Marten boot first,' said Eric.

'And then Eric used the shovel,' Mum put in. 'That's when he *smashed* the skull.'

'Thank you, Mrs Stanford, but please allow the witness to answer the question,' Mallory said. 'And you can identify the deceased?'

'Well, maybe,' said Eric. 'I mean, I thought his jacket looked familiar. But I really can't be sure now.'

'You were very sure five minutes ago,' Mum put in. 'You said it was Charlie Green and that he'd had an affair with your wife.'

'Mrs Stanford!' Mallory protested.

Eric glowered at my mother. 'I only said I thought it might be him. And it was hardly an affair. It was just a bit of fun, like.'

I felt like I was watching a farce.

'Can you describe the jacket, please,' said Mallory.

'Clive already did,' Eric mumbled.

Mallory rubbed his forehead. 'But Clive – I mean DS Banks – did not find the body. You did.'

'I mean anyone can have a leather jacket,' Eric said.

'I don't have one,' Mum chimed in.

'Mrs Stanford. *Please!*' Mallory turned back to Eric yet again. 'And you say that's how you were able to identify the deceased. From his jacket.'

'Clive knew that jacket was Charlie's,' said Eric. 'In fact, everyone knew Charlie.'

'It seems that everyone knows everyone around here,' Mallory said.

'Or is related,' Mum put in. 'Although we're not. Kat and I moved down from—'

'I get the picture,' said Mallory. 'So who *was* the deceased related to?'

'Certainly not above stairs,' Mum said. 'And not one of the big five.'

Mallory frowned. 'The big five?'

'There were just the five main families who worked below stairs,' said Mum. 'Pugsley, Banks, Stark, Cropper and Jones. They all either lived on the estate or in the village – most of the village is owned by the Honeychurch estate. If you are interested, Inspector, then I'm more than happy to show you the family trees. His lordship – that's the fifteenth Earl of Grenville, Lord Rupert Honeychurch – has appointed me the family historian.'

Mallory just blinked. His eyes met mine again. I gave another sympathetic smile and this time was rewarded with a flicker of mock despair.

'And when was the last time you saw the deceased, Mr Pugsley?' Mallory asked.

'Kat and I have never met him,' Mum said.

'I'm not asking *you*, Mrs Stanford!' Mallory exclaimed. 'Mr Pugsley?'

Eric shrugged yet again.

'You told us that it was seven years ago,' Mum said. 'The night before the beating of the bounds.' Sensing Mallory's confusion she launched into a detailed explanation of the old custom, adding, 'Eric was very specific. You said Charlie Green came to see you and that it was all your fault that he died.'

Eric looked at my mother with pure venom. 'I said no such thing!'

'Of course he's going to lie about it *now*,' Mum said smugly.

'I see.' Mallory's voice was cold. 'And what else did Mr Pugsley tell you?'

Mum opened her mouth but I got in first. 'That's not strictly true, Mum. Eric told us he thought that Charlie was living in Dublin because one of his aunts—'

'That would be Violet and Lavender Green,' said Mum helpfully. 'Now *Violet* runs the tearoom and *Lavender* dabbled in car boot sales – although she passed away—'

Mallory blinked again.

'Lavender had been receiving postcards from Charlie,' I said. 'Isn't that right, E—'

'But did you *see* the actual postcards?' Mum cut in.

'No,' said Eric.

'He didn't!' Mum crowed. 'And besides, it's only Dublin. Charlie could easily have jumped on a plane and popped back.'

'Or perhaps he never left the country at all,' Mallory said quietly.

There was a horrible silence.

'Mr Pugsley, I'd like you to show me where you found the deceased,' said Mallory. 'And then we will be continuing our conversation down at the station.'

'We should all go,' Mum declared. 'Kat and I have had some experience in this sort of thing. Will you be able to set a time frame once you've seen the state of the corpse?'

'I'm afraid I'm not at liberty to say at this stage,' said Mallory. 'I appreciate your willingness to help,

Mrs Stanford, but your presence and input could confuse the witness.'

'What witness?' Eric said. 'It was Mr Chips who dug up the body.'

Mum rolled her eyes. '*You're* the witness, Eric.'

Eric gasped. 'But I didn't see anything! I was at home that night.'

'And what night would that be?' Mallory said sharply.

'A-ha!' Mum was exultant. 'You see. He's not telling you everything.'

Clive knocked on the kitchen door and opened it. He was wearing a white overall and blue disposable booties and gloves.

'Ambulance is here, guv,' he said. 'I've set up the cordon to the entrance to the pine— I mean Honeywell Wood.'

'Don't forget there is another entrance. There's a little gate opposite *Eric's* cottage,' Mum said pointedly. 'You'll need one of those cordon things there, too.'

'Thank you, Mrs Stanford,' said Mallory wearily.

'Oh – and let's not forget the original driveway,' Mum went on. 'In fact, you really should take a map.' My mother snapped her fingers at me. 'Give him the map for beating of the bounds, dear.'

I jumped to it and handed the map over to Mallory who gave it a passing glance before snapping his notebook shut and putting both into his top jacket pocket. 'Let's go,' he said.

'Wait a minute,' I said. 'What about Violet Green? Someone should tell her about her nephew.'

'Violet won't be sorry. As I told you, she couldn't stand

Charlie,' Clive said. 'It was the other one, Lavender, who thought the sun shone out of Charlie's backside.'

The tick in Mallory's eye started up again. 'We're presuming that the deceased is indeed Charlie Green, in which case I need to know the names of all his next of kin and notify them first.'

'Violet Green,' said Clive. 'She's the only one.'

'Fine. Good,' said Mallory. 'We will be sending a bereavement counsellor to break the news.'

'I wouldn't bother, guv,' said Clive dismissively. 'The news will already have got to Little Dipperton by now. You're forgetting. This is a village. Not one of your big cities.'

'And that's where you're wrong, Banks,' said Mallory. 'I am very much aware of that fact. And I must remind you that we will be doing things very differently from now on. The proper, official way.'

As they left the kitchen, Mallory gave an exaggerated duck through the door. Mum and I waited until we were quite certain that the trio had left the building.

'Well!' she declared. 'I always knew there was something odd about Eric.'

'Mum,' I scolded. 'Did you have to make your dislike of Eric so obvious? This is serious stuff. You know as well as I do that Eric isn't guilty.'

'Do you?' Mum said. 'Do you really? It's common knowledge that his relationship with that dreadful Vera was bordering on psychopathic.'

'Mum!' I exclaimed. 'For heaven's sake. We don't know

that at all. This isn't one of your romance novels. This is real life.'

'Speaking of romance, what do you think about that new policeman?' Mum said. 'So tall and handsome,' she went on. 'And with that chiselled jaw, I'd say he's a cross between John Cleese and Desperate Dan.'

'Well, he's not Shawn, that's for sure,' I said sadly. 'What should I do about seeing Violet today? It seems a bit insensitive.'

'Rubbish,' Mum exclaimed. 'Clive said she couldn't stand Charlie. You should go. See what you can find out. I have a feeling that our new inspector is going to need our help.'

'No,' I said firmly. 'I think he's doing very well on his own.'

'All I'm saying is that he's not going to get anywhere with the villagers with his city attitude,' said Mum.

'Promise me that you won't interfere,' I said.

'Cross my heart and hope to die,' said Mum.

And with that, I left, knowing full well that when she made that promise her fingers would be firmly crossed behind her back.

Chapter Four

The minute I got into my car I called Shawn on his mobile but, per the norm these days, it went straight to voicemail. I left him a short message asking him to call me back but then changed my mind, redialled and left a more detailed message. Given the speed with which bad news travels fast, I wanted to be one of the very first to tell him about the murder.

As I made my way to Little Dipperton along the winding country lanes flanked by towering hedgerows, I couldn't stop thinking about Charlie Green. Since he didn't live on the estate or in the village, how had he ended up in the pine forest – or rather Honeywell Wood? I'd have to get used to calling it by its official name.

Mum was right. We didn't really know Eric, but he had seemed genuinely distraught when he turned up this afternoon – hardly the behaviour of a guilty man.

Even in the short time that Mum and I had lived on the Honeychurch estate, certain incidents and scandals always seemed to have been deftly covered up by Shawn. Mum was right again. Things were going to be very different with Detective Inspector Mallory.

I cautiously approached the next hairpin bend and slammed on the brakes. A flatbed lorry transporting a pale green shepherd's hut with a cheerful yellow trim had attempted to make the corner but got wedged diagonally across the lane.

What idiots! Why on earth would anyone attempt to come this way!

Devon hedgebanks are deceptive. They may be covered in foliage and flowers but behind that is solid earth and more often than not, stone walls.

The lane was one of the many narrow arteries to Little Dipperton but the entrance to this one displayed a large blue warning sign with the width restriction of 6'6" and No Access to HGVs.

It wouldn't be the first time that a stranger to the area had thought that the rules didn't apply to them.

A man with a buzz cut and wearing a wife-beater T-shirt, jumped down from the cab and strode up to my car. He was sweating profusely. I opened my window.

'You'll have to turn back,' he said rudely.

'Yes, I can see that,' I said. 'Have you called for help?'

'There's an hour wait.' He gestured to the cab where I could make out another man sitting in the passenger seat. 'Old clever clogs there said we could get through because the satnav says so. Cuts off a fair few miles.'

'I know,' I said. 'But even if you get pulled out, the lane

gets even narrower further up. You'll have to reverse all the way back to the main road.'

'Main road!' The driver laughed. 'It's only got one lane.'

'Welcome to the South Hams,' I said. 'Where are you heading?'

'Honeychurch Hall,' he said.

A shepherd's hut at Honeychurch Hall! 'Are you sure?'

'Yeah,' said the driver. 'Lady something. Lydia? Lisa?'

'Lavinia,' I said, wondering what on earth Rupert's eccentric wife was up to now. 'You should have taken the top road to Dartmouth. It would have brought you in on a wider road.'

'Thanks. I could kill him, I really could.' He turned away and stomped back to his lorry without a thought to the fact that I had to reverse at least half a mile myself.

The narrow country lanes in Devon were notorious. Even though there were passing places and the occasional gateway to pull into, trying to get from A to B in one go was a bit like running the gauntlet. I was getting proficient at reversing and usually did it with good humour. Not so my mother. Many a time she'd stared down the opposition if she felt their passing place was closer than hers. Once, she flatly refused to budge, turned off her car engine and took out a newspaper to read until the exasperated motorist gave in.

To get to the village now meant taking an even narrower route where grass grew up the middle and the hedgebanks were so high it was like driving through a trench. It was my least favourite route to Little Dipperton since it meant passing the burnt-out shell of Bridge Cottage. As well as attracting fly tippers, the place held a lot of bad memories for me.

As I slowly descended the steep hill through a leafy tunnel of trees, my eye was caught by a shimmer of silver dancing in the sunlight among the laurel. Tucked into the mouth of a partially hidden bridleway peeped the bonnet of a Rolls-Royce Silver Cloud bearing the number plate Monty1.

It was such an odd place to see Sir Monty's car that I stopped a few yards further on and wondered if I should go back to check that he was all right. But then, as I glanced in my rear-view mirror, a bicycle with a pannier basket cautiously emerged into the lane. At the handlebars was none other than my mother's best friend.

Delia Evans looked summery in a bright yellow sleeveless summer dress and sandals. Her synthetic aubergine-coloured bob brought out the colour of her tanned arms and legs.

Delia looked back over her shoulder and waved, presumably to Sir Monty. A surreptitious adjustment of her underwear confirmed my suspicions.

Delia had been meeting my mother's boyfriend.

I hit the accelerator and sped away.

Since Sir Monty cheated on the auction circuit it was hardly surprising that he cheated in the bedroom. Ugh – and who on earth chooses a romantic rendezvous so close to a fly-tip?

I couldn't wait to tell my mother and hoped she wouldn't be too upset. This was the perfect ammunition to get Sir Monty out of our lives once and for all.

For a moment, Sir Monty and Delia's betrayal made me forget poor Charlie Green until I passed the sign, 'Welcome to Little Dipperton', and it all came flooding back.

The little village boasted one narrow road lined with whitewashed cottages, some in dire need of re-thatching, others with slate stone roofs, and all desperate for a coat of paint. They formed a crescent around the Norman church of St Mary's that was currently undergoing renovations to the church tower and covered in scaffolding. A low stone wall fronted the graveyard where lichen-covered headstones commemorated the names of the families who had been born and died in a village mentioned in the Domesday Book – and immortalised on my mother's family trees.

Most of the cottages still belonged to the Honeychurch estate and bore a distinctive blue trim. Their low front doors opened directly onto the road and what small gardens they did have were at the rear.

With only one spot in front of the post office and general store now called the 'community shop', parking was either in the church car park or at the local pub, the Hare & Hounds. Despite it being a Sunday, the village was busy since Little Dipperton was an AONB and attracted a lot of visitors during the summer months.

Luckily, Violet had a dedicated space of her own – 'Parking Only for Rose Cottage' – in the alley between the community shop and her tearoom. Sometimes I managed to squeeze in behind her green Morris Minor Traveller but today there was no room. Two beautiful antique oak backless benches stood side by side on the hard-packed mud in the brilliant sunshine.

Resigned, I retreated to the church car park and left my Golf there, cutting back through the churchyard. The lychgate was plastered in posters for the upcoming beating of the bounds and village treasure hunt with a reminder to pick up maps from the community shop.

I hoped that the weather really did break by next weekend. My mother was mad to consider the twenty-mile hike just to keep up with Delia. But now I suspected that Delia's weight loss wasn't due to training at all. She was in love.

Suppressing another wave of nausea at the thought of Sir Monty and Delia in flagrante, I stepped into Violet's alley.

Now I was up close to the oak benches my stomach gave the peculiar jolt that it always did when I recognised something unique. The pair was about ten feet long and reached my mid-thigh. I took in the single-board top with the square-rounded edge, applied under-edge moulding and the eight baluster-turned legs joined by capped stretchers on turned feet. On the underside of each bench was the date 1674 – Charles II's reign.

The joined oak benches were exquisite. I knew a fake when I saw one and these were the real thing. I could tell by the patina, the cut of the wood and the flat hand-beaten nail heads.

And they were rare.

I had noticed the oak furniture in Violet's tearoom – the refectory table, various gate-leg tables and ladder-back chairs – but the tables were always covered by her signature rose-pattern tablecloths and the chairs either had someone sitting on them or were tucked under the tables.

Eric's comment about the demise of the Green fortunes hit me afresh. Now I was beginning to wonder if all the oak furniture was antique and not reproduction after all.

Doreen Mutters, the landlady from the Hare & Hounds, emerged from the side door dazzled by the sunlight. 'Oh good, you're here. Wait – I can't see.' She shielded her eyes. 'Who is it?'

'It's Kat.' I stepped out of the shadows to greet her. Doreen was Violet's closest friend and, although a terrible gossip, was a well-loved member of the village. She and her husband Stan – Mum had nicknamed them Tweedledum and Tweedledee due to their rotund shapes – knew everything that was going on.

'I suppose you were there when Eric dug Charlie up?' Doreen said getting straight to the point.

'You've heard already?' I smiled. 'That was quick even by Little Dipperton standards! How is Violet taking it?'

'She couldn't stand Charlie,' said Doreen. 'He was the one thing she and Lavender argued about. If I were you, don't say "sorry for your loss", because she's not.'

'Oh,' I said.

Doreen leaned in. 'And I can tell you, I'm not surprised he came to a bad end.'

'Oh,' I said again.

'Always asking to borrow money,' she said. 'Always roaring through the village on his motorbike at top speed.'

'Oh,' I said yet again.

'He was nothing like poor Charlotte,' Doreen went on.

'And Charlotte is . . . ?'

'His sister,' Doreen declared. 'Died a few years ago on one of those parachute things. You know, up behind a boat.'

'Parasailing?' I suggested.

'Out in Ibiza. Naturally Charlie was at the helm.' Doreen shook her head with disgust. 'So who do you think did him in?'

'I have no idea,' I said and started to edge towards the back door but Doreen blocked my move.

'Eric Pugsley?' Doreen cocked her head. 'His Vera and Charlie were having a bit of a fling at one time.' She gave a heavy sigh. 'And no Shawn to sort things out now. Sorry. That was tactless of me. He'll be back, luv. Just you see. He'll soon tire of London.'

I gave a polite smile. This was the one thing I didn't like about village life – everyone knowing everyone else's business.

'Speaking of the police,' Doreen began again. 'What do you think of our new Inspector Mallory?'

'Well, he's certainly different.' I attempted to edge towards the back door again but Doreen edged along with me.

'Clive says that he does things by the book,' Doreen declared. 'That won't sit well with us locals. We like to sort out our own problems.'

Even when it comes to murder?

I made an exaggerated check of my wristwatch. 'Goodness! Is that the time?'

'It's very kind of you to offer to clear out Lavender's bedroom,' said Doreen.

'Well, not clear it *out*,' I said quickly. 'I'm just going to take a look at a few things.'

'You'll need a big van, but perhaps you can slip Luxtons ten pounds and ask them to drop off the stuff when they pick up those.' She pointed to the oak benches.

'I wondered what they were doing outside,' I said.

'Sir Monty is helping Violet sell her old furniture,' said Doreen.

'Sir Monty?' I was taken aback.

And seeing my surprise, Doreen added, 'He's organised everything. They're going into the Luxtons sale on Wednesday.'

I knew that Luxtons was holding an important sale of fine arts and furniture this coming Wednesday because the catalogue was already out and I was planning on going. Lady Caroline Manners of Stone Park had been a well-known collector of seventeenth-century oak furniture, tapestries and oil paintings. It promised to be an exciting sale.

Doreen cocked her head again. 'I'm amazed you didn't know – what with your mum walking out with his lordship.' Suddenly the church bell chimed three times. 'Good grief, dear. You are a chatterbox! I really must get on with my day.'

And with that, Doreen ambled away as if she had all the time in the world.

I was instantly suspicious of Sir Monty's motives. It wouldn't be the first time that he had made a last-minute entry into a sale. With just a description and no photograph, pieces such as these often escaped the notice of serious collectors. I suspected that Sir Monty would then buy the items himself, mark them up and sell them on, making a handsome profit in the process. It wouldn't surprise me in the least if he were trying to cheat Violet out of their true value, but not this time. Not if I had anything to do with it.

I would have to warn her.

Chapter Five

I stepped down into Violet's kitchen and was assaulted by the usual smell of bacon. Clouds of steam were pouring out of the top of an enormous industrial-sized water boiler.

The low-beamed ceiling and small leaded light windows made the tiny room claustrophobic. In the background, BBC Radio Devon was playing Sheryl Crow's 'All I Wanna Do' on an old-fashioned transistor radio.

Violet didn't hear me come in. She was standing over the kitchen table carefully removing a Victoria sponge cake from a Morrisons' supermarket box and, with painstaking slowness, placed it on a frilly doily on a china plate.

I knew she was around the same age as my mother but Violet's choice of attire – a drab print dress and faded cardigan, and an old-fashioned perm – made her seem so much older. The thick bottle-top glasses mended with Sellotape didn't help.

I took in the kitchen with its array of teapots of all shapes and sizes lined up on the wooden shelves. Hanging above the leaded light window over the kitchen sink were strips of sticky paper stuck with flies. I doubted Rose Cottage Tearoom would get an A for hygiene.

Violet picked up a wooden spatula and slammed it onto the top of the supermarket cake. 'There. Not so perfect now.'

Suddenly, the music was interrupted by a news bulletin.

'And just in from the sleepy hamlet of Little Dipperton,' said a chirpy female voice. 'The body of a man has been found on the Honeychurch Hall estate. Police are treating this as suspicious. We'll keep our listeners posted. But up next it's Barry Manilow with "Can't Smile Without You"!'

I was shocked. It wasn't the first time that this quiet corner of England had had to deal with a suspicious death or two but it rarely made a news bulletin or, if it did, it was after the fact, not during an active investigation.

Mallory really was doing things differently.

Violet's face crumpled. Perhaps there was some sadness about her dead nephew after all. 'Oh dear, oh dear,' she said. 'This is terrible. Terrible. Terrible.'

Despite Doreen's advice, I knew I had to say *something*. 'I'm so sorry for your loss.'

Violet bristled. 'I'm not sorry about *him*. I'm sorry for the dowager countess. Lady Edith is going to be so upset! She hates this sort of thing. And the publicity! She's so private and—' Violet clutched at her throat, her face a picture of anguish. 'You don't think she will blame me, do you?'

I wasn't sure if I had heard correctly. 'The dowager countess? Blame you? Why would she?'

'I would be so upset if she blamed me.' Violet's admiration of Edith was legendary. 'I told her Charlie had moved to Dublin. This is so typical of him. He's always causing trouble.'

I thought it unlikely that Charlie had deliberately got himself killed.

There was a rustle and clatter as a young girl of about eighteen pushed her way through a red and white plastic door fringe that separated the tearoom from the kitchen. She had strawberry blonde hair swept back in a ponytail and carried a tea tray stacked with dirty cups and saucers. She looked worried. 'Oh, Miss Green! Have you heard? There's been a murder!'

'This is Doreen's niece, Willow,' Violet said by way of introduction. 'And you must recognise Kat Stanford because she used to be on the telly. Willow is taking a gap year and helping me out in the tearoom and up at the pub in the evenings.'

Willow just stared. 'But . . . Miss Green. Didn't you hear what I said? There's been a murder. It's on the news. Everyone is talking about it.'

'Yes. I know,' said Violet.

'But . . . who is it?'

'My nephew Charlie.' Violet picked up the icing-sugar shaker and sprinkled the cake, sending up clouds of white powder. 'And I can assure you that whatever happened to him was well deserved.'

Willow's brown eyes widened. 'But . . . that means there's a killer on the loose.'

'And I can assure you it won't be anyone from the village,' Violet said firmly. 'Now stack all the dirty dishes on the draining board. We'll have to do them later but they *must* be done before we close up this afternoon. A tidy kitchen is a tidy mind.'

'Don't you mean a tidy house is a tidy mind?' Willow ventured.

'I don't want you getting into bad habits at university,' Violet went on. 'Always, always wash up and put everything away before you go to bed. Never leave anything on the draining board!'

'Yes, Miss Green.'

'Stay here for a moment,' Violet continued. 'I'm going to show Kat my sister's bedroom. She's going to be clearing out all her things so I can rent that room out properly.'

Violet headed to a latch door that opened into a dark hallway with a red and brown swirl-patterned carpet. She stopped at another latch door that revealed a steep staircase.

I seized my moment. 'I hear Sir Monty is helping you sell those beautiful oak benches outside. I don't think I've ever noticed them before.'

'My customers complain they are too hard to sit on,' Violet declared. 'And I could do with the money. Of course, everything went to our brother when our parents died – the house and the land. But Mummy left Lavender and me some nice jewellery and a few antiques that she had inherited from Grandpa.'

Hearing Violet speak of 'Mummy' and 'Grandpa' made me smile.

'And then when Bunty – that's my brother – died, Charlie got the lot and we know what happened there.' Violet pursed her lips with disapproval.

'And Doreen tells me that Sir Monty is helping you put them into the Luxtons sale *this* coming Wednesday?' I wanted to be certain that Doreen had got her facts right.

'Yes. He managed to squeeze them in at the last minute.' Violet nodded.

My suspicions as to Sir Monty's intentions deepened.

'I hope he advised you to set a high reserve,' I said. 'They're very valuable.'

'Oh yes, I know.' Violet nodded again. 'Sir Monty thinks they could fetch at least five thousand pounds each.'

'Oh.' I was surprised. It was what I had thought, too, but I had expected him to come in low. 'And what's the reserve?'

'Five thousand,' Violet said. 'And if they sell, he's going to help me shift all the other antiques. People prefer Ikea these days.'

Now I heard the alarm bell. 'That's very kind of him,' I said carefully. 'And I assume he's charging you commission?'

'Two per cent because he knows I am financially strapped.'

'*Two* per cent?' I exclaimed. 'Are you sure?'

Violet stopped and turned to face me, a look of defiance on her face. 'I wasn't born yesterday, dear,' she said. 'I don't know how much longer I can keep the tearoom going and frankly, I can't eat the furniture, can I?'

'I was just surprised,' I said. 'It's so low.'

Even if I believed that Sir Monty was helping Violet out of the kindness of his heart, it still didn't explain why he was putting the oak benches into Luxtons so late. Why not wait for the next important sale? What was the sudden rush?

Violet gestured to the staircase. 'You go ahead and mind your step. I always have to hold on to the handrail.' The handrail in question was a long piece of rope threaded through brackets screwed into the wall.

I just couldn't let the Monty thing go. 'When did you decide to sell them?' I said mildly. 'Was it Sir Monty's idea?'

'Mrs Clayton – that's *Pearl* Clayton – came into the tearoom recently,' said Violet with a hint of pride. 'I couldn't believe it! She came all on her own and was so kind. Mrs Clayton said that if I changed the furniture, I could get more tables in. She's sponsoring the refreshments and had all the maps made for the beating of the bounds.'

'Ah yes, I seem to be hearing her name a lot,' I said.

'Mrs Clayton is going to run for Mayor,' said Violet. 'She's bought the Priory out Modbury way and wants to furnish it with antiques.'

'Why don't you sell your antiques directly to her?' I said. 'That way you won't have to pay any commission at all!'

'I couldn't possibly *haggle* with Mrs Clayton.' Violet pulled a face. 'And then when Sir Monty came in last Thursday with your mother, I asked what they thought and Sir Monty said he'd help me do it.'

Perhaps Sir Monty had been trying to impress my mother, but I still wasn't convinced.

'I assume you have a written agreement with him.'

Violet glared. 'Of course I do,' she said. 'My father taught me to keep records of everything. I have cashbooks and ledgers. I don't trust computers. You hear about catching viruses and I haven't had a cold in years.'

There was nothing more that I could do – although I would still talk to Michael Luxton, who owned the auction house, about the benches just to make sure the reserves were exactly what Sir Monty said they were.

I reached the small upstairs landing with the only source of light coming from a dirty window that was shut. Clusters of flies buzzed or lay dead on the peeling windowsill. The walls, as well as the ceiling, were papered in a rose-patterned wallpaper in keeping with the theme of the cottage.

Three more latch doors led off the landing; two were closed but the one opposite stood ajar. I caught a glimpse of pink tiles and a toilet.

Violet gestured to the door on the left. 'That's my bedroom,' she said. 'When I have B&B guests I move into Lavender's room. Hers is the bigger room because she was the oldest.'

'That must be inconvenient,' I said, thinking why not just move into Lavender's room and be done with it? But when Violet opened the door to our right, I could see why.

Even the stench of mothballs couldn't cover the smell of a stale room. A large mullioned window looked out over the churchyard, but just like the landing, it was coated in grime and home to a gazillion flies.

Every conceivable surface was packed with open boxes of knick-knacks, pictures and crockery. Some were draped over with heavy blankets. Clothes hung on wire hangers from rope stretched from wall sconces. Empty picture frames, broken terracotta pots, metal cooking sheets – you name it, it was there.

A quick glance confirmed my fears that there was absolutely nothing here I wanted. But I could hardly be rude and say so.

I took in a beautiful seventeenth-century oak linen press with one door open to reveal pillows and blankets and what looked like striped deckchair fabric. A large chest of drawers and a coffer of the same period were also filled to capacity and neither could be closed properly. On the opposite wall, an old velvet curtain covered a waist-high sideboard.

Violet surveyed the room. 'It may look cluttered but my sister was very organised,' she said. 'She kept detailed ledgers too. I know we haven't settled on an amount yet, but as you will see from Lavender's records, I only want what's fair.'

'Why don't you leave me here for a bit so I can have a proper look,' I said tactfully.

'All right,' Violet said. 'But I want it all gone. I've been reading a very good book about tidying up.'

'Oh?' I said. 'Is it *The Life-Changing Magic of Tidying* by Marie Kondo?'

'No, not that one,' said Violet. 'It's called *Swedish Death Cleaning* by a Swedish lady. Her message is clear. You don't want to bother your family cleaning up when you're dead and gone so you should do it now. And since I don't have any family, that frightful job would fall to Doreen. But if Doreen goes before I do . . .'

'How thoughtful you are,' I said.

'I hope you've brought your chequebook and a big enough van.'

And with that alarming comment, Violet left me to it.

Chapter Six

I went straight to the window and managed to prise it open with a letter opener that I found in a pot of pens and scissors on a shelf by the door. I had to let in some air. From Lavender's bedroom I had a good view of the churchyard and was surprised at the number of tourists wandering around enjoying ice-cream cornets from the community shop.

Turning back to the room I noticed a handful of silver-framed colour photographs arranged along the mantelpiece above the Victorian cast-iron fireplace.

One showed Violet and Lavender – both redheads – dressed in long-sleeved dresses with cinched-in waists, standing arm in arm with two very handsome men in army uniform. I'd known that the sisters had lost their fiancés in the Korean War and had never married. They all looked so young and carefree. It made me feel sad. Life rarely turned out the way one expected. It certainly hadn't for me.

Two years ago, if someone had told me that David and I would split up, my job as the host of *Fakes & Treasures* would be over and – even more shocking – a city girl like me would be living in the middle of the Devonshire countryside, I would have thought them mad. But despite all the turbulence – usually surrounding my mother – I couldn't be happier.

Another photograph was of Lavender – dressed in a nineteen-sixties mini skirt, bouffant hair and heavy eyeliner – with a boy and a girl with red hair. I guessed they must be Charlie and Charlotte. They looked about seven or eight and were dressed very smartly in navy school uniforms – a cap for Charlie and a straw boater for Charlotte. She was a pretty little thing. Out of her clenched fist poked the head of a tiny doll.

As I picked up the photograph to take a closer look, a sheaf of postcards fluttered to the floor.

They were all from Ireland and pictured stone churches, lush green landscapes, plenty of sheep, and a few leprechauns thrown in. These must be the postcards from Charlie that Eric had mentioned.

Curious, I turned the first over and read: 'Dear Auntie, Thanks for your letter. I hope you will come and visit. Don't forget I love you! Charlie x'. I skimmed the others. All had variations of the same message.

I took out my ever-ready jeweller's loupe from my tote bag to study the dates of the postmarks. It looked like Charlie wrote to his aunt every three or four months. But it was the very last postcard – a leprechaun drinking a bottle of whiskey – that made my heart miss a beat.

It had been dated just six weeks ago. Charlie must have come back to Devon after all. And yet, why hadn't anyone seen him? There was something else that bothered me. Since the pair had been so close, why hadn't Charlie come back for his Aunt Lavender's funeral?

Baffled, I sank down on the edge of the candlewick bedspread and sifted through them again.

Was it possible that Mallory was right when he said that perhaps Charlie had never left Little Dipperton at all? In which case, someone had gone to a lot of trouble to make out that he was still alive – sending postcards from Ireland for starters.

On impulse, I decided to take photographs of the postmarks on my iPhone before setting them back on the mantelpiece behind the framed photograph where I had found them. This was something the new detective would definitely want to see.

It took a monumental effort to switch my focus to Lavender's boxes of junk but I quickly realised that she was extremely organised and it wasn't as bad as it looked. Yes, there were many, many boxes but each one was labelled along with a detailed list of the contents. There was a lot of china and porcelain and of those, many were odd saucers or cups with no handle. I saw china figurines, ornaments, souvenirs from abroad – an entire box of plastic dolls in national dress – and random boxes of assorted knitting wool and fabric off-cuts.

It looked like the chest of drawers and linen press only contained textiles, so I didn't bother to look inside.

I gave the room a last look, but the label on a cardboard box tucked under a wingback chair caught my attention. It said 'Furniture for Charlotte's doll's house'. Curious, I pulled it out. It was a large shallow rectangular box that could have been used to store wrapping paper. The pieces were not plastic or cheap. They were handmade from an assortment of wood and metal. There were four-poster beds, armoires, a refectory table set with a dozen chairs. Little tins contained candelabras and tiny sets of silverware, crockery and pots for the kitchen. There were even handwoven rugs. This was quality stuff! So where was the doll's house?

I peered under the wingback chair again and saw, right at the very back, a small wooden decorative cigar box with 'Charlotte's Frozen Charlottes (8)' written in black Sharpie on the lid. Inside were seven small white porcelain corpses. These ghoulish porcelain dolls had earned their name from Seba Smith, an American journalist, who had written a poem in 1843 called 'A Corpse Going to a Ball'.

Although they weren't particularly valuable, they would make a nice addition to my doll collection. I thought of the doll clutched in Charlotte's fist in one of the photographs on the mantelpiece and went to take another look. It was a Frozen Charlotte.

I renewed my search for the doll's house and, by chance, moved the old curtain that was covering the sideboard.

I was thrilled! Not only had I found Charlotte's doll's house, it turned out to be a waist-high perfect replica of Honeychurch Hall!

The doll's house was built of solid oak and extremely heavy. Somehow I managed to drag it out from under the windowsill so that I could access the rear winged double doors.

The replica – although it couldn't possibly be the entire Hall, that was far too large – had all the main features I knew so well – the black and white marble chequered reception hall, the sweeping main staircase and two-storied galleried landing under the two domed atriums and the Great Hall. The kitchen had the iron range and the back passage led to the various larders – Meat, Dairy, Dry Larder, Still Room, Lamp Room and Flower Room. Two smaller staircases, painted a dull green, led to the attics for the servants' quarters.

The Earl of Grenville coat of arms and Honeychurch motto, *ad perseverate est ad triumphum* – 'to endure is to triumph' – were displayed above the marble fireplace in the Great Hall where the walls were stencilled with weapons as a nod to the Honeychurch armoury. But it was here in the Great Hall, with its minstrel gallery, hammer-beam roof and stained-glass windows, that something struck me as odd.

Among the stencilled swords and shields was a pair of oval-framed miniature portraits. They couldn't have been more than a couple of inches long, but they were not only out of proportion – they were also out of place.

Gently, I removed one from the wall, surprised that it had been stuck on with Blu-Tack. The subject wore a beard and was dressed in a scarlet doublet with an elaborate Elizabethan ruff collar, slashed sleeves and a brilliant red jerkin. He was holding a scroll with a name in gold lettering that said, 'Golden Hind'. The sitter had to be Sir Francis Drake; I was sure of it.

Years ago, I went on a school trip to Brixham to view the replica of the *Golden Hind* before she was moved to Southwark. I'd always been fascinated by one of the most renowned seamen of the Elizabethan age who, in 1577, was the first man to successfully circumnavigate the world. He also played a huge role in defeating the dreaded Spanish Armada.

Drake was also a Devon man. He was born in Tavistock around 1540 where a statue stands to commemorate his astonishing accomplishments. He has deep connections with Plymouth too.

Drake's home, Buckland Abbey, is now owned by the National Trust and a mere ten miles from Little Dipperton. Mum and I had been there several times. It was filled with Drake's seafaring memorabilia and artefacts including the legendary snare drum that he took on his incredible voyage.

Curious, I reached in for the second miniature that was also stuck with Blu-Tack. This time, Drake's clothing was slightly different, with the doublet being a rich plum colour, but again, he was holding a scroll. The lettering on this one said, 'Pelican'.

I tried to think back to that school trip but gave in to Google, which revealed that the *Pelican* had been renamed the *Golden Hind* in August of 1578 in honour of Drake's patron, Sir Christopher Hatton, whose family crest was a golden hind.

This was intriguing. Why have two miniatures with banners of the same ship? Were they copies? It wouldn't be unusual since an artist was often asked to paint the same portrait to give to other family members. Regardless, they were stunning and, if authentic, could be quite valuable.

I studied the *Golden Hind* and *Pelican* banners again. In the corner, barely visible, was a red dot. In fact it was a tiny poppy.

My heart began to beat a little faster. Isaac Oliver and Nicholas Hilliard – Queen Elizabeth I's court painters – were the two best-known artists of portraits in the sixteenth and early seventeenth centuries but there was another, the Dutch painter Svetlana Winkler, who signed her work with a poppy. *Anything* by Winkler was rare. The only way to be certain was to take the miniatures to my showroom, remove the backs and have a proper look under my microscope.

The door opened and Violet appeared with an armful of leather binders.

'Here are Lavender's ledgers,' she said. 'Why don't you take these with you and tally up the total? Lavender was very meticulous. You'll see what she paid for them – oh, I see you've found Charlotte's doll's house.'

'Yes,' I smiled. 'I love it.'

'Her ladyship had it specially made for Charlotte's eighth birthday,' said Violet. 'Did you find the doll's house furniture?'

'Yes,' I said. 'I definitely want to take the doll's house and the furniture – and, of course, I'll give you a fair price.'

I gestured to the cigar box marked 'Charlotte's Frozen Charlottes'. 'And I'd like to take those too.'

Violet pulled a face. 'Horrible things.'

I brandished the Drake miniatures. 'What about these?'

Violet set the ledgers down on the bed and took the miniatures over to the window. 'Isn't that Sir Francis Drake?'

'Yes,' I said.

'He was a pirate, you know,' Violet went on. 'He only lived around the corner. I always thought him rather naughty.'

'Do you know where Lavender found them?'

'No.' Violet gave them back to me. 'They'll be listed in one of those ledgers. As I said, my sister was *meticulous* with her record keeping.'

'Lovely,' I said. 'I'll have to come back tomorrow with her ladyship's Defender to collect the doll's house. It's too big for my Golf.'

'I think you'll need more than a Land Rover, dear.' Violet made a wide sweep of the bedroom. 'You'll need a lorry.'

'I need to talk to you about all these boxes,' I said. 'I think a house clearance—'

'Take the ledgers home,' Violet cut in. 'I'm sure we can settle on a figure. Perhaps five hundred pounds?'

'I'll take a look,' I said firmly.

Violet drifted over to the mantelpiece. 'Oh, how young we were,' she said wistfully and picked up the photograph of the foursome. The postcards fluttered to the floor again.

I darted forward to pick them up. 'Postcards from Charlie,' I said. 'It seems that he was very close to his aunt.'

Violet scowled. 'Close?' she spat. 'He didn't even come to her funeral!'

'One was sent just six weeks ago,' I said. 'I wondered what it was doing in your sister's bedroom. Do you think he might have come back without telling you?'

Violet shrugged.

'Wouldn't he have wanted to see you?' I persisted. It was very odd. How did the postcard get into Lavender's bedroom if he hadn't come to visit?

'The last time I saw my nephew was the night before the beating of the bounds,' she said. 'I caught him emptying out my petty cash tin. Then he dashed upstairs to use the toilet. Lavender was very upset.'

'He stole *money* from you?' I was appalled.

Violet scowled again. 'No. He just wanted the cash tin. He promised he'd replace it but, of course, he never did.'

'Miss Green!' came a shout from downstairs. 'Luxtons are here to pick up those oak benches.'

'Good,' Violet said and left me to carry what I could. I popped the miniatures and the cigar box of Frozen Charlottes into my tote bag, then, realising I couldn't carry the box of doll's house furniture and the ledgers at the same time, decided to take the ledgers home and return for the doll's house stuff tomorrow.

I navigated the steep staircase, swept through the kitchen and stepped outside into the sunshine.

Chapter Seven

A white Transit van was parked in the alley. Although it displayed the Luxtons logo – the letter L suspended from a gold coronet – it wasn't one of their regular vans in a classy shade of hunter green.

Violet's oak benches had been moved to one side so that the van could reverse in. The rear doors were open and I could see other furniture inside – an oak gate-leg table and two oak chests.

I could hear BBC Radio Devon playing in the background. Cliff Richard was telling everyone they were going on a summer holiday.

Ronnie – wearing the Luxtons' hunter-green overall – appeared with an armful of padded removal blankets. I immediately felt reassured. I knew him well from the saleroom. In his late twenties, Ronnie never said much. He wore his sandy hair in a neat parting on one side and was of stocky build with huge biceps and hands like hams. His eyes were so small they made him seem mean, although he was always nice to me.

Ronnie gave a nod of greeting before dumping the blankets in the space between the wall and the van, blocking my exit.

Another man emerged from the rear of the van who I hadn't seen before. I guessed he was in his mid-sixties. He wore a checked flat cap, jeans and an orange polo shirt that had the word 'Sunday' embroidered on the top pocket. He gave me a broad smile and extended a hand in greeting. 'Gavin, at your service. And I know who you are – Kat Stanford. Yeah? *Fakes & Treasures.*'

'That was a while ago now,' I said and smiled back. It was hard not to. He reminded me of a London black cab driver – chatty, friendly, but at the same time couldn't really care less.

I asked if he worked at Luxtons but he said he was helping Ronnie out because it was a Sunday and he'd much rather be working on his allotment. Out of the corner of my eye, I could see that Ronnie was getting agitated. He'd started to move one of the benches by himself, pushing it along the hard-packed mud towards the rear of the van. Gavin launched into a conversation about the weather and the possibility that Devon was going to get a hosepipe ban. Ronnie attempted to lift the end of the bench into the van on his own.

'I think Ronnie wants to go,' I said, thinking, so did I, but it was hard to get a word in edgeways as Gavin started to talk about his upcoming holiday to Portugal.

'Don't move it by yourself, you stupid boy!' shrieked Violet as she brought out three more leather binders that were presumably for me.

Gavin doffed his cap. I noticed he had incredibly long fingers, almost as if he were a pianist. 'Oops. Don't shout at poor Ronnie, luv,' he said cheerfully. 'It's my fault.' He sprang to help Ronnie manhandle the oak benches into the van under Violet's watchful eye.

'Don't forget the furniture blanket,' Violet said. 'That furniture is Charles II! They're extremely valuable. I don't want them getting scratched.'

Gavin waved a hand of acknowledgement but it was Ronnie who sorted out the blankets.

'Do you need a hand with those books?' Gavin offered gallantly. 'They look heavy. Where's your car?'

'I'm parked in the church car park,' I said. 'But I can manage.'

'Perhaps you can help her tomorrow?' Violet chimed in. 'She's going to be clearing out my sister's room – apart from the furniture, of course. Sir Monty is in charge of that.'

'No, please don't worry,' I said quickly. 'I'm already sorted for tomorrow.' Which was a lie but the thought of all Lavender's boxes being loaded up in this van and dumped at the gatehouse just filled me with horror.

'Where do you live, luv?' said Gavin.

'I'm fine, honestly,' I protested.

'Honeychurch Hall,' said Violet.

'Honeychurch Hall, eh?' Gavin looked to Ronnie who

looked unhappier by the minute. 'Wasn't that where that body was found? It's all over the news.'

As if on cue, Cliff Richard's summer holiday was abruptly cut short with a news bulletin. 'The body of the man who was discovered earlier today on the Honeychurch Hall estate in Little Dipperton has been identified as Charlie Green. We'll keep you updated as more information comes in. And now, let's hear it from Rod Stewart who asks us if we think he's sexy.'

'Well, really,' Violet grumbled. 'Now we'll have the press flocking to the village! This would never have happened when Detective Inspector Cropper lived here. There would be none of this nonsense!'

Gavin raised an eyebrow.

'We have a new policeman,' I said by way of explanation. I had a sudden thought. 'I assume you will be taking the benches to Luxtons' warehouse?'

'I'm just following orders— Hey! Ronnie!' Gavin called out.

Ronnie's face peered out from the rear of the van.

'Where are we taking the stuff? Newton Abbot warehouse, right?'

'Warehouse,' he grunted and disappeared from view again.

Violet turned to me. 'Now don't forget,' she said. 'My sister made *meticulous* records of her stock. It's all in there. I think those Drake portraits might be worth something. When you come back tomorrow, don't forget to bring your chequebook.'

Finally, I managed to escape. I only got halfway across the churchyard when my heart sank. Sir Monty was striding towards me and what was worse, he'd seen me coming. I attempted to forget the image of Delia Evans adjusting her underwear just a few hours earlier.

'Saw your car in the car park.' He fixed me with a glare through his monocle. Like most English country gentleman, he sported the usual green tweed jacket with leather elbow patches, moleskin trousers and a flat cap. He had to be sweltering. 'Couldn't park anywhere,' he went on. 'Just popping in to see Violet Green.'

'Yes, she told me that you were helping her sell her furniture,' I said pointedly. If he knew I knew, then hopefully whatever he was up to would make him think twice. 'That's very kind of you.'

Sir Monty gave a dismissive wave. 'Frightful business about that chap being found in your woods. Frightful. Heard it on the radio! Do they know who did it? Iris must be terrified!'

I thought of how gleeful my mother had been at the prospect of Eric being found guilty. Terrified, she wasn't.

'She's fine,' I said.

Sir Monty shook his head. 'I don't like her being alone there. Don't like it at all.'

'That's so sweet of you to be concerned.' I forced a smile. 'And poor Delia is all alone, too.'

Sir Monty reddened. 'Excuse me?'

'Delia Evans,' I said. 'My mother's best friend.'

'We're all alone really, aren't we?' Sir Monty said, neatly

avoiding my question. 'And you are even more isolated than your mother. Don't you get nervous living all the way up at Jane's Cottage with a killer on the loose?'

'I don't think we have a killer in our midst,' I said.

Sir Monty nodded. 'You're right. I heard it was something to do with a gambling debt.'

'*Gambling?*' This was news to me. 'Where did you hear that?'

Sir Monty looked startled. 'I thought . . . doesn't everyone know—?' He pulled a handkerchief from his top pocket and wiped his brow. 'My housekeeper's son works in the Winning Post restaurant at the racetrack and heard it from someone—'

I jumped in. 'You go to Newton Abbot racetrack. My mother told me. You *must* have known Charlie Green.'

'No. No. I didn't know him,' he blustered. 'Never met him. Not sure why you would think that – excuse me.'

And with that extraordinary denial, he stepped off the path and onto the grass and scurried away. I made a mental note to mention the Winning Post restaurant and racetrack connection to Mallory. What's more, it made the location of Charlie's body in Honeywell Wood even more mysterious.

I reached my Golf and was further irritated at just how close to my car Sir Monty had parked his Rolls-Royce. Since the passenger side was against a wall, I had to climb in through the hatchback. It was then that I realised I'd forgotten to pick up a map from the community shop for my mother. I would have to pick one up tomorrow. For now, I had a long evening ahead going through Lavender's ledgers.

Happily, the shepherd's hut on the flatbed lorry had been moved from the lane but, as I drew closer to Honeychurch Hall, my heart sank for the second time.

Eric's red Massey Ferguson and a trailer were parked across the entrance blocking access to the drive. In front of that was a black Escalade with tinted windows. Emblazoned on the side was 'Western Times' in silver lettering. Violet was right. The press had begun to flock.

A man and a woman got out of the car. I recognised twenty-something Ginny Riley straight away. I hadn't seen her for over a year. Ginny was dressed in a smart sleeveless shift dress and heels. She had cut her hair and wore it in a sleek brown jaw-length bob. In fact, everything about her was sleek.

It hadn't been that long ago when I'd regarded Ginny as a younger sister. Then, she had been a fresh-faced and eager trainee reporter with the *Dipperton Deal* with big dreams. Even when she'd narrowly escaped death on Dartmoor it hadn't put her off her chosen vocation and one she would definitely succeed in. I noticed her byline was now Senior Reporter and I often saw her name in the national tabloids where she was a regular stringer.

Ginny waved. 'Long time no see.' Turning to her older colleague who was sporting designer stubble and wearing a leather jacket and jeans, she introduced us. 'This is who I was telling you about, Troy. Kat, meet Troy Barnes, my partner in crime.' She gestured to Eric's tractor and added, 'Looks like Eric is holding back the hordes. He left another trailer blocking the tradesmen's entrance as well.

But you know me. We'll find out what happened one way or another.'

'Bad news travels fast,' I said for the second time that day.

'Yeah,' she grinned. 'We got a tip, but frankly, with news bulletins every half an hour how can anyone miss it? Bet the Honeychurch lot are freaking out!'

'I don't think anyone is particularly thrilled,' I said drily.

'Shawn would have kept it under wraps,' said Ginny. 'But you have a new sheriff in town – the gorgeous Detective Inspector Greg Mallory.'

'You know him?' I said.

'You could say that.' Ginny gave a sly grin. 'I should watch out for him if I were you. He was a big shot in Plymouth. Always did things strictly by the book. I heard talk of an affair with the wrong woman and that's why he got transferred. A cop with an axe to grind isn't going to turn a blind eye.'

I had wondered why Mallory had transferred to Little Dipperton. Hopefully this meant that his transfer would be temporary.

'So let's have a comment from Kat Stanford.' She thrust her iPhone – switched to record – under my nose but I gently batted it away. 'How does it feel knowing that someone was murdered in your backyard?'

'No comment,' I said.

'Where was the body found? Near your place? The sunken garden? What about the walled garden?' Ginny persisted. 'I can see the headline now. Celebrity Kat Stanford caught up in the cold case of the century – if it *is* a cold case?'

'No comment,' I said again.

'Charlie used to run his aunts ragged. Went through the family fortune – tin, I think it was, or maybe slate? I can't remember. Anyway, he left the old ladies destitute but Lavender – the one who died earlier this year – doted on him. I know this because my mum told me. Thing is, Charlie never showed up for the funeral. So you see, my theory is that he must have been killed all those years ago and never went to Dublin at all.'

'That's quite some theory,' I said mildly, having wondered the exact same thing.

'Apparently Charlie Green was last seen seven years ago, the night before the beating of the bounds,' said Ginny.

'The beating of the what?' Troy said with a laugh.

'It's a local tradition for the villagers to walk the boundary of the Honeychurch Hall estate—'

'It's the parish boundary actually,' I said.

'Takes all damn day,' said Ginny. 'There's a treasure hunt. Charlie and Eric used to make up the clues. And get this, lunch is served at Gibbet Cross.'

'Gibbet what?'

'He's a townie.' Ginny rolled her eyes. 'Gibbet Cross is on the north boundary close to Moreleigh Mount. Back in the day, one of the earls was the Justice of the Peace and used to string up the poachers. Maybe that's where that family got a taste for delivering their own sense of justice. That's the thing. That lot have always believed they're above the law. Right, Kat?'

'Stop this, Ginny—'

'I mean, let's face it,' Ginny plunged on, 'all the evidence points to Charlie's death being down to one of them.'

'Them?' Troy said.

'The bloody Honeychurch lot,' Ginny said exasperated. 'They close ranks whenever there's the slightest whiff of a scandal.'

'Like the royal family, you mean,' Troy said with a sneer.

'You can't dis the Royals in front of Kat,' Ginny teased. 'She's a diehard monarchist.'

I didn't bother to answer. Of course, I knew exactly what Ginny meant. At one time she had planned on doing a series of exposés about the Honeychurch family. The problem was, she was right. They did manage to put a lid on any scandal; that is, they *could* when Shawn was around.

Ginny snapped her fingers. 'Eric! I bet he's got something to do with it. He'd throw himself under a train to protect Lord bloody Rupert.'

'Eric was in shock. He was distraught,' I protested and immediately realised what I'd done.

'So *Eric* found the body?' Ginny was triumphant. 'Thanks, Kat. That's very helpful.' She gave Troy a nod. 'Did you get all that?'

To my annoyance, Troy showed me his mobile. 'Yep. Every word.'

Ginny thought for a moment. 'How is the old bag Violet taking the news? I can't believe she's still in business. Don't you remember how much we hated her tea?'

I suppressed a smile as I remembered the very first time

we'd met there for tea. Ginny spat it out and we laughed so hard that we had to make a hasty exit. Sometimes I missed the old Ginny.

'Let's go there now,' said Troy. 'We're not getting anywhere here and I could do with a cup of tea, even if it's a bad one.' He got back into the Escalade but Ginny took my arm and pulled me into a brief hug.

'Don't hate me,' she said lightly. 'I'm just doing my job.'

I relented a little bit. 'And one you are very good at.'

She stepped back and to my surprise her eyes were full of concern. 'Just be careful,' she said. 'I know I said I thought the family had something to do with this but the truth is, I don't think they do. Call it my reporter instinct. Something isn't right.'

Troy beeped the horn.

'We must have a drink sometime,' she said and I believed she meant it.

The Escalade drove away. I retrieved my tote bag and the ledgers from the Golf and let myself into the gatehouse, dumping them on the desk before dashing to turn off the alarm.

Ginny's visit had unsettled me. I felt a shudder of foreboding. Why had she warned me to be careful? What did she know? If the new detective was going to do everything by the book, then I had an awful feeling that there could be more skeletons tumbling out of the closet at Honeychurch Hall.

Chapter Eight

Back in my showroom-cum-office, I opened the three bay windows that looked out over the drive. I didn't have air conditioning and of course, with all my stock, I would never risk leaving a window open.

With a gabled ceiling and standing one and a half storeys high, the eighteenth-century gatehouse was light and airy. A pleasant breeze soon began to circulate.

I headed straight for the galley kitchen to pour myself a glass of Peggy Cropper's homemade elderflower cordial and topped it up with Perrier. A quick peep in the fridge reassured me that I had lots of healthy snacks – celery sticks, carrots and fruit – to keep me going, although I now wished that I'd not left the banana bread at my mother's. It had turned out quite well!

I cleared a space on my desk and set out my tools – my exam light, my hands-free magnifier OptiVisor headband, a Rumold stainless steel ruler and a pair of tweezers. Much went into the process of identifying whether a painting was authentic or fake. I always started with these four elements – the frame, the technique, the sitter and the signature.

Within minutes I knew my initial reaction had been right. Although the frames looked identical, the ruler revealed that there was just one and a half millimetres difference in size. When I looked at the miniatures, they fitted the frames exactly, confirming that these were handmade specifically for these paintings. I removed the frames to inspect the back. The artist had painted the portraits on vellum that was stuck to a playing card, the normal backing for that period. So far, so good.

Next, I looked at the painting technique.

Copies – even good ones – tended to appear flat. Yet these had richness and depth – not exactly three-dimensional, but something I liked to call the artist's essence painted onto the canvas. This was something ethereal and impossible to replicate – rather like trying to paint Peter Pan's shadow.

I examined the details through my OptiVisor. I was getting excited. The artist had painted Drake's wart on the tip of his nose – this was a detail that had only come to light in the last few years and was not often captured in the hundreds, if not thousands, of portraits that existed of Sir Francis Drake.

I then turned to Winkler's trademark signature – the poppy. It was miniscule and yet, thanks to my OptiVisor, I could clearly see the four red, crepe-like petals and stigma.

Yes, I was sure of it. These two Drake miniatures were authentic.

I grabbed my laptop and googled Svetlana Winkler and learned she was born in 1565 and died in 1617.

Winkler sounded like a fascinating woman. She was fiercely independent and never married. She travelled extensively, especially to Africa and the Middle East. It was rumoured that she'd even painted Shah Abbas who ruled Persia, although none of that work has ever been recovered. Winkler was often shunned in female society since her beauty made her a constant threat to other women, but she didn't care. She was definitely a woman ahead of her time. The profile went on to explain the significance of her unusual signature with some historians claiming that she was no stranger to opium.

And then I did a double take.

Although her last miniature had sold for seventy-five thousand pounds twenty-five years ago, it was the Drake Six miniatures – six miniature paintings of Drake holding a scroll bearing the name of each of his favourite ships – that had brought her recognition at the court of Queen Elizabeth I.

I was stunned. In my hand I held the *Pelican* and the *Golden Hind* and yet Google also named the *Judith*, *Pasha*, *Swan* and *Marigold*.

Where were the other four miniatures? And how did two end up stuck to the wall of a doll's house in a tearoom in Little Dipperton?

I had to think. Boot sale enthusiasts dream of such a discovery and since Lavender recorded everything that she bought and sold, the miniature portraits must be logged in one of the eight ledgers.

I picked up the first one.

Time just flew by as I painstakingly toiled through Lavender's ledgers. Violet was right. Her sister was incredibly neat. She often made little pencil sketches to accompany an item along with the measurements. The Frozen Charlottes were noted – property of Charlotte Green, valued at £150 – and Charlotte's doll's house, 'Gift from Lady Edith Honeychurch. Not For Sale'. As I turned the final page on the last ledger there was no mention of the Drake miniatures. It was really odd.

The only explanation I could come up with was that these had been part of the fake robbery that Edith's husband had engineered in June of 1990 to avoid crippling inheritance tax. Some of the villagers – specifically the Croppers – were in on it and had hidden items from the insurance investigator. Fortunately, David had had access to the case and given me a copy of the list of 'stolen' items. I kept it in the safe.

I reassembled the miniatures, found two velvet pouches and popped a miniature into each. I took David's list out of the safe, and put the miniatures inside.

Back at my desk, I went through the list item by item. The Drake Six weren't recorded on there either. Next, I logged on to the Art Loss Register thinking they could have been stolen, but drew a blank there too. I was at a loss.

I'd have to talk to Edith in the morning. Perhaps she knew something about them; after all Rose Cottage belonged to the Honeychurch Hall estate. It was worth a try.

It was seven thirty and I was ready to go home. I decided to take the ledgers back to Jane's just in case I had missed something. But just as I returned from cleaning up the galley kitchen, I was startled. A pretty woman in her twenties was standing in the middle of my showroom. Dressed in cream capri trousers, a Breton striped top and navy ballet flats, she wore her dark brown hair swept off her face in a high ponytail.

'Can I help you?' I said.

'Oh, I'm sorry!' she exclaimed. 'I didn't mean to make you jump.' The woman extended her hand. 'I'm Wren Fraser and you must be Kat Stanford. You used to be on the telly.'

I immediately went on guard. She had to be another reporter.

'I asked for directions at the community shop and was told that you lived here.' Wren flashed a smile and seemed nervous. 'I couldn't believe the shop was still open. It's crazy. They sell everything,' she gabbled on. 'I picked up a few things, too, since I doubt if there is food laid on in the shepherd's hut.'

I regarded her with surprise. 'The shepherd's hut?'

'Oh yes. I'm so excited! I've rented it.'

That was quick! I'd only seen it myself a few hours ago.

'I'm a writer, you see, and I'm on a deadline,' Wren continued. 'I always shut myself away when I'm finishing a book.'

I thought of my mother and the frantic last weeks to make her deadline when she rarely emerged from her writing house at all. 'Yes, I hear that's what writers tend to do,' I said. 'Perhaps we should call and make sure everything is ready for you? And find out where they've put the shepherd's hut. The estate is very large.'

'That would be so kind,' Wren gushed. 'Thank you. I hope they won't be cross. I was expected hours ago.'

I picked up my mobile and dialled the Hall. 'I hope you haven't driven too far.'

'London,' she declared. 'Shepherd's Bush.'

I could feel her watching me whilst I waited for what seemed like ages for someone to pick up the rotary dial telephone. Edith didn't believe in answering machines. She maintained that if something were important enough, whoever it was would keep on trying.

'Can I use your loo?' Wren said suddenly. 'I'm desperate.'

I pointed to the archway that led through to the galley kitchen. 'The door is on the left.'

Finally, Rupert answered. I explained that their guest had arrived and asked where she should go, to which there were a lot of grumbles that included 'ridiculous idea', 'police everywhere' and 'walled garden'.

Wren returned clutching a handful of toilet paper. She was dabbing her nose. 'Allergies,' she said. 'I'm just not used to all the pollen.'

'Oh dear,' I said. 'I'm afraid the shepherd's hut is in the Victorian walled garden. There is going to be a lot of pollen about. Will you be all right?'

'I've got my inhaler,' she said. 'Where is the walled garden? It sounds lovely!'

'If you wait a moment, I can show you. I'm going that way. I just have to lock up.'

'I'll help you,' said Wren. 'I take it you want all the windows closed, yes?'

I felt I had to tell her about Charlie Green. In fact, I was surprised that she hadn't mentioned it to me, especially since she'd stopped in the village where there would have been talk of nothing else.

I took the plunge. 'I'm assuming you listened to the radio on your drive down so you know that a body was found on the estate.'

'Yes. Very sad,' she said. 'I thought about changing my mind but the couple who run the community shop told me it happened years ago and not to worry. Some family feud or something.' She cocked her head. '*Should* I be worried?'

Family feud? I regarded her bright-eyed enthusiasm. 'Well, I live on the estate and I'm not worried.'

'Good,' Wren declared. 'Then I shan't be either.'

I set the alarm, picked up the ledgers and my tote bag, and we walked to our cars. I was glad to see that Eric had moved his tractor and trailer although I hadn't heard him do it.

Wren pointed to the stone hawk that topped each granite pillar. 'It's so grand here.'

'Honeychurch Hall can be traced back to the 1400s,' I said. 'The title of the Earl of Grenville was created by Henry V and has been passed down the male line ever since. Lord Rupert Honeychurch is the fifteenth Earl.'

'Wow! It's just the sort of place I write about,' she enthused. 'Upstairs and downstairs.'

'What kind of books do you write?'

'Love stories,' Wren said. 'But not under my name and don't ask me to tell you what that is.' She gave a mischievous grin. 'My parents would be disgusted if they knew!'

I remembered how embarrassed I'd felt when I read one of my mother's novels for the first time. 'Ah. The bodice-ripper type.'

'They used to call them penny dreadfuls in the old days.' Wren hesitated for a moment before adding, 'You could say that I write like Krystalle Storm. Have you read anything of hers?'

'Yes,' I said all innocence. 'You must have seen her books for sale in the community shop.'

Wren nodded. 'Actually, the woman behind the counter even asked if I *was* Krystalle Storm!'

I raised an eyebrow. 'And are you?'

She laughed. 'I'm afraid I can't tell you otherwise the world's best-kept secret would be out.'

'It certainly would,' I said drily.

For a start, Krystalle Storm, aka my mother, was at least forty-five years older than Wren Fraser, but if she wanted to play let's pretend, that was fine by me. I thought Mum would find it hilarious.

Wren pointed to a dusty navy-blue Honda CR-V that she'd parked bumper-to-bumper behind mine. I noticed a child seat and a dog gate in the back.

'You should have brought your dog with you,' I said. 'There are some beautiful walks around here.'

'Oh, that's not my car,' Wren said hastily. 'It belongs to my sister. Mine is being repaired.' She smiled again. 'I'll follow you! I can't wait to see my little writing house.'

Chapter Nine

I turned into the tradesmen's entrance and took the pot-holed service road very slowly, mainly to save the shock absorbers on my own car. Wren was lucky to have an SUV.

Flanked by dense laurel, one side bore evidence of the flatbed lorry's attempt to navigate the narrow drive with its wide load. There was a continuous line of broken foliage that littered the ground with sticks and leaves. The drive curved and at one bend an old stone gatepost had been reduced to a pile of rubble.

We passed the entrance to Mum's Carriage House on my left and Eric's scrapyard – thankfully hidden from sight behind another thick laurel hedge – on my right.

Ten minutes later the terrace of three stone cottages came into view. I thought they looked particularly pretty this evening with their window boxes full of red geraniums. Next to them, another set of granite pillars topped with hawks flanked the open wooden gates that were bleached silver grey with age.

I pulled up behind a pale green Fiat 500 that displayed the logo 'Pansy's Jamborees'. It was then that I spotted the crime scene tape across the latch gate on the opposite side of the lane, which barred entrance to Honeywell Wood. A large blue road sign said 'Police! Accident!' It was a chilling reminder of what had been discovered within.

Wren joined me. 'Is that where the body was found? I didn't . . . I didn't realise it was so close!'

Although I didn't know the exact location of the body, I tried to reassure her. 'The woods are quite large,' I said. 'There is a footpath that runs from here to the Carriage House. But don't worry. You have neighbours.' I gestured to the cottages.

'Oh, phew,' said Wren. 'I was a little bit worried for a minute. Do they work here?'

'Peggy Cropper is the cook, Delia Evans is the housekeeper and Eric is a sort of a jack-of-all-trades and owns the scrapyard.'

'Hello! Hello! You made it!' trilled Lady Lavinia as she strode through the gates. Dressed in her usual attire of jodhpurs and faded polo shirt, Lavinia had discarded her heavy hairnet and allowed her long blonde hair to flow. I also noticed a smudge of bright red lipstick.

'Welcome, welcome!' Lavinia thrust out her hand in greeting. 'You are our very first guest! I hope you aren't going to be put off by the murder,' she went on cheerfully. 'Let me help you with your luggage.'

'I can do it.' Wren returned to her Honda to retrieve a

small suitcase, a satchel – that presumably held her laptop – and a paper carrier bag of groceries.

Lavinia sprang forward. 'Can I help you carry something?'

'Thank you, but I can manage, your ladyship,' she said.

'Oh, just call me Lav,' said Lavinia. 'Everyone else does. Is this all you have? What about your laptop?' Lavinia caught my eye. 'Did Wren tell you she is a famous writer?'

'She did,' I said.

'We only got the shepherd's hut set up properly about an hour ago.' Lavinia was expiring with excitement. 'But there is a shower. I expect you must be frightfully hot after your long journey.'

'I hope there is electricity,' I said.

'Oh yes,' Lavinia said. 'There's a leisure generator. Pansy's sorted out everything—Paaaaaan!' she shrieked.

A young woman with red hair held back by a colourful yellow bandana and wearing dungarees stepped into view. She was tall and thin and spoke with the same strangled vowels of the upper classes as Lavinia.

'This is my friend Pansy, or should I say, Lady Pansy Forbes-Mathers. She lives at Huntsham Place,' Lavinia burbled on. 'They have heaps of shepherd's huts to rent there. She's a whiz on Airbnb and is building our website. Pan, this is our first guest – oh, and this is Kat Stanford.'

Pansy beamed and shook hands with Wren who gave a squeak of pain. When Pansy took mine I knew why. It was like having my hand squeezed in a vice.

'And as I said to Lav,' said Pansy, gesturing to the crime scene tape, 'there's no such thing as bad publicity!'

'I'll say,' Lavinia said, nodding. 'Come on. Let's go.'

I followed the trio into the overgrown garden. There were two main central paths within the ivy-clad walls. One ran north to south, the other east to west. A wide border bounded a perimeter path that divided the old garden into four equal sections. On one side ranged glasshouses in varying states of decay. Rows of empty slatted shelves and broken clay pots were visible through the cracked panes. Behind the glasshouses and hugging the boundary wall stood abandoned hothouse furnaces, potting sheds, tool rooms and a hen house. In the far corner, steps led down to a beehive-shaped building partially below ground.

I watched Wren as she gingerly picked her way through the weeds, pausing every few moments to sneeze or swat a fly.

At first I couldn't see the shepherd's hut, although deep wheel tracks left marks through the stinging nettles, ragwort and thistles to indicate that it had passed this way.

Lavinia and Pansy pointed to a fence of hazel-woven panels about twelve feet tall where the top of a green bow-topped roof and flue could just be seen.

Lavinia and Pansy waited for us to catch up. 'It's behind here. *Frightfully* private.'

Wren's face fell, her disappointment plain. 'Oh dear. It's a bit um . . . well . . . wild.'

'Today yes,' Pansy said with gusto. 'But we'll be landscaping next month. Get the digger in.'

Lavinia looked worried. 'We weren't expecting anyone so soon. But when you're behind the fence it's *frightfully* cosy. Just you see.'

We stepped around the panel.

The shepherd's hut was surrounded by a flattened mess of what would have been the remains of the vegetable garden as well as a wire cage for raspberry canes, but despite everything, it was utterly charming.

Pansy explained how the lighting worked and that the water hose was connected to the water supply in the glasshouse.

'Unfortunately you'll have to use the old icehouse for your fridge.' Lavinia winked at Pansy who sniggered.

Wren looked blank. 'I don't follow.'

Lavinia grinned. 'It's the little beehive building over in the corner. It was used in the old days to make ice.'

'Oh, don't be cruel, Lav,' laughed Pansy. 'You're frightening her. Don't worry, you've got a proper fridge.'

Wooden steps led up to a stable half-door that opened into the living space. There was a small wood-burner, a tiny cooker and stone sink. A two-seater sofa in a cheerful yellow print stood opposite a small fold-out table and two chairs. At the end, spanning the width of the hut, was a raised bed framed with carved wood and painted with primroses and violets.

'It's lovely!' I said. And it was.

Wren frowned. 'But where is the bathroom?'

'Just you wait!' Lavinia was thrilled. 'Let me show you the shower.' We trooped around the side of the hut to a space in the rear that was just feet away from the boundary wall. Pansy had rigged up a shower with hessian matting that had been put directly onto the hard-packed mud. There was no drainage.

'You'll have heaps of hot water,' gushed Lavinia. 'Pan has thought of everything.'

Wren did not look impressed. 'But where's the loo?'

'Ah. Slight snag but it's okay. I promise.' Lavinia pointed vaguely in the direction of the potting shed. 'You'll have to use the old gardener's loo.'

'We're going to build a compost loo,' Pansy chimed in as if this would be any consolation to Wren's current situation.

Wren pulled a face. 'Oh.'

'You sort of caught us on the hop,' said Lavinia desperately. 'I do hope you haven't changed your mind.'

There was a silence as we all held our breath. Wren looked around. She went back inside the shepherd's hut. After another minute or two, she reappeared and smiled. 'Well. All I can say is thank heavens I brought lots of wine.'

Lavinia clapped her hands. 'Oh, hurrah!'

'Hello?' came a cry. Delia popped her head around the corner of the panel. 'I come bearing gifts!' She was carrying a basket filled with goodies. I spied freshly baked bread, homemade blackcurrant jam, Sharpham Brie, a box of Cornish Smugglers breakfast tea and a pint of milk. 'That should keep you going until the morning.'

'Lovely,' said Wren.

'Wren is a famous writer, Delia,' Lavinia declared.

Delia smirked. 'Yes, and I know who. It's all over the village but don't worry, we're very discreet here.'

I heard a snort of disdain and realised that it was actually coming from me. 'Excuse me,' I said. 'It was lovely to meet you, Wren – and you too, Pansy. I'm sure I'll see you again soon.'

'Oh, definitely,' Wren said. 'We must have a glass of vino one evening.'

I left everyone to it, but Delia thrust the basket at Lavinia and hurried after me. 'Kat! I must ask you something.'

We made our way back to the gate. Delia had to dance around the stinging nettles to avoid her bare legs getting stung. Now I was seeing her close up, she had definitely lost weight. Not only that, Delia was positively glowing in her sleeveless summer dress. Usually Delia wore shapeless baggy clothes. I knew that her hair was a wig, but even that seemed shinier than usual. But most of all, she was extremely friendly towards me, even praising my pots of hydrangeas at Jane's Cottage and asking my advice on window boxes – both of which I knew nothing about.

'And what do you think of the writer?' she asked.

'Wren? She seems nice.'

'It was all so last minute,' Delia went on. 'Her ladyship got a phone call and even though she wanted to turn her down, *Wren* insisted.' Delia emphasised the name Wren. 'She's nothing like her photo, is she?' Seeing my confusion she plunged on. 'Krystalle Storm!'

I tried not to laugh. 'I don't think for a moment that Wren Fraser is Krystalle Storm. For one thing, she's far too young.'

Delia thrust out her jaw. 'Well, we all know what lengths celebrities go to if they want to fly under the radar. Mark my words. It's her. Everyone in the village says so.'

We'd reached my Golf. Delia deftly stepped in front of the driver's door preventing me from leaving. I was immediately hit by the distinctive smell of Reine de Nuit. It seemed that Sir Monty had even bought Delia the same perfume as he had bought my mother!

'You smell nice,' I said pointedly. 'Isn't that Reine de Nuit?'

Delia flushed pink. 'My son . . . my Guy bought it for my birthday.'

'Guy did. How generous. It's so expensive,' I said.

I waited for the inevitable snippy comment that Delia always managed to throw in ever since Guy and I had broken up, but all she said was, 'I'm trying to get hold of Iris.'

'As far as I know, she should be home,' I said.

'I wondered if she was upset with me,' Delia said slyly. 'Not that I've done anything for her to be upset with me for.'

Only sleep with her boyfriend, I wanted to say but didn't. It was none of my business.

'Have you tried to call her?'

Delia nodded. 'And I went over this afternoon and her car wasn't there. The new detective has put a mobile police unit in her courtyard. I couldn't believe it. I am to report there tomorrow morning. I mean, what do I know about this Charlie Green's death? And then I went back to the Carriage House an hour ago and Iris still wasn't there.'

'Perhaps she's gone out with Sir Monty?' I said.

A flush crept up Delia's neck. 'Oh. Is she still seeing him? I thought . . . that they weren't getting along.'

'Really?' I said. 'Whatever gave you that idea?' I flashed her a smile. '*If* she comes home tonight and *if* I see her, I'll tell her that her *best* friend is looking for her.'

Delia's flushed deepened. 'But . . . why wouldn't Iris be coming home tonight?'

I shrugged. 'I'm sure she's told you what Sir Monty is like. Maybe he's decided to whisk her off to Paris for a surprise weekend.'

Delia looked as if she was going to be sick.

Suddenly I felt awful. What a horrible thing to say especially as I knew it wouldn't be true. 'Is everything all right?'

'Oh yes. Fine. Fine.' Delia looked over to the police cordon tape across the entrance to Honeywell Wood. It occurred to me that she lived alone and perhaps she was a little nervous.

'Are you okay staying at the cottage on your own tonight?' I said gently.

'I've got Peggy Cropper on one side – not that she'd be much use in a crisis – and Eric on the other. That is, if he isn't arrested.'

'Arrested?' I said sharply.

Delia cast a look over my shoulder as if to make sure no one was listening. 'Clive told me that they're searching Eric's scrapyard tomorrow with that old police dog Fluffy. Who calls a police dog Fluffy? It should be something like . . . Bullet or Killer.'

'Is it about the missing motorbike?' I asked.

Delia nodded. 'When I was in the village this afternoon, Doreen Mutters said that Charlie used to have a lot of motorbikes. He restored them as well. So it stands to reason that he would have ridden his motorbike to Honeychurch Hall and if he rode it there . . . where is it now?'

I had thought the exact same thing although there was always the chance that the body had been dumped there, but I wasn't about to share my thoughts with Delia.

'The new detective seems very thorough,' Delia continued. 'I suppose you'll throw yourself at him now that Shawn's gone and left you.'

I was wrong. Delia hadn't changed towards me at all. I swallowed the insult. 'I just might do that.' It was meant as a joke but I could see Delia had taken it literally.

'I don't blame you,' she said. 'Pity things didn't work out between you and Shawn. But never mind. My mother used to say, "There's plenty more fish in the sea, Delia." And you know what I'm going to say—'

'Yes, I think I do,' I said. 'And please don't.'

'You really missed out on my Guy,' she said quickly. 'He's such a catch! So— Ouch!'

Delia gave a cry of pain and sprang away from my car door. 'That was my foot!'

'Oh! I am so sorry.' Although it had been deliberate I had forgotten that Delia was wearing open-toed sandals, but it had done the trick.

I got into my car and drove home.

As I crested the brow of the hill that dead-ended at

Jane's Cottage, the answer to Delia's question about my mother's whereabouts lay ahead.

Her red Mini was parked outside my front door.

Chapter Ten

Mum was sitting out on the little terrace. She gave a wave from the wicker two-seater but didn't get up. As I walked over, I noticed an empty glass tumbler and a plate of crumbs. On her lap she held a yellow legal pad that was covered in scribbles.

'What a nice surprise,' I said. 'And I'm glad you've made yourself at home.'

'Hiding the front door key under the flowerpot is hardly rocket science.' Mum gestured to my planters of hydrangeas and window boxes of red geraniums. 'You've made this very pretty, darling. I love the little fairy lights on the fence over there. And the view is just astonishing. It's very *Titanic*.'

'*Titanic?*'

'On top of the world.' Mum smiled. 'You seem settled and happy here.'

'I am,' I said. And I realised that I was.

Jane's Cottage had been built as a summerhouse in the 1800s on the original site of Warren Lodge where – back in the day – the warrener lived to keep an eye on the Honeychurch rabbits. Poaching was a serious crime, as evidenced by the warning signs that still peppered the estate.

The cottage was built from red brick under a pyramidal slate roof with two bay windows that flanked the Venetian entrance and ionic pilasters. A fanlight over a pediment door was the finishing touch. I loved it.

I'd transformed the front area to an outside flagstone terrace with a panel of woven hazel to enclose the east end where I'd hung the fairy lights. The terrace was my favourite place to sit of a summer's evening, enjoying a glass of wine and taking in the beauty of the South Hams. To the north was wild, beautiful Dartmoor with its magnificent tors that were outlined on the horizon; to the west lay Honeychurch Hall, the grounds and woodland surrounding Mum's Carriage House; and to the south stood the gatehouses and, in the distance, the village of Little Dipperton. There was very little to see to the east since the walled garden, stable block and Honeychurch Cottages were hidden by dense woodland along with – thankfully – Eric's scrapyard.

How different my life was now! I thought of bustling London where the view from my bedroom window was the platform at Putney Bridge tube station. My thoughts turned to Shawn and the twins again. London! Giving up all this for that?

'Do you want to stay for supper?' I said. 'It's just salad, new potatoes and cold salmon but I've got enough for two.'

'That would be lovely,' said Mum. 'I'm not keen on going home anytime soon. That new inspector has installed a mobile police unit in my courtyard. I can't get to my writing room undetected.'

'Ah yes. Delia told me about that,' I said.

'I can't possibly work in my writing house until they leave and Mallory' – she made air quotes – '"isn't at liberty to say" how long they are going to be.' Mum gave a heavy sigh. 'Do you mind if I work from here tomorrow?'

'Of course you can. Did you bring the Olivetti?'

'I don't want to lug that typewriter all the way up here,' she said. 'Besides, I'm still developing the story and I like to do that longhand.'

'Shall we go inside?' I suggested.

She stood up. 'I could do with a top-up.'

As we headed indoors, Mum said, 'Clive said that the new inspector is furious about the news bulletins on the radio.'

I was surprised. So they hadn't come from Mallory after all. I told Mum about Ginny Riley staking out the main entrance.

'She knew everything already but wouldn't say who her source was.'

'They never do,' Mum said. 'How was Lavender's junk?'

'Interesting.' I wasn't ready to tell her about the Drake Six until I had spoken to Edith, but I did tell her about Charlotte's doll's house.

'A copy of Honeychurch Hall!' Mum enthused. 'How lovely of her ladyship to do such a thing.'

'It's gorgeous,' I said. 'There is a box of doll's house furniture too. I'm going to borrow Edith's Defender and pick it up tomorrow.'

'Why don't you go and change, dear,' said Mum. 'You look exhausted. I'll meet you in the kitchen.'

Having taken off my make-up and splashed my face with cold water, I threw on a pair of linen trousers and a long-sleeved T-shirt and pulled my hair up into a bun.

When I returned Mum had put the supper together. 'Do you have a tray? I thought we should eat outside by fairy light.'

We fell into a comfortable silence as we ate our supper.

'I just can't understand all the drama. A mobile police unit!' Mum grumbled again. 'It happened years ago so we're off the hook – not that we were ever on it.'

'Well, maybe not,' I said and went on to tell her about the postcards from Ireland that I'd found on Lavender's mantelpiece.

Mum's jaw dropped. 'And you're saying the last one was postmarked *six* weeks ago?'

I nodded. 'I don't know what to make of it either,' I said. 'Violet swore that the last time she'd seen Charlie Green was the night before the beating of the bounds.'

Mum frowned. 'What I find interesting is the connection with the Honeychurch family and Charlie Green's sister, Charlotte.'

I shrugged. 'It's not like living in London, is it? Everyone seems to know everyone around here.'

'Well,' said Mum, 'that inspector will soon flush out the

culprit. He's really got the bit between his teeth. I told him there's no need to go overboard. There are only eight of us on the property – nine counting little Harry, but isn't he still off on that trip with the Totnes Sea Scouts?'

'He'll be home on Friday,' I said. 'But there aren't nine of us. There are ten if you count Wren Fraser.'

'Who on earth is Wren Fraser?'

'I'll tell you all about it,' I said. 'But first let me take these things inside. I'll top up your glass too. You're going to need it.'

'I'm intrigued,' said Mum.

I cleared the table and took the tray back to the kitchen, returning moments later with the wine bottle and a fresh gin and tonic for my mother.

Mum raised an eyebrow. 'So?'

'Wren Fraser is a writer,' I said. 'She writes romance like you. Cheers!' We clinked glasses.

Mum frowned. 'Never heard of her. Does she write under a pseudonym?'

I tried to keep a straight face. 'You could say that.'

'And?' Mum prompted. 'What's the matter with you? Why are you giving me that funny look?'

'Her name is . . .' I gave a dramatic pause. 'She's Krystalle Storm.'

Mum's jaw dropped. Her expression started with amusement then morphed into disbelief and finally, suspicion. 'Does she look like me?'

'If you mean, does she look like the photograph on your website that does not look like you,' I said. 'No. Besides, she's in her twenties. In fairness, she didn't exactly say she *was* you, but she certainly implied it. And, according to Delia, everyone in the village believes that she is.'

Mum gasped. 'Well, I'll be blowed!'

I filled her in on the shepherd's hut and Lavinia's new hospitality business expecting a few derogatory comments but Mum didn't seem to care, not even when I mentioned a holiday rental business and the possibility of hosting weddings.

'But I don't understand. Why would this Wren person say that?' Her frown deepened. 'And you say she's renting the shepherd's hut that literally just arrived this *afternoon*?'

'It was all very last minute,' I said. 'It's very charming. I was really impressed. It has all the mod cons – lights, a little cooker and a fridge, all run off a leisure generator. There's a shower and hot water. Times have changed since you were a girl.'

I waited for the usual rush of nostalgic memories about my mother's childhood when she lived in a gypsy caravan and toured the country with Bushman's Travelling Fair and Boxing Emporium.

There were none. Just a long silence until Mum said, 'Delia never mentioned anything about a shepherd's hut coming to the Hall.'

'Ah. I want to talk to you about Delia,' I said.

Mum dismissed my request with a flap of her hand. 'I can't think about Delia now.'

'Surely you're not upset about the Krystalle Storm thing.' I was amazed. 'I thought you'd find it funny.

Looking on the bright side, it means that no one knows that Krystalle Storm lives here, so your secret is safe.'

Mum suddenly put down her drink and scrabbled in her handbag. She pulled out her iPhone and started tapping the keyboard – using only one finger.

'Do you want me to look for whatever you're looking for?' I suggested.

Mum shook her head.

I drank an entire glass of wine waiting for her to finish whatever she was doing.

Finally, she stopped tapping. Her expression was grave. 'Wren Fraser does have a website but it's only a home page. Google says she lives in Devon and is very private. None of her books are listed. She doesn't subscribe to Twitter, Facebook or Instagram.'

'Nor do you,' I pointed out. 'And your website is very basic too.'

'But mine has my backlist,' Mum protested.

I remembered the first time I saw it. I couldn't believe how many books my mother had written before her *Star-Crossed Lovers* series propelled her to international stardom. I remembered too, that her profile mentioned a manor house in Devon, a villa in Italy and – the kicker – a caramel-coloured Pekinese dog called Truly Scrumptious. Pure fiction. Not only that, Mum's headshot with her perfectly coiffed platinum hair and a white shirt, dripping with diamonds, bore no resemblance to the mother I knew.

I regarded Mum with concern. She had turned pale. 'What's the matter?'

'Oh, Kat,' she whispered. 'Oh my God. What if this Wren person works for HMRC – the tax people!' Her eyes widened in horror. 'What if she knows that *I'm* Krystalle Storm?'

'You *are* Krystalle Storm, Mum,' I said wearily. 'And that would make no sense. Wren's only staying here for a couple of weeks – actually, I don't know how long she's staying – but it's to finish writing her book. Maybe she's a young writer just starting out and is getting a thrill out of pretending to be famous? Personally, I think you're overreacting.'

'*Overreacting?*' Mum exclaimed. 'She's a *spy*! I can feel it in my water!' She downed her gin and tonic. 'She's a tax detective. That's what your father did. You do know that, don't you? He was investigating the fair for tax evasion. That's how we met!'

I rolled my eyes. 'I know! You're constantly reminding me.'

'And that's how they do it! They infiltrate the community!' Mum's voice was growing shrill. 'Oh my God. I'm going to go to prison.'

The awful thing was that Mum had every reason to be afraid of HMRC – and perhaps she was right about Wren. There was something strange about her. Even though I wanted to reassure my mother that she was imagining things, I couldn't.

My mother had not declared any of her earnings since the year dot. To this day I have no idea why she felt the need to keep her writing accomplishments a secret. True,

Dad had been a little uptight and old-fashioned and from what I had read of my mother's work, her bodice rippers made *Fifty Shades of Grey* read like *Winnie the Pooh*. But, according to Mum, that's what fans expected these days.

'Well, there's only one way to be sure,' I said. 'Wren already suggested she and I have a glass of wine—'

'*Wine!*' Mum exclaimed. 'Who has time for being social when you're on a deadline!' She shook her head vehemently. 'No. If a writer has taken the trouble to rent somewhere because they have a drop-dead deadline, the last thing she's going to think about is getting plastered with a stranger.'

'Perhaps not all writers are as tortured as you?' I suggested.

Mum's phone pinged an incoming text. She glanced down and groaned. 'Monty. Again. He's worried about me living alone with a killer on the loose. He wants to come and spend the night—'

'I bet he does,' I muttered. 'It's after ten. It's a booty call.'

'Don't be disgusting,' Mum said primly. She switched off the ringer. 'I shan't reply. This will be his fifth text today. I saw him yesterday! I don't want to see him every day! The more I ignore him, the more persistent he gets.'

I was in a dilemma – should I tell Mum about Delia, or not. Yes, I should.

I took a deep breath. 'What would you say if I told you that Sir Monty might be cheating on you?'

Mum seemed incredulous. 'Cheating . . . on *me*?'

For a moment I hesitated but then I thought of how much I disliked the man and how I just didn't trust him. I took another deep breath. 'And I think it's with Delia.'

A tide of red rushed up Mum's face. 'You mean my *best* friend. The one and only friend I have in the world?' I looked for a sign that she wasn't serious but to my dismay, saw genuine hurt in her eyes.

I felt terrible. Deep down I had always thought she and Delia just tolerated each other, but clearly it didn't seem to be the case at all.

'Don't take my word for it,' I said hastily. 'I just . . . well . . . I saw them together.'

'What do you mean, *together*? Together how?' Mum demanded. 'Where?'

'Near Bridge Cottage.'

Mum's eyes widened. 'At the *fly-tip*? Perhaps it was a coincidence? I mean . . . who would arrange to meet someone at a fly-tip?'

'Not exactly the fly-tip,' I said. 'He'd reversed his Rolls into the bridleway and I saw Delia come out pushing her bicycle and looking furtive. That's all.'

Mum just sat there. Mute.

'I may have imagined it,' I said desperately.

'No,' Mum said slowly. 'You didn't. Do you have yesterday's copy of the *Dipperton Deal*?'

I jumped up. 'I'll get it.'

I flew inside, cursing my stupidity. The way Mum had talked about Sir Monty had led me to believe that their relationship was all a bit of light-hearted fun, too.

Grabbing the local paper, I returned and gave it to my mother who opened it to the Dear Amanda problem page.

'There!' she said. 'Read it out.'

So I did.

'Dear Amanda,'" I began. 'I should have been promoted! I hate my new boss—'

'Not that one, the second one down!' Mum exclaimed.

"'Dear Amanda,'" I began again. "'I've fallen in love with my best friend's boyfriend. Although he is with her, he told me that if he weren't with her, he'd be with me. Their relationship is strictly platonic but he told me he has manly needs—" Good grief! "Manly needs"! Eew!'

'Read on,' Mum said tightly.

"'Am I wrong to accept his advances? We are mature and time is running out."

'Signed: "Confused".

'Amanda says: "He's a snake. Move on."'

'Well, it sounds like he's having his manly needs met,' Mum said bitterly. 'No wonder she's lost all that weight.'

I put the newspaper down. 'We don't know for sure the letter is from Delia,' I said, although I was convinced that it was. I wondered if this was why Delia had been trying to talk to my mother.

Mum picked up her legal pad and pen and suddenly got to her feet.

'Where are you going?' I said.

'I don't feel well,' she said. 'I've got a migraine coming on.'

'Trying the old excuse, are you?' I teased. 'Do you remember when you pretended to have a migraine when I was growing up but really you were writing your novels?'

But Mum's face was a picture of misery. 'I think I want to be alone.'

And with that, she walked somewhat unsteadily back to her Mini and fumbled with the car keys, dropping them twice before successfully opening the door.

'Mum!' I called out again. 'Do you want me to drive you home?'

She waved a hand as if to say, clear off, got into the car and turned the ignition. There was a nail-biting graunch of gears and she revved the engine half a dozen times. Executing a very bad five-point turn, the Mini kangarooed down the service road.

Although I felt guilty for being the bearer of bad news, I told myself it was for her own good.

A glance at the clock reminded me that my own love life wasn't straightforward either.

It was nearly time for my daily FaceTime with Shawn. I brushed my hair, added a dab of Burt's Bees tinted lip balm, threw on my pyjamas and climbed into bed with my laptop.

Chapter Eleven

At first I didn't think Shawn was going to answer but after what seemed like forever, there was a ding and he morphed onto my screen.

Straight away I could tell that he was distracted. He was sitting in his kitchen wearing a navy sweatshirt bearing the slogan 'Rolling Stock', a nod to his passion for trains. Behind him I could see the fridge covered in his kids' drawings. It made his domestic situation in London seem permanent. I felt a pang of insecurity.

After the usual exchange of hellos, I got straight to the point. 'There's been a murder in Honeywell Wood.'

'Where? Oh. Yeah. Honeywell. I forgot that it's the official name for the pine forest,' said Shawn. 'Gran told me about Charlie and even if she hadn't, it's been all over the news.'

'Oh.' I felt put out. 'I thought I might have heard from you.'

'We're talking now,' said Shawn somewhat rudely.

'Eric said you went to school together.'

'We did,' said Shawn. 'Why?'

I was surprised by Shawn's curt response. 'Wasn't he a friend? You don't sound upset about it.'

Shawn didn't comment.

'Violet definitely wasn't upset,' I plunged on.

When Shawn still didn't comment, I added, 'It sounded like Charlie caused his aunts a lot of heartache.'

'And why do you think that?'

'I went to Rose Cottage to clear out Lavender's bedroom and Violet told me everything,' I said. 'It seems that Charlie mixed with a bad crowd.'

'Kat,' Shawn said exasperated, 'promise me you and your mother aren't going to play detective.'

My hackles went up. 'Of course not, but aren't you concerned? Worried?'

'About you? You're in good hands,' said Shawn. 'Greg Mallory is an excellent police officer.'

This was not the answer I was expecting.

'Let him do his job,' Shawn went on. 'And all I can see is your neck. Are you in bed?'

'Yes.' I dragged myself into a better position and readjusted the screen on my laptop. 'Mum says there is a mobile police unit parked in her courtyard and tomorrow Mallory is doing one of those grid-search things with Fluffy. They're going to search Eric's scrapyard.'

'As I already told you,' said Shawn firmly. 'Mallory knows what he's doing. Can we talk about something else?'

'Something *else*?' I said with disbelief. 'Other than the fact that a man had his skull smashed in where I live?'

'I didn't mean it like that. I just don't want to talk about *that*,' he said.

'Okay. Then we won't talk about *that*,' I said.

'Gran mentioned that Lavinia wants to get into the holiday business,' said Shawn. 'Apparently she's installed a shepherd's hut in the walled garden and the first guest has already arrived.'

'Yes. She's a writer,' I said sulkily.

'What's this writer like?' he asked.

'Her name is Wren Fraser. She's in her twenties and she's pretending to be Krystalle Storm,' I declared.

'She's doing *what*?' Shawn exclaimed.

'Mum is freaking out,' I said. 'She thinks this Wren person is working undercover for HMRC. I think she's an under-cover reporter. Ginny Riley has been skulking about too. Someone has been leaking stuff to the media and even though Wren only just got here, there's something weird about her.'

'Weird?' said Shawn. 'In what way, weird?'

'For a start, the shepherd's hut only arrived this after-noon,' I said. 'It nearly didn't arrive at all.' I told him about the delivery lorry getting stuck in the lane. 'Lavinia even tried to put Wren off because they weren't ready for guests but apparently she insisted on coming.'

Shawn didn't say anything. He ran his fingers through his curly brown hair making it stand on end. I felt a twinge of guilt. He looked shattered.

'Are you okay?' I asked. 'You look tired.'

Shawn gave me a small smile. 'It's a new case I'm work-ing on.'

'I wish you were here now,' I said suddenly.

'I will be,' said Shawn. 'On Thursday night.'

'Good,' I said. 'Because Mallory does things very differently from you and the villagers don't like it. He's asking too many irrelevant questions. You need to tell him that we don't do things like that here.'

'It's his case,' said Shawn. 'I can't get involved, Kat.'

'Well, Clive obviously doesn't like him,' I said.

'Clive is going to have to like him,' Shawn said.

I was getting frustrated. 'But . . . what if the family are involved in some way? I mean, why would Charlie Green end up in Honeywell Wood? I know that Eric fell out with him over Vera – he told me – and then I heard that Charlie was a gambler—'

'Kat! Stop!' Shawn protested but I couldn't help myself.

'And what if Eric is covering up for . . . for . . . someone else – like Rupert, for example. You know how loyal Eric is to the family.'

'I refuse to discuss this any further with you.' Shawn's tone was cold. It was so unlike him. 'Let Mallory do his job.'

'Let Mallory do his job,' I echoed. 'Fine. I shall.'

'Oh – and Kat,' said Shawn.

'Yes?' There was a silence. He was going to apologise now for being so short with me.

'Was there anything else at Rose Cottage that you found interesting?' he asked.

'Such as what? Violet's teapot collection?' I knew I was being childish.

Shawn rolled his eyes. 'I don't know. But clearly you were snooping around.'

'I wasn't *snooping*, as you put it,' I said. 'Violet is clearing out her sister's bedroom and asked me if I wanted to buy any of her sister's stock. She used to do car boot sales.'

'Oh yeah, that.' Shawn stifled a yawn. There was *another* silence.

I felt miserable and sank down further into my pillows.

'Your top button has come undone,' said Shawn. 'I can see your cleavage.'

I knew it was an attempt to offer the proverbial olive branch but I wasn't amused. I didn't answer.

'Well, I can see that this conversation isn't going anywhere,' said Shawn tightly. 'You're tired. I'm tired. Let's just FaceTime tomorrow. Nine thirty?'

'If you can spare the time,' I said equally tightly.

'Kat – I love—'

But my laptop had slid off my knees and by the time I'd righted it again, Shawn had gone. I called him straight back but he didn't answer.

Damn and damn!

Sleep was out of the question. Was this the end of our relationship? I was so confused. What was he about to tell me? He loved me or maybe my cleavage?

I knew that Shawn would be here in four days' time. We couldn't go on like this. We needed to have an honest conversation about our future.

I flipped off the light but just lay there in the dark playing out what I would say to him. Then I started thinking about Charlie Green, the Drake Six and Sir Monty and my mother.

I got up, grabbed my pale-blue cashmere wrap and went into the kitchen to make some chamomile tea to take outside. I walked to the edge of the hardstanding and, as my eyes adjusted to the darkness, took in the view.

Everything was picked out in silhouette – the outline of the tors on Dartmoor, the multiple chimneys at the Hall and the church spire in the village.

I knew where to look for Jupiter, Mars and Saturn now. The night before Shawn left for London he brought the twins up to Jane's along with a fancy StarSense Explorer telescope because the kids had discovered the joy of stargazing and Elon Musk's Starlink satellites were scheduled to pass over the South Hams district. Harry had come up to Jane's, too, and the three boys had all made a pledge to become astronauts and travel to Mars.

Shawn had asked if he could leave the telescope with me, so it lived in the corner of my sitting room as a constant reminder of that special evening. It was the first – and last – time that the twins had slept in my spare bedroom at Jane's. Just days later they left for London.

The silence was broken by the sound of a car engine in the distance mingled with the strangled cry of a mating fox.

I began to feel maudlin but as I turned away to go back inside, I saw a solitary light slowly skirting Honeywell Wood near the old drive to Mum's Carriage House.

I darted indoors to fetch the telescope and within moments I had it set up. But, to my astonishment, caught *another* light entering Honeywell Wood from the other entrance next to Honeychurch Cottages.

Two lights!

I stepped away from the telescope and watched each light move towards the other. But before they met, both lights suddenly went out. I took to the telescope again but try as I might I couldn't find the source of either. It was extraordinary.

I must have searched for a good ten minutes before I heard a car engine start up.

I swung the telescope towards the sound but couldn't see anything until a pair of car headlamps suddenly flared and went out. Zooming in, I was able to make out the dark shadow of a vehicle crawl past the gatehouse and through the main gate where it turned right and vanished into the night.

Was it Mallory? Perhaps he'd come back for a second look? But why use the old drive? The entrance to Honeywell Wood was from my mother's courtyard. I doubted that Eric would want to go back into the woods – but Wren Fraser might.

My suspicions as to her being an undercover reporter deepened.

Sleep was impossible. I started to go through Lavender's ledgers again but couldn't concentrate. In desperation I made myself an amaretto and brandy nightcap – one of my dad's remedies for insomnia. The chamomile tea just wasn't cutting it. I dragged my duvet into the sitting room, put *The Thomas Crown Affair* into the DVD player and settled on the sofa.

I must have fallen asleep eventually because I was rudely awakened by the sound of someone hammering on the front door. I grabbed my blue cashmere shawl to wrap around my pyjamas and went to answer it.

It was Detective Inspector Mallory. He flashed his ID card. 'Mind if I come in?'

Chapter Twelve

Mallory didn't wait for my answer. He ducked through the doorway and stepped into my sitting room. He looked immaculate.

'Come right on in,' I muttered.

He raised an eyebrow. 'Rough night?'

I saw exactly what he saw – the duvet on the sofa, the remnants of my nightcap – a bottle of Amaretto and one of brandy – a half-eaten bowl of popcorn, an empty tub of ice cream and the *Thomas Crown Affair* DVD tossed on the carpet.

I ignored him. 'Coffee?'

'That would be nice, thank you.'

'Why don't you go and take a seat outside on the terrace,' I suggested. 'Give me a few minutes.'

Mallory gave a nod and ducked back out of the front door.

I went straight to the kitchen and whilst the kettle was boiling, raced to my bedroom and threw on a pair of jeans and a top. A glimpse in the mirror showed that my morning-hair was wilder than ever. I scrunched it all together and dragged it back into a low ponytail. I felt flustered. I hated being caught off guard. How had I overslept? But then I remembered that sometime in the early hours I had woken up and turned off my alarm that was always set to 7.30 a.m.

The croissants I'd bought yesterday were a bit dry so I decided to abandon them and grabbed an unopened packet of chocolate digestives. The milk was way out of date but hopefully he drank his coffee black like me. Ten minutes later I emerged into the morning sunlight with a tray holding the cafetière, the expired milk in a jug, some sachets of sugar and the packet of biscuits.

Mallory got to his feet and took the tray. He set it down and then waited for me to sit before sitting himself. It was old-fashioned but I liked it.

'The weather is supposed to break tomorrow,' he said. 'Thunderstorms.'

'I hope so,' I said, thinking how English it was to talk about the weather. 'But today is going to be another scorcher. Milk? Sugar?'

'Just black,' said Mallory. 'And tempting though they may be, no biscuits for me. If I start eating sugar at this time of the morning I'm doomed for the rest of the day.'

'Me too.' I smiled. 'I don't know why I even brought them out here.'

'I sometimes have that effect on people,' he said. 'They eat so they can't answer my questions.'

I wasn't sure if Mallory was joking but he did seem different this morning – despite flashing his ID card. Not so formal.

'I wanted to talk to you,' I said. 'I was at Violet Green's yesterday and—'

'All in good time, Ms Stanford – or should I say Miss? I never know these days.'

'Kat is just fine,' I said.

He took a sip of coffee and gave an appreciative nod. 'Not too strong and not too weak.'

'Thanks,' I said.

'You're very isolated up here,' he began. 'I should imagine this is quite a change from London.' Noticing my surprise, he added, 'I do my homework. I think I prefer Steve McQueen and Faye Dunaway however.'

'Excuse me?' I was confused.

'*The Thomas Crown Affair*,' he said. 'I saw the DVD on your floor. I find art theft investigation a fascinating topic – but then, of course, you know all about that because of your years spent with one of the leading art investigators in the country, David Wynne.'

'Yes,' I said looking him straight in the eye. 'We were together for a very long time.'

'And your mother is a widow?' It was said as a question but of course Mallory knew she was.

'Mum had always wanted to move to the country,' I said. 'So of course I decided to move with her.'

He gave a smile. 'And your mother? Is she glad she did?'

'Very much so,' I said.

'I believe the South Hams is very expensive,' Mallory said. 'But presumably she got a good price for the three-bedroom semi-detached in Tooting.'

'Gosh. You really do your homework,' I said. 'Although I'm not sure what this has to do with Charlie Green.'

'And your father worked for HMRC?' he said. 'The Carriage House is a stunning property.'

What other homework had Mallory done? Did he know the truth about my mother? Was he asking these questions because he wanted to know how she could have afforded to buy the Carriage House? I started to feel anxious.

'My father was always very careful with his money,' I said and promptly picked up the packet of digestives and tore it open. 'Are you sure you don't want one?' And then I remembered his comment, so I put the packet back on the tray. 'You're right. It's far too early for chocolate.'

'That must have been a big decision for you,' he said changing tack. 'Leaving such a popular television show.'

'I had wanted my own business for a long time,' I said. 'In fact, Mum and I had originally planned to open an antique shop together in Shoreditch but . . .' I shrugged. 'Sometimes life doesn't go the way you expect, does it?' When he merely nodded, I plunged on. 'I mean, it must be quite a change for *you* moving from Plymouth to the countryside.'

He didn't answer. I plunged on again. 'It must be a huge adjustment from being a city cop to a village bobby. You won't have much use for a Taser here.'

'Perhaps. Perhaps not.' Mallory cracked a smile. 'But

you will find my investigations – although likely to be Taser free – will be very different from my predecessor.' Mallory paused. 'First of all, I like to get straight to the point. Why did you tip off the media?'

'Excuse me?' I felt a flash of annoyance. 'You think it was *me* who did that?'

'I know Ginny Riley,' said Mallory. 'I've had dealings with her before. She mentioned you are friends.'

'*Were* friends,' I corrected him. 'Before she moved away. But I definitely didn't tell her anything she didn't already know.'

Mallory stroked his jaw. Mum was right – it was very chiselled. 'And yet your name was mentioned in this morning's news bulletin, Kat. I quote: *Home of TV celebrity Kat Stanford who runs a flourishing antique business in Little Dipperton and from the Dartmouth Antique Emporium*,' he said. 'Don't they say that there is no such thing as bad publicity and with your new enterprise . . . ?'

'I'm ignoring that comment because it's insulting,' I said stiffly.

Mallory topped up my coffee, and then his. 'I believe you and Detective Inspector Shawn Cropper were very close.'

Were very close? 'We still are,' I said firmly. 'And my private life has nothing to do with this.'

'It might, if you are deliberately hampering my investigation.'

Mallory was beginning to irritate me. 'Trust me, I have far more important things to do than hamper your investigation,' I said. 'I have no idea where Ginny got her information but I deeply resent you assuming it was from me.'

'I just had to ask.' Mallory smirked and, for a moment, I saw a flicker of amusement in his eyes. 'You know . . . sometimes it's not good being too close to something – or someone. This is a very tight-knit community and often you can't see the wood – no pun intended – for the trees. Don't you agree?'

'Then we're lucky to have you,' I said not bothering to disguise my sarcasm.

Mallory brought out his police notebook. I wondered if he had memorised my answers to his questions but then I realised that I hadn't told him anything he hadn't already known. It looked like his Q&A had just been a warm-up.

He turned to a fresh page. 'You mentioned you had seen Violet Green yesterday?'

I said that I had and went on to tell him about the postcards from Charlie with one of them being postmarked just six weeks ago. 'Does that mean he was murdered years ago or just recently?' I asked.

'I like to keep an open mind,' said Mallory. 'I follow the A, B, C rules of policing. Assume nothing, believe nothing and challenge everything.'

'Won't you be able to get a sense of when Charlie was killed from the autopsy?'

'Perhaps,' Mallory said again. 'In the meantime, we're putting together a timeline of the deceased's movements when he was last seen in the area.' He thought for a moment. 'Did you leave the postcards at Rose Cottage?'

'Yes,' I said. 'But I did take photographs of the postcards – front and back. Excuse me, I'll go and get my mobile so I can show you. It's in my bag.'

I headed back inside, grabbed my tote bag and returned to the terrace. I gave Mallory my loupe and selected the photos from the photo feature for him to view on my iPhone.

Mallory scrolled through them, enlarging the images with his thumb and finger, but all he said was, 'And what was your reason for visiting Rose Cottage?'

I told him that Violet was clearing out her dead sister's bedroom and had offered me Lavender's car boot sale stock. 'It's a mixture of bric-a-brac, plates and mismatched objects,' I said. 'The type you'd find at—'

'A car boot sale?' Mallory suggested. 'So nothing of interest for you.'

'Yes and no,' I said. 'There was a doll's house that was custom-made for Charlotte Green – she was Charlie's sister. She died—'

'Yes, so I heard,' Mallory interjected, nodding. 'Your speciality is dolls and bears, I believe.' He reached inside his jacket pocket and brought out a plastic bag marked 'Evidence'. 'I'm afraid you can't remove this from the bag but I'm interested in what it is.'

Curious, I smoothed the plastic out and gave a cry of surprise. It was a Frozen Charlotte. This one wore a pale blue dress and white lace cap but around her neck was a piece of string fashioned like a hangman's noose. It was horrible.

'You've seen it before,' said Mallory sharply.

'Not this one.' I took out the cigar box of Frozen Charlottes and gave it to Mallory. 'Take a look.'

He opened the lid. 'What curious things.'

'They're called Frozen Charlottes and actually belonged to Charlie's sister,' I said. 'Charlotte's Frozen Charlottes.'

'The same Charlotte who had the doll's house?' said Mallory.

'Yes,' I said. 'They were part of Lavender's stock.'

Mallory's expression was hard to read. 'Are they valuable?'

'To a collector, yes. They're easy to pick up on eBay,' I said. 'They were listed in one of Lavender's ledgers.'

Mallory turned to a fresh page. 'Tell me about these dolls.'

'They're pretty macabre,' I said. 'Frozen Charlottes were very popular during the Victorian era. Sometimes they were known as pillar dolls, solid chinas or bathing babies. Most had glazed china fronts with unglazed stoneware backs so that they could float on their backs in the bath. Their hair was nearly always human hair.'

Mallory continued to scribble.

'Originally, the dolls were naked,' I went on. 'But with time they became more elaborate. Some were even made into jewellery— Wait. Is that *shorthand*?' Mallory's scribbles were in fact squiggles, lines and dots. 'I didn't think anyone used that any more.'

'Well, some people do,' he said mildly. 'So these Frozen Charlottes are a Victorian gimmick, if you like. But where did the name come from?'

I told him about 'A Corpse Going to a Ball'. 'Charlotte's mother pleaded with her daughter to bundle up against the horrific cold that she and her escort would be facing on their fifteen-mile sleigh ride into town but the young girl was vain and refused to do so. She thought it would crumple and ruin her dress. When she and Charlie—'

'Charlie!' Mallory said sharply. 'You said Charlie?'

'Yes.' My stomach lurched. I hadn't connected the Charlotte and Charlie in the poem to the real siblings at all. 'When the pair reached their destination, Charlotte is dead. She has frozen to death.'

'What a gruesome story!' Mallory exclaimed.

'I know,' I agreed. 'And the moral of the story is always to do what your mother tells you. They used to put Frozen Charlottes in Christmas puddings . . .'

'Christmas *puddings*?'

'Kids loved finding them,' I said. 'It served as a playful reminder to always do as your mother tells you.'

Mallory made some more notes and then looked up. 'And where does the noose fit in?'

I felt a shiver of foreboding. 'It doesn't,' I said. 'I've never seen a Frozen Charlotte with a noose. Where on earth did you find this one?'

Mallory hesitated. He looked uncomfortable. My heart began to race erratically, as if I already knew what he was going to say.

'In the deceased's pocket,' said Mallory.

I pointed to the label on the side of the cigar box. 'There should have been eight Frozen Charlottes but there were only seven. D-do you . . .' I began to stammer. 'Do you think someone put it in Charlie's pocket?'

'Or he put it there himself.' Mallory held out his hand for the evidence bag. 'In which case it suggests that the deceased must have visited his aunt to have taken the doll.'

'He did,' I said. 'Violet told me the last time they saw Charlie was the night before the beating of the bounds. He also took a petty cash box but didn't take the money inside.'

Mallory nodded. 'I shall be speaking to Miss Green later. And you mentioned the cigar box was listed in a ledger. Can I see it?'

'Violet gave me all of Lavender's ledgers. I left them at the gatehouse,' I lied. They were sitting on my kitchen counter. I wanted to take another look for the Drake Six. 'I can show you later. There was nothing unusual in the listing.'

Mallory's eyes bored into mine. 'How many ledgers?'

I shrugged. 'Eight.'

'You went through eight ledgers just to look for the Frozen Charlottes?'

'I thought I might have missed . . . missed something,' I stammered and reached for the biscuits but then saw Mallory watching and stopped myself again. 'Shall I make another pot of coffee? I'm sure you must need it having been up all night.'

'Excuse me?'

'In Honeywell Wood,' I said. 'I saw headlights and heard the sound of a car around one in the morning and assumed it was you.' I hadn't assumed, I'd only wondered. 'There was a second light too. It was coming from the direction of Honeychurch Cottages.'

'Please show me where you saw the lights.' Mallory put his notebook away and got up without waiting for my answer. He walked over to where he'd parked his black Peugeot on the hardstanding and I followed.

It was a beautiful morning. A thin layer of mist was still floating above the rolling hills.

Mallory scanned the area. 'What an incredible view.'

'You can't quite see the drive from here, of course, because of the trees,' I said. 'But I definitely saw headlights and I heard the sound of a car engine starting up and driving away.'

Mallory pulled out the map from inside his jacket pocket. 'Show me on here, please.'

I pointed out where I'd seen the lights. 'And that's the old drive – it's marked on here because it's an old map. But it's overgrown now.'

'Then let's go and see just how overgrown it is,' said Mallory.

'What?' I said. '*Now?*'

'Yes, Kat. Now.'

'Can I at least clean my teeth?'

Chapter Thirteen

As we set off in convoy with me leading the way, I thought how crazy it was that as the crow flies, my home was about five minutes from the rear of the Hall, but because one of Rupert's ancestors didn't want the staff to accidentally wander onto the main drive, he'd created an elaborate network of service lanes. It usually took me fifteen minutes to travel down the drive, exit right at the tradesmen's entrance, skirt the estate boundary wall along Cavalier Lane, turn into the main gate and drive the mile up to the Hall.

Even though I saw the hawks with their outstretched wings on top of the granite pillars engraved with the words 'Honeychurch Hall' every single day, I always felt a stirring of pride. If Eric *was* protecting something or someone, wasn't I doing the same by wanting to talk to Edith *first*, about the two Drake miniatures I'd found in Lavender's bedroom?

I parked my car in its usual spot outside my showroom and Mallory's black Peugeot pulled up alongside.

I gestured to the passenger door, opened it and slid inside. 'It's a ten-minute walk so it'll be quicker by car.'

Mallory's Peugeot was immaculate. I thought of Shawn's car with its children's toys, sweet wrappers and empty water bottles. His police panda was like that too. The two men couldn't have been more different.

We drove by the wrought-iron archway topped by a metal cast of a galloping horse.

'What's that all about?' Mallory asked.

'The equine cemetery,' I said and went on to give him a history lesson. 'The dowager countess's father created it the day that Queen Victoria died. It's where all the family horses are buried.'

He glanced over. 'You really like it here, don't you?'

I was a bit taken aback by the question. 'Of course I do. Why?'

'In the short time I've been living in the area I've noticed a fierce loyalty to the Honeychurch family,' Mallory remarked.

'Don't you get that kind of thing in Plymouth?' I teased.

He grinned. 'No, but it means I don't get blinded by sentiment and misguided loyalty.'

I was about to disagree when I suddenly saw the gaping entrance to the old drive that was usually hidden by dense and overhanging laurel.

My stomach did a little jump. 'Oh! On the right—'

'What's wrong?'

'The entrance is usually hard to find but . . . yes . . . a car must have come this way last night. And look.' I pointed to the wooden sign that said 'Carriage House' which lay broken in the undergrowth.

Mallory pulled over, mounting the grass verge. He turned off the engine and we got out. Grass was flattened and marked by tyre tracks and the hedge on one side was a mass of crushed and broken branches.

He made a beeline for the tyre tracks. 'Someone thought they could get through.' He looked down the old drive. 'When was the last time you came here?'

'Gosh,' I said. 'The first day I arrived. My mother had tried and got her Mini stuck.' In fact, that day was still vivid in my memory. I had just met seven-year-old Harry dressed as his hero, Squadron Leader James Bigglesworth, and he had brought me this way insisting we could get through. It had been a disaster.

'Let's see, shall we?' Mallory set off with his impossibly long stride. I had to break into a jog to keep up.

Grass had long grown over the surface but due to the weather, much had died, exposing glimpses of the old cobbled drive.

It was no wider than the width of a horse-drawn carriage. As time moved on and vehicles got bigger, the Devon lanes remained the same width. On many occasions I'd seen beautiful historic medieval bridges lose ancient bricks to the SUV gas-guzzlers or – as the locals liked to call them – Chelsea tractors.

After a few minutes, the drive narrowed. I was even more shocked at how much the laurel had crept into every available space, creating a sense of claustrophobia, choking whatever trees had been there before and enveloping the rusting iron fence that lined the old drive.

And then Mallory stopped and pointed to the decimated undergrowth where a mangled fence was exposed. The bottom stretcher had been completely torn away.

Mallory bent down to take a closer look. 'No sign of rust at the break,' he said. 'And I would think there'd be a fair bit of damage to someone's bodywork.'

'And that someone was rubbish at reversing.' I gestured back to the way we had come. There was an obvious snaky line carving a swathe through the laurel. 'But then it *was* dark,' I said. 'The driver didn't turn the headlights on until he reached Cavalier Lane.'

'Not a local man,' Mallory said more to himself than to me. 'And an easy mistake for a stranger to make.'

'The old drive is still on the ordnance survey map,' I agreed. 'And on the map for the beating of the bounds, as you saw.'

Mallory started foraging through the undergrowth. 'Ah. Good.' He pulled out his disposable gloves and an evidence bag and bent down again.

I joined him. 'What is it?'

'Broken glass from a side mirror.' He popped it into the evidence bag, made a notation with a Sharpie pen and straightened up. 'Let's keep going.'

The drive had narrowed into nothing more than a hardened mud path. Mallory was on a mission and completely focused, eyes looking left and right. He reminded me of Fluffy the bloodhound.

We couldn't have been walking for more than five minutes when Mallory swerved and ploughed into the undergrowth. I hung back.

'Over here,' he called out.

I pushed my way through to join him. He was standing at an iron kissing gate surrounded by trampled stinging nettles and brambles that looked as if they had been beaten back and pushed aside with a stick.

'I had no idea that this gate was here,' I said.

Mallory gestured for me to step closer. 'Footprints, and fresh ones at that.' He gave a grim smile. 'Perhaps whoever leaked the story to the media has done us a favour after all. Someone must have come back for a reason.'

'You mean, the killer?' I felt sick. 'But why would he come back?'

'To check the crime scene,' said Mallory. 'Make sure that nothing was left behind—'

'Like the Frozen Charlotte?' I suggested.

'Or a small knapsack,' said Mallory. 'Yes, there was an empty bag in the shallow grave.'

A ping heralded an incoming text. 'Ah. Forensics has arrived with my team. I must go.'

We retraced our steps in silence. It was only as we got back to his car that Mallory turned to me and said, 'You've been very helpful. Thank you, Kat. I appreciate you taking time out of what must be a very busy day. If you hadn't seen those lights in the early hours of this morning, we would not have this lead. Can I drive you back to the gatehouse?'

'I'd prefer to walk,' I said.

'And if I need to look at the ledgers?'

'Just let me know,' I said.

And with that, Mallory got into his Peugeot, executed a perfect three-point turn in the tiniest of spaces, and sped away.

I checked my watch. It was almost ten. If I was going to catch Edith I needed to get to the Hall as quickly as possible. The sooner I solved the mystery of the Drake miniatures the better.

I was surprised that Mallory had shared his thoughts with me. The fact that I was hiding the Drake Six from him made me uncomfortable. There was also something very weird about the Frozen Charlottes. Why did Charlie have one in his pocket?

I let myself into the gatehouse, switched off the alarm and took the two velvet pouches out of the safe.

Moments later, I parked next to Pansy's Fiat 500 at the rear of the Hall and entered the coolness of the long flagstone corridor that led to the kitchen.

I found Peggy Cropper, dressed in her usual pink striped pinafore over a plain white linen short-sleeved dress and white mob-cap, seated at the pine table shucking peas. The kitchen was in its usual state of disarray that I knew drove Delia mad. With its old-fashioned range and stone sinks it probably hadn't been modernised since the 1970s. I didn't know how Peggy managed and yet, despite all Delia's scheming to get her to retire, the elderly cook clung on.

I said hello but Peggy didn't seem to hear me the first time so I repeated myself until she looked up.

'Oh, I thought I heard voices.' Delia limped into the kitchen surrounded by a cloud of Reine de Nuit. 'You're not still shucking those peas, are you?' Delia's eyes met mine. She mouthed, 'She really needs to retire!'

Delia looked positively glowing this morning, dressed in another sleeveless shift that exposed her tanned limbs. Unfortunately her outfit was marred by the heavy bandage she wore on the foot that I had trodden on yesterday.

I knew I should have felt guilty, but I didn't. 'I'm so sorry about your toe. Is it still painful?'

'I suppose you just don't know how big your feet really are,' Delia replied with a tinge of malice. 'What are you? A size ten?'

I forced a smile. 'I've come to see the dowager countess. Do you know where she is?'

'Dressed like that?' Delia scolded. 'You look as if you've just got out of bed. Would you like to borrow my comb?'

When I said thank you but no thank you Delia turned to Peggy and shouted, 'Peggy, they want another pot of coffee in the morning room. Peggy? *Peggy!*'

'I don't think she can hear you,' I said.

'If you want something doing then do it yourself,' muttered Delia and limped over to the range to heft the heavy iron kettle onto the boiling plate. 'Her ladyship is having breakfast with Lady Lavinia and Lady Pansy.'

'I know where the morning room is,' I said and set off, only for Delia to beat me to the door.

'Wait!' she said. 'Did you tell Iris that I wanted to speak to her?'

'I did,' I said.

'Well.' Delia pouted. 'She never called me back.'

'Mum's been busy,' I lied.

'*Busy?* Busy doing what?' Delia said with scorn. 'I can't imagine what she does all day.'

'Working on the Honeychurch family tree for starters,' I lied again. I thought how much easier it would be for everyone if I could just say, '*My mother is working on a book. She doesn't want to be disturbed.*'

Delia gave a little cry. 'I've just had an amazing idea!'

I raised an eyebrow.

'We should tell' – Delia made air quotes – '"*Wren*" about the Honeychurch family tree.'

It occurred to me that my mother must have caught the air quote habit from Delia. 'Why?' I asked.

'Their antics – especially the Turkish harem and the woman who went off and married a Sheik,' said Delia. 'Perhaps I could be Krystalle Storm's consultant!'

I rolled my eyes. 'You can't *still* think that Wren Fraser is Krystalle Storm.'

'Oh yes, I'm sure of it.' Delia nodded. 'She's paying three thousand pounds to sleep in that hut for three weeks! Three thousand *pounds*! And she paid in cash! But then I suppose she can afford to, can't she?'

'Perhaps you should ask the new detective what he thinks,' I said.

'I will,' Delia agreed. She glanced at the wall clock. 'I have an interview with him this morning in that funny mobile police unit, although I can't imagine that I'll be of any help. I didn't even live here at the time.' She nodded in Peggy's direction. '*She* did though, but when I asked Peggy about this Charlie Green chap she claimed she didn't remember him at all. Selective memory, that's what she's got— Oh! Your ladyship!'

'Ah. Good. Kat, a normal person at last.' Edith stalked into the kitchen dressed – as always – in her side-saddle riding habit, her grey hair in neat pinwheels and her lips adorned with her trademark red lipstick.

'The kettle's not boiled yet, your ladyship,' said Delia. 'I'll be just five minutes with another cafetière of coffee.'

'Not for me,' Edith declared. 'For those two babbling idiot girls – as if they haven't had enough caffeine for one day.'

'Of course, your ladyship.' Delia did a little bob. 'And just to be clear, their ladyships would have had their fresh pot sooner had Mrs Cropper done what I asked her and put the kettle onto the boiling plate when told to do so.'

Edith gave a dismissive wave of her hand. I glanced at Peggy who caught my eye and winked. I had to stifle a smile. If I had to work with Delia all day I think I would pretend to be hard of hearing too.

'Are you here to see those silly girls?' Edith demanded.

'Actually, it was you that I wanted to see.'

'I could do with an extra pair of hands to ride out this morning,' she said. 'Lavinia is tied up with her friend and Duchess missed out yesterday for the same reason, too.'

'That would be lovely. Although I'll need to pop home and change.' I hadn't anticipated riding but I never missed an opportunity to do so. As a child and a teenager, I had been desperate to have a pony of my own. And here I was all those years later having the best of both worlds. Edith always wanted me to think that Duchess was mine. I got to ride her as much as I liked and I didn't have the responsibility of having to take care of her 24/7.

'Excellent! Shall we say within the hour?' Edith said, which was really an order rather than a question. 'But tell me, you came here for a reason. I hope it isn't anything to do with that frightful business in Honeywell Wood?'

Delia may have been standing over the range waiting for the kettle to boil but I could tell by the way she stood – albeit slightly lop-sided because of her mangled foot – that she was eavesdropping.

'Yes,' I lied. 'But perhaps we can go somewhere private?'

'The library,' Edith said and swept out of the kitchen, but as we crossed the vast black and white chequered reception area I said, 'Actually, can we go to the Great Hall? There's something I'd like to talk to you about.'

Chapter Fourteen

I was disappointed. 'And you've never heard of the Drake Six?'

Edith handed the two miniatures back to me. I slipped them into their velvet pouches.

'Very charming, but no,' she said. 'We Honeychurches were horsemen, infantry, the army – that sort of thing. Oh, and of course, the air force too. We've never had a naval man.'

Edith and I were standing in front of the marble fireplace in the Great Hall. The walls displayed the Honeychurch armoury of pole arms and halberds, muskets, vicious stiletto knives, rapiers and basket-hilted two-edged mortuary swords. There wasn't a portrait, large or small, in sight.

'Perhaps they were tucked away somewhere and Rupert decided to sell them?' I suggested.

Edith looked doubtful. 'That's highly unlikely. One of our ancestors had a run-in with the Second Baronet – that would be Drake's son. He couldn't make up his mind which side he was on during the Civil War – for King or

Cromwell.' Edith regarded me with curiosity. 'You look concerned. Is it important?'

'I honestly don't know.' I decided there was no point being mysterious about it so I told her about Violet inviting me to look through Lavender's stock and that I had found the miniatures in the doll's house that Edith had given to Charlotte. 'There should be six miniatures, but I only found two.'

Edith looked startled. 'Good heavens. Yes, I remember that doll's house. Charlotte was thrilled to bits. Such a lovely girl.'

'Every single detail is there –' I gestured to the spectacular hammer-beam roof and floor-to-ceiling stained-glass window of knights in battle – 'the screens passage, the minstrels' gallery – the mantelpiece even has the Honeychurch motto engraved on it too,' I enthused. 'Whoever built it was a magnificent craftsman.'

'Yes, I was very happy with how the doll's house turned out,' said Edith. 'It was an exact replica of my own.'

'*Your* doll's house.' I was surprised. 'I thought it was a copy of the Hall.'

'That would be too big a job.' Edith smiled. 'Charlotte's was copied from the doll's house that my mother had made for me. Charlie and Charlotte would often play in the attics at the Hall – their mother was a friend of mine, used to ride to hounds – and Charlotte begged to have one of her own.'

I'd always wondered why Edith seemed to have a soft spot for Violet. 'You knew the Green family well?'

'At one time Rupert and Charlie were quite tight.

Rupert, of course, was older than Charlie but I always felt that Charlie looked up to him,' Edith said. 'They'd go racing together but Rupert isn't a gambler and then of course Charlie got in with the wrong crowd.'

'Where did the Greens live?' I asked.

'They were neighbouring landowners,' said Edith. 'They owned Moreleigh Manor just beyond our northern boundary. Of course, it's a holiday complex now.' She gave a shudder of distaste. 'I think they even have . . .' She seemed to struggle to find the words. 'A . . . bouncy castle and a miniature golf course!'

I stifled a smile. 'Oh, dear.'

'The Greens made their fortune in mining on Dartmoor in the nineteenth century,' Edith went on. Her jaw hardened. 'Charlie ran through his inheritance with no thought to his aunts and their future. I'm not surprised that ghastly boy ended up the way he did and I'm livid that it should have happened *here*!' She was getting upset. 'And now our name is all over the news. It's that wretched new detective's fault. If only Shawn were here. He'd know how to handle this nonsense!'

Edith reached out to steady herself on a wainscot chair. Her face was flushed.

I was alarmed. 'Are you feeling all right?'

'Yes, of course I am,' she snapped. 'It's nothing.' But even so, she sat down. Sometimes I forgot just how old Edith was. She still rode every day and bragged that she did one hundred sit-ups a day – which I seriously doubted.

Rupert stepped into the Great Hall looking furtive.

Slightly balding, with a trim military moustache and upright bearing, the 15th Earl of Grenville was the epitome of the English aristocracy. Today he was dressed in beige corduroy trousers, with a navy and white checked shirt and tie.

When he saw us he looked relieved. 'Thank God it's you and not my wife and her irritating friend.'

'Apparently they are in the north-east wing,' said Edith. 'Pansy thinks they can accommodate fourteen guests up there.' She turned to me with a pained expression. 'Lavinia's chum has put the most ridiculous ideas into her head. She's suggesting that we start a hospitality business here at the Hall. Weddings, corporate events and—'

'A bouncy castle?' I suggested.

Edith was not amused. 'She insists that's what all the big houses do these days. What do you think, Katherine?'

I hesitated. 'If it means keeping the family heirlooms, then I would consider it.'

Edith looked at me with horror. 'But . . . to have strangers stomping around our home is *outrageous*!'

'We just might have to give it a try, Mother.' Rupert sounded resigned. 'I hate it too, but one day we won't have any furniture and paintings left to sell.'

I thought that was a bit of an exaggeration but I had definitely noticed a slow seepage of antiques and artwork in the short time that I had lived on the estate.

'Hate it. Hate change,' Edith said to herself. '*Hate* progress. I'm too old for all this.'

'In that case,' said Rupert, 'you'll have to say goodbye to that wainscot chair that you are sitting on. Old Monty says it would fetch three thousand pounds at auction, but Lavinia has just let the shepherd's hut for the same amount for only three weeks. It's tucked away in the walled garden out of sight and not doing any harm to anyone.'

Hearing Sir Monty's name set off an alarm bell. 'Surely it's too late for this week's auction.'

'I didn't want to sell,' said Rupert. 'Even though he offered to handle it all for a very small commission.'

'Two per cent?' I suggested.

Rupert seemed surprised. 'Why yes. How did you know?'

'Sir Monty is selling some Charles II oak benches on Violet's behalf,' I said. 'He seems to be quite the benefactor at the moment.'

'Ask Rupert about the miniatures,' Edith said suddenly. 'Katherine wants to show you something.'

I took the miniatures out of the velvet pouches again and showed them to Rupert. He gave them nothing more than a passing glance. 'No. Never seen them before but perhaps you should talk to Pansy.'

Edith gasped. 'You can't inflict Pansy on poor Katherine?'

'Her father was a naval man,' said Rupert. 'Sort of thing he would have collected. Obsessed with Drake.' Rupert thought for a moment. 'What do you make of the new detective?'

'He's very thorough,' I said.

'I have to report to the mobile incident unit at noon.' Rupert sounded as if he couldn't believe it. 'The last time I saw Charlie was when he roared up on his motorbike the night before the beating of the—' Rupert stopped and frowned. 'Now that's damn odd . . .'

Edith and I waited for him to finish his thought for what seemed like ages. And then Rupert snapped his fingers. 'Ah. Yes. That's it.'

'Do enlighten us, pet,' said Edith.

'Charlie is still paying the lease on that farm building on Moreleigh Mount,' said Rupert. 'How odd.'

'That *is* extraordinary,' Edith mused. 'Are you certain?'

'He wanted somewhere to restore his motorbikes,' Rupert went on. 'We had no use for it. When he went off to Ireland, he kept the lease going. I wonder who is footing the bill?'

I thought of Violet and Lavender and their meticulous record keeping. It would be easy enough to find out.

'Do you think the motorbikes will still be there?' I asked.

'We'll ride that way this morning and see,' Edith declared.

But then came the sound of shrill female voices from the minstrels' gallery above. I heard snatches of, '*abso-lute-ly* terrific idea, Pan!' and 'We could knock out the linenfold panelling, Lav! Hold medieval banquets in the Great Hall!'

Edith turned pale.

'Oh yes!' shrieked Lavinia. 'Everyone can dress up.'

'I bet Rupert would look good in a codpiece!' There were screams of hysterical laughter. 'Let's go down there now and have a proper look.'

Rupert looked stricken. 'Christ! They're coming this way.'

'Quickly! Follow me!' Edith got to her feet and strode over to the far corner of the room. Rupert and I scurried after her. Edith's fingers skimmed the linenfold panelling until one of the panels popped open to reveal a secret passage.

We ducked inside. Rupert ushered me on ahead before turning to close the panel behind us.

'Forgotten about this,' he muttered.

It was dark, damp and cold and we had to feel our way along the rough walls. Rupert was right behind me, breathing heavily, which was a little creepy. After just a few moments, light suddenly flooded the passage and we followed Edith into an unfurnished anteroom with two opposing doors leading off. Faded red velvet curtains were drawn back from the casement window. The dark-red carpet bore signs of furniture long since removed and the walls, with their picture lights over empty squares, was a stark reminder of our earlier conversation in the Great Hall.

The window overlooked a range of derelict outbuildings. I couldn't find my bearings. It was yet another part of the house that I didn't know.

Rupert closed the linenfold panelling behind us again. It was flush against the wall. Unless you knew where to look, you would never know the door to the secret passage was there.

'Right then,' said Rupert, 'I'll leave you both to it,' and he left through one door.

'This way,' said Edith, and we took the other. It opened into yet another corridor, equally as stark and neglected as the anteroom. She strode on ahead before stopping at yet *another* door. This one revealed a steep, narrow staircase. The walls were painted a dark brown, the steps made of stone. We began to climb.

'How many staircases are there?' I asked.

'Six or seven,' she said. 'I must admit I'm not sure.'

'Where are we going?'

'You'll see,' said Edith.

At the top of the first flight of stairs Edith opened yet *another* door. We stepped out onto the galleried landing that overlooked the black and white chequered reception area. Light spilled from the domed atriums above.

Edith strode on ahead as we crossed to the other wing.

I wondered if she saw what I saw. A threadbare carpet bore more imprints of heavy furniture that had been sold off and, yet again, a range of picture lights sat above empty squares where once beautiful paintings had hung. It was easy to be blinded to reality when it happened so very slowly – the loss of a painting here and a chair there. It was hardly noticeable to begin with until one day, the proverbial curtains opened to reveal stark, empty rooms. It was very depressing.

Finally, after two more flights of stairs we came to a long narrow corridor under the eaves with just the natural light from a range of dusty dormer windows to show us the way. At the end was another door. We had finally reached the attic.

Edith flipped on the light switch. 'Good heavens. I haven't been up here for a long time.'

I stood there taking in all the clutter. It was overwhelming and, unlike Lavender's organised chaos, this could only be described as a hoarder's paradise.

'Perhaps after you've cleared out Lavender's room you could come and make a start here,' said Edith with a smile.

'I'm glad you are joking,' I said.

There were plenty of tennis rackets and golf clubs in old leather bags; huge mirrors rested against steamer trunks – I counted five and I wasn't even looking very hard; dozens of moth-eaten curtains tossed over broken chairs, sagging sofas and partial bedsteads – even an abandoned Hotpoint Twin Tub, circa 1955.

On top of a cracked chest of drawers were at least a dozen boxes labelled 'Hornby' – Rupert's famous train set – and still in the original boxes too. A nineteenth-century dapple-grey rocking horse – minus its mane and tail – rested on a chipped wooden stand, the leather bridle and saddle long since rotted away.

'Oh!' I exclaimed. 'Poor thing.'

'Her name is Starlight,' said Edith wistfully. 'I learned to ride on her. She was very fast.'

'Let me have her,' I said suddenly. 'I know an excellent restorer who specialises in rocking horses. I'll even pay for Starlight myself! Perhaps she can live in the gatehouse!'

'We'll see,' said Edith. She sounded just like my dad who often used that phrase, which, in my experience, meant 'No'.

We picked a path through more boxes of old gramophone records and LPs, gas lamps and empty glass jars, but were stopped by a forbidding wooden lectern on a plinth that blocked our way.

'Is that what I think it is?' I asked.

'That used to be in the Justice Room next to the library,' said Edith. 'The gavel is somewhere.'

'My mother told me all about the sixth Earl of Grenville,' I said.

'He was a tyrant and anyone caught poaching rabbits was immediately sentenced to be hanged at Gibbet Cross. We'll be going past there this afternoon on our way to Moreleigh Mount. Help me move it aside.' We pushed it out of our path.

Edith pointed to an octagonal window at the far end of the attic. 'The doll's house should be over there.'

Edith's doll's house was much larger than Charlotte's. 'It's . . . it's . . .' I tried to find the right word to describe it. 'Magnificent.'

'And it's no good up here,' said Edith briskly. 'Clearly Harry isn't going to be playing with it. Why don't you take it – and yes, you can take Starlight too. I know you will look after them.'

I was thrilled. 'You have my word that both will be well looked after.'

'Let's move the doll's house into the middle of the room so that you can take a proper look.'

'It's very heavy . . .'

'I'm not an invalid!' Edith declared and, sweeping her long habit to one side, grasped two of the corners and I took the other two.

We managed to slide the doll's house just far away enough from the window to open the rear doors.

It was fully furnished inside – albeit a muddle. Our efforts to move it had knocked over all the freestanding pieces. But there were so many treasures! I felt like a kid myself. I gave a passing glance at the Great Hall in the wild hope that there could be a pair of Drake miniatures stuck to the wall with Blu-Tack, but, of course, there wasn't.

I spied a family of small dolls in Victorian dress – a father, mother, two children and a baby – nothing unusual there, but when I looked in one of the bathrooms, I gave a cry of surprise. Lying in the empty claw bath was a naked Frozen Charlotte.

Edith seemed to be enjoying my reaction. 'I trust you know the poem about Charlotte freezing to death on the way to the ball?'

'Yes,' I said. 'As a reminder to always obey your mother!'

'Charlotte was obsessed with that story and those dolls,' said Edith. 'In the end I gave her my collection – except for just this one.'

'I have seen your collection,' I said. 'It's in a cigar box. But . . . there's something you should know.'

'What's the matter, dear?' Edith's concern grew as I told her about the Frozen Charlotte that was discovered in Charlie Green's pocket.

For some moments, Edith didn't comment. She sat down on the edge of a trunk. 'I'm afraid I don't believe in coincidences. Charlotte loved those dolls but Charlie thought they were silly.' She frowned. 'There must be a reason why he had one in his pocket. He must have been trying to send a message.'

'I think so too,' I said.

'Charlie was always fond of riddles,' Edith went on. 'He loved creating the clues for the treasure hunts. All so long ago now.'

I closed the doors behind the doll's house and we left it where it was. It was going to be a bit of a job lugging the doll's house and rocking horse down from the attics but I'd hire Eric's muscle if I had to.

Edith checked her wristwatch. 'Go home and have lunch and we'll meet at the stables at 1.30 p.m.'

Outside in the courtyard I found Pansy closing the boot of her car. At her feet was a WHSmith shopping bag. 'Supplies for Lav's new office,' she said happily. 'Oh – can I have a quick word?'

'Of course,' I said.

'You have Edith's ear, so to speak, don't you?' she said.

'I'm not sure if anyone does,' I replied.

'Do you think you can have a chat with her about our plan?' Pansy went on. 'Lav says Edith won't have any of it and Rupert is too much of a wimp to insist, but honestly, Edith's got to move into the twenty-first century to keep this place going if she wants Honeychurch Hall to survive.' Pansy looked at me keenly. 'Don't you agree?'

'It's hard for Edith—'

'It's not enough to have an open day where people can stroll around the grounds,' Pansy continued passionately. 'These stately homes have to pay their way. I mean, the

Duchess of Rutland says it costs two hundred thousand a year just to break even at Belvoir!' She pronounced it the correct way as 'beaver'.

'I had no idea but—'

'I haven't sold a *single* stick of furniture or a painting since I started Jamborees – I keep telling Lav that with every heirloom that Edith sells she is *ripping* the soul out of their home. Don't you think?'

'It must be very difficult . . .' I started edging my way to my car but Pansy followed so closely I could smell stale coffee on her breath.

'And of course attracting A-list celebrities is *excellent* publicity,' Pansy gushed on. 'What a coup to get Krystalle Storm— Oh yes. Don't look at me like that. Of course it's her. See it all the time. Checking in under aliases and whatnot. Even that awful business'– she pointed vaguely in the direction of Honeywell Wood – 'can be attractive to the right client. We absolutely must think *inside* the box, I say – *Lav!*'

I turned to see Lavinia scurrying over.

'Lav!' Pansy shouted again. 'I was just telling Kat we must think *inside* the box—'

'I think you mean outside the box,' I said.

'Inside, outside!' Pansy said. 'Get the celebrities here in droves.'

Lavinia was out of breath. 'Like Krystalle Storm.'

'Yes, so you say,' I said. 'I was there when she arrived – but she's not Krystalle Storm.'

'Of course she is,' Lavinia said. 'Everyone knows it's her.

We're so lucky that she heard about it. I hadn't even put the postcard into the post office – I mean community shop or whatever it's called these days.'

'That was pure fluke, Lav darling,' Pansy said. 'Anyway, you won't need to do all that old-fashioned stuff. Once your website is up and running you'll be swamped with bookings.'

I thought of how often Edith described her daughter-in-law as thicker than two short planks and I was inclined to agree. I wasn't too impressed with her friend Pansy either.

'Wren Fraser mentioned that she'd heard about your shepherd's hut from a friend,' I said.

'Yes.' Lavinia nodded. 'But I don't know who it was and anyway, who cares! She paid in cash.'

Pansy frowned then brightened. 'I have another brilliant idea! Bell tents are becoming popular now – ninety pounds a night and you just shove them in the park. I bet we could pitch at least twenty.'

Lavinia pulled a face. 'I don't think Edith will go for that. She kicked up a fuss about the shepherd's hut, which is why it's stuck out of sight in the walled garden.'

'Well, this is all very interesting,' I said. 'But I need to go.'

'Thanks for riding out,' said Lavinia. 'Pan's time is money, so to speak, and she's showing me all the ropes.'

'Yep.' Pansy nodded. 'Otherwise Lav will be all at sea.'

'Speaking of ropes and the sea,' I said. 'Can I show you something, Pansy?'

I pulled out the velvet pouches yet again and withdrew the miniatures.

Pansy gave a squeal of surprise. 'Oh! Oh! I *love* these so much! Why have you got them?'

This was not the answer I was expecting at all. 'You recognise them?'

'Of course I do!' Pansy exclaimed. 'They were ours.'

Chapter Fifteen

Pansy was in raptures. She turned to Lavinia. 'These are called the Drake Six miniatures, Lav – you know, Sir Francis Drake. Greatest seaman ever.'

'Oh yes, my brother Piers is chums with one of his descendants,' said Lavinia. 'Can I see?' She looked politely over Pansy's shoulder and muttered, 'Nice beard.'

'The *Pelican* was renamed the *Golden Hind*,' said Pansy. 'There should be four more miniatures to make up the set. Daddy hadn't wanted to sell them but we were in such a pickle. Dry rot.'

I couldn't believe my luck. 'You sold them? They weren't stolen?'

'Sold. Can't remember how we got them. Always been in the family.' She gave another squeal of delight and nudged Lavinia. 'You see that red speck? It's actually a poppy. Daddy used to say it should be a pansy because I'm Pansy . . .'

Pansy rambled on as I tried to come to grips with this extraordinary turn of events.

I finally managed to get a word in edgeways. 'Where did you sell them?'

'Auction,' said Pansy. 'Luxtons. Huge nautical sale.'

Luxtons again. 'Was Sir Monty involved in any way?' I said mildly.

Pansy shrugged. 'No idea. Daddy handled it. But it was absolutely yonks ago. I can't believe Perry sold them without telling me!'

I was stunned. 'Wait!' I exclaimed. 'You know who *bought* them?'

'Commodore Peregrine Fitzgibbon,' Pansy declared. 'I expressly told him that should he ever want to sell them I would absolutely buy them back from him. What a swizz.'

At last I felt that I was getting somewhere. 'Perhaps they were stolen from this friend of yours?'

'I'm going to phone him right this minute!' Pansy thrust the miniatures into Lavinia's hands and whipped out her mobile. As she scrolled down her contact list and hit a button she continued muttering under her breath, 'Can't believe he'd do that. He promised.'

The phone couldn't have rung more than once. 'Good morning, Jennifer,' said Pansy. 'Is the Commodore in?'

Apparently he wasn't but that didn't stop Pansy forging ahead with the reason for her call. 'Can you tell him I'm frightfully upset about the Drake Six – he'll know what I mean,' she declared. 'He must phone me back immediately. Got it? Good.'

Pansy ended the call. 'I know Perry's there. Jennifer is his frightful secretary who screens his calls.'

'Where does the Commodore live?' I asked.

'Dartmouth, of course,' said Pansy. 'Naval Academy.'

'Pansy knows everyone important,' Lavinia chimed in.

'Perry was a chum of Daddy's.' Pansy pulled a face. 'I can't believe he'd sell them. Perry's *obsessed* with Sir Francis Drake. Even called his cat Judith – that was Drake's first ship. But wait—' She cocked her head. 'You didn't tell me where *you* got them from.'

I hesitated. What was I to say? I found them in a doll's house in Lavender Green's bedroom and I think they may be stolen?

'A client,' I said. 'When did your father sell them? You mentioned it was a long time ago but how long are we talking about?'

Pansy frowned. 'Six, maybe seven years – oh.' Her phone rang. She glanced down and smirked. 'Calling me back already.' She jabbed a button. 'Perry!' There followed a long conversation on his end, punctuated by the occasional 'Ah-ha' and 'Seriously?' from Pansy.

After promising to have lunch soon, Pansy ended with a triumphant, 'Yup. I thought so. Of course, darling. Yup. Yup. Byeeee.' And disconnected the call.

'Well?' I said.

'You're going to have a very unhappy client,' Pansy declared. 'Your miniatures are fake.'

I did my best to keep my expression neutral. 'How can you be so sure?'

'I told you Perry would never sell the set.' She thought for a moment. 'You, of all people, should be able to tell a fake from the real thing.'

'You're right,' I said lightly. 'They must be very good fakes.'

'Can I see them again, Lav?' asked Pansy.

Lavinia handed the miniatures back for Pansy to inspect. 'It would be terrific fun if we could compare them with Perry's!' Pansy seemed to finish every sentence with an exclamation mark and she was beginning to wear me out.

'That would be super fun,' Lavinia agreed.

'We'll go today— Damn. I can't,' Pansy moaned. 'I've got a wedding meeting this afternoon and you're coming with me, Lav. And tomorrow – we're going to inspect the parkland for the bell tents.'

'Oh, that's a shame,' I said. 'Perhaps I could see the Commodore on my own? It's actually very important. I will need to tell my client that he has, er . . . fake Drakes.'

'Fake Drakes!' Lavinia sang. 'That rhymes.'

Pansy nodded. 'I'll see what I can do.'

We exchanged contact information and, with Pansy promising to text me to let me know, I headed for home.

I was more puzzled than ever about the Drake Six. Were they fakes? Was I losing my touch?

As I headed back down the drive, Clive – in a dazzling fluorescent high-visibility vest – stepped out and flagged me down. He looked very hot.

I noticed that the entrance to the old drive to the Carriage House had been cordoned off with crime scene tape. I opened my window.

'Got to stop all cars coming and going to the Hall and ask for their movements,' he said with an eye roll. He brandished his notebook and pencil and checked his wristwatch for the time.

'Well,' I teased, 'I've just come from Honeychurch Hall and now I'm going back to Jane's and then I'm going riding with the dowager countess. How long do you think this is going to go on for?'

'They're doing a grid search in Honeywell Wood right now,' he said. 'His high and mighty knows people in the right places and got some extra coppers on the job. They're interviewing everyone who works on the estate today and moving the mobile police unit into the village tomorrow.'

'And you? Why aren't you involved in the search,' I said.

'The boss said it was a conflict of interest and got Malcolm to assist,' said Clive, clearly not happy. 'He's a desk sergeant! Can you believe it?'

I actually couldn't. I thought of mild-mannered Malcolm manning the tiny satellite office that was being thrust out into the field.

'Malcolm is more worried about not being able to stop for snacks,' Clive went on but then his eyes widened. 'Speaking of snacks . . . now . . . *that's* a sight for sore eyes.'

I glanced in my rear-view mirror. Wren was approaching carrying the same wicker basket that Delia had dropped off to the shepherd's hut yesterday. Wren looked very pretty in a pale-blue linen skirt, white short-sleeved shirt and flip-flops.

Clive broke into a broad smile. 'Bless her. I thought she was joking when she said she'd bring me some lunch.'

I was instantly suspicious. 'How did you manage that?'

'My charm,' Clive said with a wolfish grin. 'I was watching the other gate this morning and she came out for a chat – brought me a cup of coffee in fact.'

'Clive,' I said quickly. 'Be careful about telling her anything.'

'Why?' he said. 'She's that famous writer Krystalle Storm. The most she'll do is put it in a book. Maybe I might be in the next one as . . . what do they call them? A love interest?'

At that, I had to laugh. 'It's highly unlikely that she is Krystalle Storm – if anything, she could be an undercover reporter. As you know, someone has been leaking details to the media.'

'No! Really?' said Clive. 'Okay. Mum's the word.'

Wren was soon upon us with her bright smiles and cheerful hellos. 'Ham and cheese with an apple and one of Peggy Cropper's flapjacks.'

'You're bloody gorgeous,' he blurted out, clearly infatuated.

Wren laughed. 'And you are too cute for words.'

I stifled a groan. 'How is the writing coming along?'

Wren sneezed. 'I had to get away from the garden,' she said. 'I took some antihistamine but it's that yellow stuff in there that's killing me.'

'Ragwort,' I said.

'Oh, I saw your mother this morning,' said Wren. 'She's invited me for drinks this evening at six.'

'But what about your deadline?' I said all innocence.

Wren cracked a smile. 'It will be my reward. Now, Clive

– you should be in the shade. It's far too hot in the sun.' And, taking him by the arm, she steered him into the shadows.

I turned the ignition and saw I had missed a text from Pansy. It read: *Perry can meet you tomorrow at noon! Pass at gate! Give him kisses from me!*

Even her texts had exclamation marks. I texted a reply – outdoing her: *Great!!!!*

Tomorrow would work well. I had planned to view Luxtons in the afternoon, so I would go to Dartmouth first.

As I pulled up to Jane's Cottage, Mum's Mini was there. I had forgotten that she was using my house as a temporary office.

I found her perched on a bar stool at the kitchen counter. A yellow legal pad was covered in writing. She waved at me with her pen. 'I didn't expect you here this morning.'

'Don't worry,' I said. 'I'm not staying long.'

'It's madness in my courtyard,' she said. 'The place is crawling with police. It's like one of those murder investigations that you see on the telly.'

'That's because it *is* a murder investigation,' I said.

As I made myself a piece of toast and added lashings of Peggy Cropper's blackcurrant jam, I filled Mum in on last night's mysterious lights in Honeywell Wood and Mallory's early-morning visit.

'A Frozen Charlotte in Charlie Green's *pocket*?' Mum said with amazement. She sat back and tapped her pencil on her top front tooth. 'That's a clue if ever there was one.'

'But a clue to what?' I said. 'I found seven Frozen Charlottes in a cigar box among Lavender's stock. There should have been eight.'

'How do you know?' Mum said.

'Because Lavender was meticulous to a fault and it had eight written on the side of the box.'

Mum shrugged. 'Charlotte can't have the monopoly on those hideous dolls,' she said.

'True,' I said. 'But I think that Charlie must have gone to Lavender's to get it before he was killed.'

'And then he came to the Hall where Eric killed *him* in a jealous rage,' Mum said.

'You and Eric!' I sighed. 'But that would make no sense as to why Charlie deliberately put a Frozen Charlotte into his pocket. What could that possibly have to do with Eric?'

Neither of us spoke. I finished my piece of toast and popped in another.

'Should you really have two, darling?' Mum said.

'Yes,' I said. 'And there is something else that I found odd.' I filled Mum in on the Drake Six and Charlotte's doll's house.

'Let me have a look at those,' said Mum.

I showed her.

'Very pretty,' she said. 'And stuck to the wall with Blu-Tack? That sounds to me as if they were deliberately hidden.'

'I think so, too,' I agreed.

'Drake was quite the rogue, you know,' Mum said. 'A lot of people thought of him as nothing more than a pirate. He was a slave trader and he even had his cousin's head cut off over a disagreement somewhere out in the Pacific Ocean – so the story goes.'

'Well, these six miniatures are extremely rare and very valuable,' I said. 'They were painted by a Dutch artist called Svetlana Winkler.'

Mum raised an eyebrow. 'Winkler? Never heard of her.'

'Have you met Lavinia's friend Pansy?' I asked.

'I've seen her striding up and down the drive in dungarees,' said Mum.

'The Drake Six have been in Pansy's family for generations,' I said. 'But they were forced to sell them – dry rot – and the Commodore of Dartmouth Naval Academy bought them at auction.'

'So you're saying you have the originals and the Commodore has the fakes or vice versa?'

'I just don't know,' I said. 'But I only have the two that I found in the doll's house in Lavender's bedroom.'

'Do you think you missed the other four?' Mum asked.

'It's possible I missed them,' I said. 'There was so much stuff in that bedroom. I'm going to have to take another look. I'm going to see the Commodore tomorrow at noon.'

'Well, make sure he doesn't get the wrong idea,' Mum sniggered. Seeing my confusion she added, 'When you ask him to show you his Winkler.'

'Mum!' I protested. 'You are incorrigible.'

She brightened. 'We should definitely let Alfred take a look at these. He's very good at forgeries.'

'Yes, I know,' I said drily. 'Which is why he spent so much time in prison.'

'On second thoughts, maybe not,' Mum said. 'He's got terrible anxiety about the police being here as it is.'

I finished my toast and took my plate to the sink.

'Of course I'm quite familiar with the Elizabethan *limnings*, as they were often known, or' – she made those annoying air quotes – '"pictures in little".'

'I am impressed!' I exclaimed.

'I do write historical fiction, dear,' Mum went on. 'I need to be up to speed on this kind of thing. In a way, the Elizabethan miniature was today's version of Instagram. Many of the female objects of desire were men, scantily clad, exposing their hairless chests for their ardent admirers. Often the artist would paint flames in the background to symbolise desire. Things haven't changed *that* much when it comes to love.'

'Speaking of love,' I said. 'What did you decide to do about Sir Monty?'

Mum's face fell. 'I'm not sure.'

'Oh, Mum!' I wailed. 'What are you waiting for?'

'Don't rush me. I have my reasons,' she said. 'He's taking me out to lunch today.'

I was disappointed. I had hoped that Sir Monty would have been given the boot, but then I was struck by a great idea. 'When you talk to your boyfriend, can you discreetly find out why he suddenly decided to help Violet sell her furniture for a staggeringly low two per cent commission and—' I made a dramatic pause. 'Guess what? He extended the same gesture and low commission to Rupert!'

'He *can* be kind,' Mum said as if she didn't believe it herself. 'And I was there when he saw Violet. We went in for tea.'

'Violet mentioned that you had,' I said. 'Why the sudden interest in her awful tea?'

'Monty was dropping me home and said he'd never been there before and wanted to support the local community,' said Mum. 'I told him that Violet's tea tasted like dirt but he didn't care.'

My suspicion as to what Sir Monty was up to deepened.

'It's not just the visitors who risk her refreshments,' Mum went on. 'Violet told us that even Pearl Clayton had stopped in last week.'

'I know,' I said. 'Violet told me about that too but you know it's because Pearl Clayton wants to run for Mayor. She's touting for votes.'

'She's got my vote,' said Mum. 'I like her.'

'So what are these so-called reasons to see Monty anyway?' I said.

Mum hesitated and then said, 'I'm going to ask him outright about *her.*'

'Violet? Pearl Clayton—?'

'No, my best friend Delia,' said Mum. 'I want to hear what he has to say and I'm going to record him saying it.'

I was appalled. 'You can't do that,' I said. 'It's an invasion of privacy!'

'No, I'm determined,' said Mum firmly. 'If things do get ugly, I don't want it to be a case of he-said-she-said. This way I'll have proof. The only problem is that I can't find my mobile. I left in a bit of a hurry when the Keystone Kops turned up waving their batons.'

'Don't you have the Find My app?'

Judging by my mother's expression, she had obviously never heard of this genius invention.

'Follow me,' I said and went to the sitting room to get my iPad from the coffee table. 'I'll log out of my account and into your Cloud. I know your email address but what's your password?'

'Exposed.'

'Ah, the title of your next book.' I typed it in. Mum hovered over my shoulder as the app worked its magic and Little Dipperton began to morph onto the screen, growing larger and larger until it zeroed in on Honeychurch Hall, the gatehouses . . . zooming in and in until . . . a blue dot blossomed right outside my front door.

'It's in your car,' I declared.

Mum looked to me in amazement. 'Now *that's* an invasion of privacy! Good grief! Let's see where Sir Monty is right now.'

I laughed. 'It doesn't work that way. You have to know his passwords.'

'I'll bear that in mind,' she said. 'What time are you going riding?'

I gave a cry of dismay. 'In . . . ten minutes' time! I can't be late!'

Chapter Sixteen

The moment I stepped under the archway and into the peace of the stables, I immediately felt better. Built around a stone courtyard, three sides of the quadrant housed four loose boxes, with the fourth side being divided by the main archway that was topped with a dovecote and clock.

It never ceased to amaze me how different it was here. As the condition of the Hall continued to deteriorate, the yard remained in pristine condition with not a piece of straw out of place.

I spied Mum's stepbrother, Alfred Bushman, carrying a bucket of fresh water in each hand. With his thatch of white hair, steel-rimmed glasses and a jaw like a French bulldog, he had been a professional boxer and was not a man to be trifled with.

He set one bucket of water down outside Jupiter's loose-box and another by Duchess.

'She's already tacked up for you,' said Alfred. 'She's feeling a bit skittish today. She knows there's a storm coming.'

'Today?' I said doubtfully.

We looked up at a cloudless blue sky.

'Within the next twenty-four hours, I reckon,' he said. 'Her ladyship is in with Tinkerbell.'

'Are you all right?' I asked. 'Mum mentioned the police—'

'I've got to talk to that inspector this afternoon,' he said anxiously. 'I already told them it's a waste of time. Do you think they'll do background checks?'

Alfred had every reason to be worried. My mother had managed to get him the job as Edith's stable manager under false pretences. Mum had told the dowager countess that he had been working with retired circus horses in Spain, when in reality, he'd been serving time at Wormwood Scrubs prison in Hammersmith.

'Alfred!' came a shout and Edith's face peered over the half-stable door. 'Do you think Tinkerbell's shoe will hold?'

We went to see.

Alfred let himself into the box to change places with Edith who was holding up Tinkerbell's off fore fetlock. The pair inspected the underside of her hoof.

'I reckon so,' said Alfred. 'Farrier's coming on Thursday. Are you taking the dog with you?'

'Not today,' said Edith. 'We're going too far. I locked Mr Chips in the kitchen. You can let him out when we've gone.'

Ten minutes later, Edith and I clattered out of the yard and down the drive side by side.

'I thought we'd follow the boundary line of the parish,'

said Edith. 'It'll take us past the building Rupert was talking about at Moreleigh Mount. No one has ridden that way for a long time, so it will be a good opportunity to check the fences.'

My heart sank. We'd be gone for hours! Although I never passed up a chance to ride, Edith's invitation had taken me off guard. I hadn't planned on going to the Emporium today and there were no valuations to do in my diary. But I had wanted to get back to Violet's to collect the doll's house and take another look at all the items in Lavender's bedroom. I hadn't checked the armoire or chest of drawers, and the remaining four Drake miniatures could be tucked away somewhere in those.

'Can I borrow the Defender?' I said to Edith. 'I want to pick up the doll's house from Violet's this afternoon. I need to figure something else out to pick up yours and the rocking horse.'

'Of course,' said Edith. 'Take Alfred to help you.'

'He's got to talk to Mallory,' I said.

'Oh, for heaven's sake,' Edith grumbled. 'That frightful man wants to talk to me too. Mrs Cropper was *interrogated*! Apparently she saw Charlie and Vera in the walled garden the night the police think he was killed.'

'Wasn't Eric there too?' I asked.

'Not at first,' said Edith. 'Mrs Cropper was watching from her upstairs bedroom window. And . . . well . . . something was going on in the icehouse.'

'The *icehouse*?' I exclaimed. 'But it's so small.'

'It was most inappropriate. Most inappropriate indeed.'

My curiosity got the better of me. 'What was inappropriate?'

Edith looked at me. 'Do I have to spell it out for you?'

I wanted to scream, *Yes! Please spell it out!*

'He caught them,' said Edith. 'And that's all I'm prepared to say.'

My heart sank. 'Are you thinking that Eric is responsible for Charlie's death?'

'People do all sorts of foolish things when they are in love,' she said and kicked Tinkerbell into a trot. The conversation was obviously over.

I was reminded of Edith's own foolish love affair that my mother knew about all those years ago when she used to come to Honeychurch Hall with the Travelling Fair and Boxing Emporium. That, too, had ended in tragedy.

Forbidden was Mum's second *Star-Crossed Lovers* novel and one that – albeit heavily disguised – featured a young Lady Edith Honeychurch and her liaison with the gamekeeper that would make Lady Chatterley's adventures seem dull.

Edith didn't speak again until we had left the woods and rolling valleys of the Honeychurch Hall estate well behind and the terrain had changed to rough moorland. We followed well-worn grassed-over trails of flint and granite. At times, narrow ditches fell away to be lost among boulders and rough scrubland. Sheep grazed and I was thrilled to see a handful of wild Dartmoor ponies. Not so far away was Haytor, a distinctive hill capped with its twin-peaked granite rock formation.

Edith drew rein where an upright post stood on a grassy knoll. Four mud beaten tracks went off in different directions. It was a bleak corner of the Honeychurch estate and I said so.

'This is our northern boundary,' said Edith. 'It used to be a busy route centuries ago with horse-drawn coaches and foot travellers. It was a known haunt for highwaymen and although dangerous, the site of the gibbet' – she pointed to the upright post with her whip – 'was a stark reminder of what might lie ahead for those who did not follow the law. The cross bar rotted away years ago.'

'*This* is Gibbet Cross?' I couldn't think of a worse place to sit and have a picnic!

'You saw the lectern in the attic,' said Edith. 'Being a judge was no small thing. Under the old act, the lord of the manor had the right to hold what was called a court leet. Only ten manors in the old hundred of Haytor – are you familiar with the term "hundred"?'

'A hundred was the ancient name for a specific area of a shire – not a parish or a county, which can seem confusing,' I said. 'The idea being that a hundred had enough land to sustain one hundred households.'

'You know your history, dear.' Edith seemed impressed. 'And what else?'

I smiled. 'It was introduced by the Saxons purely for administrative, military and judicial purposes.'

'Exactly,' said Edith. 'And as I was saying, only ten manors were granted permission to possess their own gallows.'

'Own gallows!' I echoed.

'Honeychurch Hall was one of those manors,' Edith said. 'The Murder Act was introduced in 1751 that gave judges the power to sentence criminals – particularly those who had committed murder, stole sheep, indulged in highway robbery and, of course, poached rabbits. As you know, Honeychurch used to have its own rabbit warren, so poaching was a big temptation.'

'I find it astonishing that the decision to condemn a man to death was down to one person,' I said.

'Most of the time, yes,' said Edith. 'Although my ancestor was ruthless in his choice of the hangman's noose, it was at least quick – others favoured the metal cage. Rather than be hanged, the prisoner was left to die of starvation.'

'Who was the hangman?' I said. 'Surely not the sixth Earl of Grenville?'

'It was a Pugsley,' said Edith.

I gasped. 'Oh! Good grief. My mother is going to love hearing about that!'

Edith gave a small smile. 'Let's hope the thirst for blood doesn't run in Eric's genes.'

There wasn't anything to say after that. We sat there on our horses just taking in the magnificent vista. It was then that I saw the top of a chimney in a small basin among the low hills.

'Where is that?' I asked.

'Moreleigh Manor,' said Edith. 'That was where Violet, Lavender and Bunty – their brother – grew up. The mines are beyond there, although of course long abandoned.'

So this was the manor and mining business that Charlie

had inherited and then sold off, causing so much financial hardship for his two aunts.

'Where is the building that Rupert leased to Charlie Green?'

Edith pointed her whip towards the east. 'Moreleigh Mount. Not far from here. It's on our way back but I thought you would enjoy a tour of the boundary.'

I followed her in single file as we descended a narrow track through a small wood of dwarf pedunculate oaks – a regular sight on Dartmoor. The stunted and gnarled trees always seemed sinister to me.

The track opened into a green lane, one of many hundreds that threaded their way through the South Hams. The surface was rough with slate and granite slabs, rutted with the wear of centuries. The horses found it hard going and struggled to keep their balance. I was worried about Tinkerbell's shoe. I could hear it clink on the granite. It was definitely coming loose. The idea of walking a lame horse back to Little Dipperton did not fill me with joy.

Edith drew rein again at an open rusty-iron gate. The mud-hardened trail showed two well-worn channels that suggested the constant use of a farm vehicle.

'This way.' Edith set off through a leafy tunnel of arching treetops. Tinkerbell's shoe wasn't so loud on the mud and, so far, she didn't seem lame. I wondered why Edith – who adored that horse – had been so determined to see this building on horseback. It would have made much more sense for Rupert to drive here.

The trail curved gently and we emerged from the dappled canopy of overhanging branches onto a hardstanding in front of a purpose-built farm building made of cinder blocks and topped with a corrugated-iron roof.

Even though the surrounding yard had the usual rusting machinery that seemed to be the norm in any farmyard, the building looked as if it was still in use. I felt a strange prickle of unease.

Edith stopped. 'Why don't you go and have a look.'

Having a look was the last thing that I wanted to do. I urged Duchess forward but she wasn't having any of it and started backing away as a gust of wind sent up sheets of discarded black plastic. I dismounted and handed the reins to Edith and set off on foot.

It was then that I noticed that the range of windows just beneath the roofline had all been painted out. The door was padlocked and the padlock looked fairly new. Something didn't feel right here at all.

'It's padlocked,' I called out.

'Go around the back,' Edith shouted.

I followed the line of the building to the rear where there was a set of double doors, but they were padlocked, too. I looked up and saw a tiny red light. My heart turned right over.

It was a CCTV camera.

I hurried back to Edith. 'Not only is someone using this,' I said. 'But they've installed a security camera.'

'But this is preposterous!' Edith exclaimed. 'How can Rupert not know?'

'In all fairness,' I said. 'If the rent is being paid, then surely the tenant can do whatever they like?'

'Well, clearly this so-called tenant isn't Charlie Green,' Edith declared.

I mounted Duchess, anxious to be away. 'I'm sure Rupert only has to look at his bank statements to see where the money is coming from.'

'One would hope so,' Edith muttered.

It was moments after we left the track and the rusting gate behind us that Tinkerbell finally cast her shoe.

'Alfred said she would be fine,' Edith grumbled. I helped her off Tinkerbell and up onto Duchess. With her riding habit and the absence of a mounting block it wasn't easy despite Edith being as light as a bird, but we did it. Edith rearranged her long skirt – or petticoat to use the correct term – and we headed for home.

Edith rode on ahead with me on foot leading Tinkerbell. We'd not gone far when we heard the sound of an approaching car and a white BMW hatchback came into view.

There was no room for the car to pass us. It was too far to walk back to the rusting gate, but luckily the BMW reversed – and extremely well, clearly a local – before pulling into a passing place so we could finally get past him.

But it wasn't a man. It was a woman in her fifties with a honey-coloured bob and wearing huge sunglasses. She opened her window and turned off her ignition so as not to spook the horses.

'Can you help? I'm hopelessly lost,' she called out. I detected a distinctive Devonian accent. 'My satnav gave up on me.'

I approached the car. Up close, the woman was much older than I thought – closer to sixty-five than fifty. She wore a crisp pale-pink pin-striped shirt and expensive jewellery.

'Where are you trying to get to?' I asked.

'Okehampton,' she said. 'I thought I'd take the scenic route across the moors.'

'We've all done that.' I smiled. 'But I'm afraid this lane is a dead-end. You'll have to go back to the main road.'

'Is everything all right? Is your horse lame?' the woman asked.

'Tinkerbell cast a shoe,' I said. 'We've got a very long walk home.'

'I'd call someone if I had a signal.' She turned away to pick up a bottle of water. 'For you. It's a new one.'

'Thank you!' I said gratefully. 'That's very kind.'

'Good luck!' she said.

'And good luck to you too!' I replied.

Edith and I retraced our steps for a few yards so the woman could turn her BMW around. Within moments she had driven away and disappeared from view.

I gave Edith the water bottle. She shook her head. 'I'm fine. I used to hunt all day and never stopped for lunch.'

'You probably started with a hearty breakfast,' I teased. 'And had nips from your hip flask to keep you going.'

Edith seemed pensive. 'Odd that she got lost here.'

'I still get lost in Devon,' I pointed out and set off again, thankful for the water.

Eventually, our lane came to a T-junction.

'Right or left,' I said to Edith.

'Left,' said Edith. 'We're on the home stretch now. We'll be back within the hour.'

I thought back to the woman in the BMW. When we'd exited the lane where we'd seen her, the No Through Road blue sign with the red horizontal bar of the T, although partially covered by buckthorn, was not difficult to see. I soon forgot her as my heels got blisters and all I could think about was getting home.

By the time we reached Honeychurch Hall, my feet were killing me.

Alfred came rushing out to greet us. 'I was so worried milady. You should have been home hours ago!' He helped Edith dismount.

Rupert appeared, which – in the stable yard – was a rare occurrence. He looked distraught.

'Whatever's happened?' Edith demanded.

'Eric's been arrested for murder!'

Chapter Seventeen

'The new inspector found Charlie Green's motorbike in Eric's scrapyard,' Rupert said.

'Planted it, didn't they,' muttered Alfred.

Rupert turned on Alfred, eyes narrowing. 'What was that you say? Planted it? Deliberately, you mean?'

Alfred met Rupert's gaze without flinching. 'He's a new copper. Wants a quick arrest. Stands to reason that's what he'd do. He hasn't got a suspect so he picks Eric.'

'Do you think so?' Rupert sounded relieved.

'Where is Eric now?' I asked.

'He's been taken into police custody,' said Rupert. 'They're taking his DNA.'

'Did Eric cough to it, milord,' said Alfred.

'Cough? What do you mean, *cough*?' Rupert demanded.

'Alfred means did Eric admit to killing Charlie Green,' I translated.

'No, of course he didn't,' snapped Rupert. 'But he admitted that he caught his wife – that would be before your time – and Charlie Green alone in the walled garden and there was an argument.'

This was news to me. Edith hadn't mentioned any argument.

'That don't mean he did it,' Alfred said stubbornly. 'That's what the cops do. Try to trick you into saying you're guilty. Talk you in circles until you admit to killing your own grandmother!'

'Good heavens, man!' Rupert exclaimed.

'You'd better go and sort the new policeman out, Rupert,' Edith said wearily. 'He can't go around arresting our servants willy-nilly.'

'I don't think they're called servants these days, Mother,' said Rupert.

'Really?' Edith said. 'Then what are they called?'

Rupert just blinked.

'Katherine wants to borrow the Defender and I said she could,' said Edith. 'Are the keys in the ignition?'

'Yes,' Rupert said with a nod.

And with that, Edith left. I passed Tinkerbell's reins to Alfred and he led the mare back to her loosebox. I was exhausted and the last thing I felt like doing was going into Little Dipperton to pick up the doll's house, especially as I had been counting on Eric's assistance.

'Katherine,' said Rupert. 'Do you know where your mother is?'

'Probably at Jane's Cottage,' I said. 'Why?'

'The police want to look in the old piggery,' said Rupert. Mum's writing house! All her awards! Her Krystalle

Storm first editions! I thought my heart would stop. 'Why? Whatever for?'

'That Mallory chap wants to understand the relationship between the Pugsleys, Starks and Croppers,' said Rupert. 'Apparently Iris had told him about the below stairs family tree.'

'But . . . but . . .' I stammered. 'Charlie Green has nothing to do with below stairs.'

Rupert just shrugged.

'Did they try her mobile?' I asked.

'I have no idea,' said Rupert. 'The piggery door is locked but I told him to go ahead and open it. Apparently among his many talents this Mallory chap is also an expert in picking locks— Are you all right? You've gone very pale.'

'Fine,' I muttered. 'The heat. Must go. Excuse me.' I darted back to my car, calling Mum's mobile on my way. There was no answer. I sent her a text: *Mallory wants to see family tree ASAP. Meet you there* and added a silent prayer that I would get to the courtyard in time.

My worst fear was happening! My mother's secret was about to be revealed!

I roared into the courtyard just as Mallory opened the door to the writing house. Clive turned and waved.

I was too late.

I ran over to join them feeling hot, scruffy. I wanted to cry. 'I really think we should wait for Mum to join us,' I said desperately. 'She'll be here at any minute.'

'But you're here now,' said Mallory.

'You heard about Eric,' Clive said with a snigger. 'I'm

not surprised. He was obsessed with Vera. Everyone knew she was a bit of a goer – at school she would show you her underwear for a pound.'

'For God's sake, Banks!' Mallory groaned. '*Please.*'

Mallory ducked through the door with Clive and I behind him. It was gloomy inside. Mum had dropped down the blinds as the rear window looked out over Honeywell Wood.

Mallory flipped the light switch.

'Well, blimey, will you look at all this!' Clive exclaimed. 'It's bloody luxury!'

A grey metal filing cabinet five drawers high stood in one corner. In another was a standard lamp and Dad's battered leather wingback chair that Mum used for reading. Next to that was a hexagonal table piled with editions of *The Lady* magazine and the weekly *Dipperton Deal*. There was a wood-burning stove in the corner that, of course, wasn't lit during the summer, and opposite that was a comfortable sofa.

Floor-to-ceiling custom-made bookshelves covered one wall. Miraculously, the green taffeta ballgown that my mother had worn to the Jockey Club Summer Ball was hanging from the top of the bookshelf. It covered nearly all of my mother's writing awards but not her first editions. Those ranged along many shelves – a tribute to her decades-long writing career.

Dad's Olivetti typewriter sat on Mum's walnut partners' desk. Thankfully there was no stack of incriminating sheets of typewritten pages ready to edit, but there was one solitary sheet of paper in the carriage.

Fortunately, Mallory and Clive made a beeline for the corkboard that spanned an entire wall.

'Well, I'll be blowed!' Clive exclaimed. 'Will you look at all this?'

I could tell that both men were impressed. As long as I kept their attention on the family trees, I just might be able to keep my mother's secret.

A third of the corkboard was covered in black-and-white photographs of Honeychurch Hall and the formal gardens in what must have been its heyday at the beginning of the twentieth century – the golden age of the English country house. Colour photographs dating from the 1950s and early 60s showed the interior of the shell-lined grotto and the exterior of the Carriage House before it was abandoned for the new stable block closer to the Hall. Unfortunately, the grotto was where I had discovered Vera's body not long after I moved to Honeychurch Hall. I saw no reason for Mallory to know.

Pinned in the top left-hand corner was a newspaper cutting of Edith riding Tinkerbell. HRH Princess Anne was presenting her with a large silver cup.

Another third was labelled 'Above Stairs' and was a family tree of interconnecting lines and circles that traced the Honeychurch clan back to when the 1st Earl of Grenville was created in 1414 by Henry V. Post-it notes were fixed to various family members with random information. Next to Edward Rupert b.1835–d.1899 was 'Crimea/Mummified Hawk'. Harold James b.1840–d.1885 was 'Explorer/Polar Bear'. Another family member perished on the *Titanic* and was the reason Edith had one of the rare *Titanic* Mourning Bears that she had given to Harry; and yet another ancestor had run a Turkish harem in London. Delia was right. The Honeychurch antics would fill dozens of racy novels.

And the remaining third – labelled 'Below Stairs' – was still in its relative infancy. There were five main families – Pugsley, Banks, Stark, Cropper and the infamous Jones clan. Mum had started the family tree at 1850 although, judging by the Post-it notes, she planned on going much further back. I noted an Alfred Pugsley, 1756–1803, and the location of his headstone in the graveyard, and wondered if he had been the family executioner that Edith had spoken of.

The five families were interlinked by birth or marriage. Clive was in raptures and went on to spill the beans about the various scandals and goings-on in the village.

'I think I get the picture,' Mallory was finally able to say. 'But this isn't helpful. Where does Charlie Green fit in?'

Clive looked blank. 'Well, he had a fling with Peggy Cropper's niece Vera who was married to Eric.'

'Banks,' said Mallory with a heavy sigh, 'this proves nothing other than the fact there is a worrying amount of inbreeding here in Little Dipperton. Please thank your mother, Kat. I think we are finished here.'

'Oh, great,' I said. As Mallory left the building I let out the breath that I didn't realise I'd been holding since the moment Rupert told me the police were breaking into the piggery! I stepped into the courtyard and watched Mallory disappear into the mobile police unit but, when I turned back to close the writing house door, Clive was still inside.

'Clive, come on!' I said and rushed back to get him.

I froze in the doorway. In one hand, Clive held the typewritten page from the carriage of the Olivetti and in the other, a crumpled piece of balled-up yellow paper that he must have found in my mother's wastepaper basket.

Bewildered and with growing excitement, Clive studied the bookshelves that were jammed with Krystalle Storm first editions.

His face was flushed. 'What's all this?'

'Mum's a fan of Krystalle Storm,' I declared.

'No. I think she *is* Krystalle Storm!' Clive's eyes narrowed. 'Look.' He thrust the typewritten page under my nose. It was the title page of Mum's next novel: *Exposed*.

'Don't be ridiculous!' I exclaimed. 'Anyway, I thought everyone around here believes that Wren Fraser is Krystalle Storm!'

'What do you make of that then?' He thrust the balled-up piece of paper at me. There were some barely legible notes: *Amanda meets C. of I. in Rose garden. Argument. He's upset with new officer. Jealousy. Humiliation. Sword fight. Remember thick ankles.* The notes had a big line across them with the word 'NO!' written in black pen.

'Bloody hell, it's true, isn't it?' he said. 'My wife reads her books and says Amanda is one of her favourite characters. Well, I'll be blowed! Bloody hell.'

I didn't know what to say. I didn't know what to do.

'I thought that Wren was too young,' Clive gabbled on. 'And it's your—'

'Mum's Dear Amanda,' I blurted out.

Clive's jaw dropped. 'What? What do you mean she's Dear Amanda?'

'She's Dear Amanda,' I repeated and took the yellow scrap of paper from him. 'You see it says Amanda right there . . . and the letter C, that stands for – Clive or Chris or something, and the rose garden is *obviously* Rose Cottage.'

Clive's complexion had turned an ugly red. I could see that he didn't believe me – and why should he?

'Where does she keep all her letters?' He marched over to the metal filing cabinets. I darted ahead and jumped in front to stop him.

'Please don't do this, Clive,' I protested. 'It's all highly confidential.'

'So your mother knows all the village secrets, does she?' Clive was furious. In fact, his reaction was not one I expected at all. When he'd believed Mum was Krystalle Storm he seemed excited, but now he was angry – no, not angry, he was scared.

It suddenly hit me. Had Clive sought Dear Amanda's counsel at one time? Why else would he be so upset?

And then my mother burst in. Her face was ashen. 'It's all a lie!'

'Hi, Mum,' I said brightly. 'I'm afraid I had to tell Clive that you're Dear Amanda.'

Mum looked blank and then her face went through a series of expressions from relief to anxiety and then finally to feigned horror. 'Oh *dear*, I was so hoping it would never come to this, Clive.'

Clive swallowed hard. He looked as if he was going to cry. 'I didn't mean what I said about destroying Mallory's career.'

Mallory's career?

'It's just that' – he swallowed again – 'with Shawn gone, I should have been promoted,' he whined. 'Instead, they send in some hot-shot detective who we all know was only transferred because he slept with the wrong woman.'

Mum caught my eye. 'Of course you were upset and I don't blame you,' she said smoothly. 'Sometimes we just want to tell someone how we feel, knowing that we won't be judged. Don't you agree?'

Clive nodded miserably but my mind was reeling. I thought of the first letter I'd begun to read from last Saturday's edition of the *Dipperton Deal*. Was it possible that Clive had been the leak and not Wren after all?

'Please don't tell anyone,' Clive mumbled. 'It would be the end of my career.'

'Confidentiality is the name of the game,' Mum said cheerfully. 'Isn't that right, Kat?'

'Our lips are sealed,' I agreed. 'And yours should be too, Clive.'

'I won't breathe a word of it.' Clive brightened. 'So is it true about Doreen Mutters hiding her credit card statements in the freezer?'

'Clive!' Mum wagged her finger. 'Don't be naughty now. I am the keeper of *everyone's* secrets. Now run along. Not a word to a soul and you'll keep your job.'

Clive left and closed the door behind him.

'What a clever girl you are!' Mum beamed.

'Not really,' I said as the impact of my mother being Dear Amanda slowly began to sink in. 'The problem is that Dear Amanda has been around for ever. Decades before we arrived.'

'All that matters is that for now, we got away with it,' said Mum.

'No. *You* got away with it. I haven't done anything to get away with.' I sank onto the sofa, extremely distressed. 'Thank God it was only Clive. This must stop, Mum. Seriously.'

'So Clive is the leak. He's the one talking to the press,' Mum mused. 'It's always good to have leverage over someone.'

'Leverage,' I scoffed. 'You've been watching too much American TV.'

Mum looked smug.

'Why?' I said slowly. 'Who else have you got leverage over?'

She brandished her mobile. 'Monty. It's all recorded here. The scoundrel told me Delia was practically stalking him and that he was only talking to her to be polite. He was actually very unkind about her.'

'What a cad!' I exclaimed. 'What are you going to do?'

'I'm not sure yet,' she said. 'But when I am, I'll let you know.'

'Did you find anything else out?' I said. 'Why he's offering such low commissions?'

'Well . . . I do think he is up to something,' Mum said. 'He was dashing off to pick up another piece of furniture in Ashburton. When I questioned who from, he said it was an elderly lady who was going into a luxury retirement home and her daughter had to sell her antiques to pay for it.'

I was intrigued. 'So . . . he's offering some kind of house clearance service?'

Mum shook her head. 'No,' she said. 'That's the thing. He said it was just an armoire and an oak settle.'

'Did you ask him how he heard about the items?' I said. 'How was he contacted? Email? Phone? A referral?'

'I didn't ask,' Mum said. 'It was a monumental effort to be civil after he denied anything was going on with Delia. I had to restrain myself from tipping my gazpacho soup all over his head.'

I couldn't help it: I laughed.

'But when I asked Monty if he had ever met Charlie Green, he got very agitated and claimed he didn't know that Violet Green was Charlie's aunt.' Mum frowned. 'Wait, isn't *Charley's Aunt* a play?'

'It's a farce,' I said. 'And I feel like I'm living one.'

Mum grinned. 'Speaking of impersonations,' she went on. 'Don't forget that Wren is coming for drinks at six.'

'I haven't forgotten,' I said. 'But first, I need to pick up the doll's house from Violet's.'

I got up to leave. 'Oh, and one more thing. Eric's been arrested.'

Mum beamed again. 'You've made my day!'

And with that, I drove *back* to the stables to switch my Golf for Edith's Defender and *finally* headed for Little Dipperton.

Chapter Eighteen

Twenty minutes later I pulled into the alley and parked behind Violet's Morris Minor Traveller. It was almost five o'clock.

I found Violet seated at the kitchen table counting out banknotes and coins – presumably the day's takings – although there seemed to be a lot of twenty-pound notes.

'I'm sorry I got held up,' I said. 'I've got the Defender outside and I'm going to ask Simon next door if he can help me move the doll's house.'

'You're too late,' she declared. 'The house clearance man came and took everything away.'

'What?' I gasped. '*Everything?* But . . . you knew I wanted the doll's house—' To say nothing of having a thorough look through Lavender's things for the other four Drake miniatures.

'You didn't take them yesterday,' Violet grumbled. 'You didn't come this morning. I assumed that you didn't want them after all.' She paused. 'And he gave me one thousand pounds!'

'One thousand *pounds*!' I was shocked. So the piles of cash that Violet was counting were not the day's takings after all. There was no way that Lavender's car boot stuff was worth that much. My surprise turned to suspicion.

'Who came to take everything away?' I demanded.

'I forget his name but he just turned up,' Violet replied.

'He wouldn't have turned up out of the blue.'

Violet blinked at me through her bottle-top glasses. I was making a superhuman effort not to show my dismay. 'Who was it? Did Sir Monty send someone?'

Violet was getting nervous. 'I don't remember.'

'The dowager countess will be very disappointed when she finds out that the doll's house she gave Charlotte as a present – something she spent a lot of money on having made specially – has been given away to a stranger. Her ladyship wanted it for the Museum Room.' I let this sink in. Of course Edith had said nothing of the kind, but I hoped this would shock Violet into remembering.

Violet gave a cry of distress. 'He was so insistent. He wanted everything or nothing at all.'

'Why don't you call him and say you made a mistake?' I suggested.

Violet bit her lip. 'I don't have his number.'

I took a deep breath. 'I'm surprised he didn't want to see Lavender's ledgers,' I said slyly.

'I told him that you had the ledgers,' said Violet. 'But he didn't care.'

I thought for a moment. 'Was it Gavin or Ronnie from

yesterday?' At least I could call Luxtons and get a number that way.

'No.' Violet frowned. 'Although he did look familiar.'

There was a clatter of plastic and Willow batted her way through the red and white plastic door fringe. She was carrying a tray laden with dirty crockery. 'That's the lot. Everyone has left. I locked the front door and flipped over the "Closed" sign.' She took the tray to the draining board and started to wash up. Violet didn't believe in dishwashers.

'Don't forget, I want everything put away in its proper place,' Violet reminded her.

'Oh, Kat,' said Willow. 'Everyone in the village is talking about Mr Pugsley being arrested. Is it true?'

'It's true,' Violet declared. 'And I'm not surprised. Everyone knew that Charlie had been carrying on with his wife – who was also no good. They'd been fornicating for years.'

Willow turned scarlet. 'Oh.'

'That's not exactly true,' I said springing to Eric's defence. 'And we don't know all the details.'

'The new detective seems to think so,' Violet declared. 'They're not doing any more interviews. Doreen Mutters says it's a closed case.'

I had a sudden thought and turned to Willow. 'Do you remember the name of the man who came to clear out Lavender's room today?'

'I think it was Leslie,' said Willow.

Leslie? I was flummoxed. I knew there wasn't a Leslie who worked at Luxtons. 'What did he look like?'

Willow shrugged. 'Old, I suppose. Not as old as Miss Green but older than you.'

I suppressed a smile. I remembered being Willow's age when anyone over the age of thirty was as good as dead.

'He was very short,' she went on. 'Like a jockey. But very strong.'

'He must have been very strong to have moved all that stuff downstairs on his own,' I said. 'Especially the doll's house.'

'He had one of those dolly things – the kind used for loading and unloading,' she said.

'Really?' This surprised me. 'And he managed to take the doll's house down the staircase using that?'

Willow looked uncomfortable. 'I helped him with the doll's house.'

'Ah! So you went outside to load it in the van?' I said. 'Did the van have the Luxtons logo on the side?'

'No,' said Willow. 'It was just white with a bit of fence stuck in the bumper. I remember that because he said he didn't do it.'

I thought of the broken stretcher that Mallory had spotted earlier. 'Did you notice if the side wing mirror was broken?'

'No, sorry.' Willow turned on the taps and started washing up.

A bit of fence stuck in the fender was too much of a coincidence. Could the white Transit van be the vehicle that I'd seen driving away in the early hours of the morning?

Violet sat in front of the piles of cash looking miserable. 'I don't want her ladyship to be angry about the doll's house.'

I pushed the pang of guilt aside. I *had* to know who had taken the contents of Lavender's bedroom. And then I had another thought.

'Do you know anything about a lease on one of Lord Rupert's farm buildings out at Moreleigh Mount?' I said. 'Apparently Charlie used it to restore his motorbikes.'

'Oh yes,' said Violet. 'Lavender insisted that we pay for it, but I never went there. The road is so narrow.' Her expression hardened. 'At least I won't have to pay for *that* any more.'

'Do you know how much you were paying?' I said.

'His lordship never put the rent up,' said Violet. 'I think it was twenty-five pounds a month. We paid by direct debit.'

'That seems very cheap,' I said.

'Twenty-five pounds is still twenty-five pounds,' Violet protested. 'Or was it twenty-five pounds? Perhaps it was twenty-six? But the arrangement was between his lordship and Charlie. I shall go through my tos and froms tonight and let you know the exact date and exact amount.'

'Thank you – and, of course, if you find this man called Leslie's phone number, that would be really helpful.'

But I felt unsettled. The farm building had looked as if it was still very much in use, especially given the CCTV camera.

'Do you mind if I just take a quick peep in Lavender's bedroom to see if Leslie has taken everything?'

I didn't wait for Violet to answer. I went straight upstairs.

Violet was right. Only the furniture was left. The room had been stripped – along with the photographs on the mantelpiece and the postcards from Ireland.

Thoroughly frustrated, I left Rose Cottage empty-handed and turned my thoughts to the next mystery.

Wren Fraser.

Chapter Nineteen

Wren was already waiting in the cobbled courtyard at Mum's Carriage House. She had parked her Honda next to the wishing well and was snooping around the range of buildings that stood in the quadrangle. Although the mobile police unit was still there it looked ready to be towed away. The metal steps had vanished and the free-standing police signs had gone.

I left my car next to Wren's and got out. She waved and hurried over.

'I would love to live somewhere like this,' Wren beamed. 'It's a writer's paradise.'

'It certainly is,' I said.

'I had to look inside every building,' she gushed on. 'Is that a still in the old hen house? Do you make moonshine?'

'Gin,' I said. 'My mother makes it for friends at Christmas.'

'I don't drink gin,' said Wren. 'It makes me depressed.'

She pointed to the converted piggery. 'And what's in there? It's padlocked.'

'The Honeychurch family archives.' I felt sick just thinking about how close Mum had come to being exposed.

It was hard to escape the irony. My mother was now Dear Amanda and Wren was posing as Krystalle Storm. If things weren't so serious, it would have been funny.

'I went to the front door but no one answered,' said Wren.

'My mother can't hear anyone at that door,' I said. 'We use the one in the carriageway. Let's go.'

'Clive told me all about the family trees – both above and below,' she said as we walked across the courtyard. 'He said his folks were gardeners and grooms.' She cocked her head. 'Where did the Green family fit in?'

'They didn't,' I said. 'They were landowners themselves.'

I picked up the pace, anxious to change the subject.

'They arrested Eric Pugsley – but of course you'd know that.' She hurried along beside me. 'Do you think he did it?'

'What does your friend Clive think?' I said pointedly.

Wren frowned. 'He's gone a bit weird on me,' she said. 'He was all friendly and then suddenly he's clammed up and isn't talking. He is married though. Perhaps he thought I was after him. As if!'

'Perhaps he didn't like your sandwich,' I said drily.

'That's why I'm asking you,' she said obviously missing my sarcasm.

I stopped in my tracks. 'Why are you so interested?'

'I'm a writer! Everything interests me.' Wren grinned.

'From what I've heard, the affair between this Charlie bloke and Vera had been over for ages.'

'Wren,' I said wearily. 'This happened way before my time.'

'And what were they doing in the walled garden?' she went on. 'It's in full view of Eric's cottage so they were bound to be seen by someone – which they were of course. Eric saw them and so did Peggy Cropper. If they were sneaking around, why sneak there? Why not sneak in say . . . the stumpery?'

She looked at me keenly. I desperately wanted to shout out, 'You're a fraud! You're a reporter!' but for now, I had to play along.

'What do you think?' Wren said.

'I don't know,' I said.

'Peggy Cropper says that at the time of Charlie Green's disappearance, Eric and Vera were in a good place together,' Wren continued. 'They were happy. So I don't think it was a romantic assignation at all. Do you?'

'To be honest, Wren, I'm surprised you're taking such an interest. Shouldn't you be thinking about your deadline?'

Wren turned pink and didn't answer.

I walked on ahead. She followed me into the carriage-way.

Wren gasped. 'It's amazing! Gosh. I love the herring-bone floor! And that skylight is awesome.'

The skylight ran the length of the arch-braced roof. Wren bombarded me with questions about the carriageway that I was happy to answer – anything to change the subject. I told her that the redbrick building had been built in 1830 and that it used to accommodate four carriages and twenty-four horses.

'Through there are the original stalls.' I pointed to the red-brick arches that stood on either side of the carriageway. The stalls still had their original metal nameplates – Fiddlesticks, China Cup, Tin Man, Lady, Briar Patch and Misty – horses long since gone but now resting in the equine cemetery.

'The housekeeper told me that there's a horse grave-yard,' Wren enthused. 'I would love to go and see that.'

'I'm sure it can be arranged,' I said.

'Is that in Latin?' Wren pointed to the first archway that, like all the archways, displayed the family coat of arms – two hawks flanking an ornate blue shield edged in gold.

'It's the Honeychurch motto,' I said. '*Ad perseverate est ad triumphum*, which means "to endure is to triumph".'

'Are the hawks significant?' she asked. 'They seem to be everywhere.'

Mum had swotted up on heraldry and told me all about it. 'The hawk symbolises one who does not rest until one's objective is achieved. Gold is for generosity and the elevation of the mind. Silver is for peace and sincerity, and blue or azure is for truth and loyalty.'

'Gosh. So much history,' said Wren. 'I can only go back two generations on my mum's side and just three on my dad's.'

'A bit like me,' I said. Much as I didn't want to, I couldn't help but warm to her enthusiasm.

Mum must have been waiting for us. She threw the door open with a big smile. 'Welcome to my humble abode!'

'It's soooooo beautiful here,' Wren said. 'It's hard to believe that someone was murdered in your back garden. I suppose you know that Eric Pugsley has been arrested.'

Mum seemed taken aback. 'Let's not talk about that sort of thing,' she said. 'I want to hear all about you. Kat, why don't you go inside and get the drinks and I'll take Wren around to the suntrap.'

At the beginning of the summer my mother had found a sheltered nook on the south side of the building and created a Moroccan-themed patio area with plenty of colourful cushions and exotic lanterns. She had also planted lush grasses in terracotta pots.

'I thought we'd have Pimm's,' Mum declared.

'Oh, just a weak one for me,' said Wren. 'I'm writing and I can't afford to lose my focus.'

'Weak? Don't be silly, dear. Pimm's is mainly fruit.' Mum's eyes met mine again and in them I caught a glint of mischief. 'Kat will make up a *weak* jug,' she said, then mouthed, '*Lots of gin.*'

I left them to it and headed to the kitchen. Mum had already set out three pretty Moroccan amethyst-coloured glasses on a decorative tray, along with a matching glass pitcher. I made up the Pimm's and added plenty of gin, sliced the fresh fruit, added some fresh mint and a couple of strawberries. I set out some Sharpham Brie and crackers and went to join them.

Enclosed on three sides by adjoining walls, the fourth

was open and looked over a field of waving corn. Wren sneezed and pulled a tissue from her handbag.

'Wren tells me she's a writer,' Mum said all innocence. 'I've always wanted to be a writer so I'm anxious to know all about it.'

'Well,' said Wren, 'there's honestly not much to tell. I just sit down at my laptop and the words just pour out of me. I can write for hours and hours. Once I'm immersed, I seem to lose all track of time.'

'How lucky,' Mum said brightly 'So all that rubbish about tortured scribes and writer's block is just to put normal people off writing. Don't you agree?'

Wren nodded and took a sip of Pimm's. 'This is delicious.'

'Do you write longhand first?' Mum said. 'Just to map out your stories?'

'I don't need to.' Wren tapped her forehead. 'It's all in here.'

'Really?' Mum said with mock surprise. 'Even the great Agatha Christie had notebooks full of her plots and characters.'

Wren shrugged. 'I don't write those kinds of books. I write love stories.'

'Love stories?' Mum cocked her head. 'Oh! You mean *romance*? Isn't that what people call it these days?'

Wren nodded and took another sip of Pimm's. 'Dashing knights and damsels in distress with a little bit of saucy stuff thrown in.'

'Like *Bridgerton*?' Mum suggested. 'What was the name

of the author?' She snapped her fingers. 'Julia Quinn. Kat and I loved the series on the telly – and that handsome Duke of Hastings . . . don't get me started on his many attributes!'

Wren looked startled. 'I don't know it.'

'*Really?*' Mum said with mock surprise again. 'Or perhaps you are a *Fifty Shades* kind of girl.'

Wren frowned. 'Fifty shades?'

'Of grey,' Mum said. 'Lots of S&M. Bondage—'

'Mum!' I protested.

My mother gave a dismissive wave of her hand. 'Wren's not prudish. Not if she writes romance. Isn't that true, dear?'

Wren nodded and drained her glass.

'Oh. I think we all need a top-up.' Mum picked up the pitcher and filled our glasses to the brim.

'It *is* just fruit, isn't it,' Wren said anxiously.

'Just fruit,' Mum agreed. 'So tell me, how *long* does it take you to write a book?'

'Oh, I can knock one out in three weeks,' said Wren.

Mum inhaled a strawberry that provoked a coughing fit.

'Three weeks,' I exclaimed. 'Wow!'

'And how many drafts do you normally do?' Mum croaked, but then reached for her glass yet again. 'Went down the wrong way.'

'Drafts?' Wren hesitated. 'Just one.'

'*One?* Good heavens. Did you hear that, Kat? *One* draft!' Mum met my eyes for the umpteenth time. She was thoroughly enjoying herself. 'How impressive!'

'Impressive,' I agreed.

'This is utterly fascinating,' Mum said. 'And how many words do you write a day?'

'Words?' Wren bit her lip. 'You mean, pages?'

'Words! Paragraphs! Pages!' Mum beamed. 'Do tell.'

Wren took another slug of Pimm's. I thought that as an undercover reporter she was utterly useless. And what possessed her to pretend to be Krystalle Storm!

'Lots of pages,' said Wren firmly. 'But I'm boring. All I do is write. Tell me about you? Kat says you're the Honeychurch family historian. You must know tons of juicy scandals and gossip.'

Instead of answering, Mum switched topics. 'I've been meaning to ask you – how did you find out about the shepherd's hut? I said to Kat, "Goodness, how on earth did that happen?" It only arrived on Sunday afternoon and just a few hours later . . . up you pop.'

'Through a friend of a friend.' Wren regarded her empty glass. 'Gosh. This has gone straight to my head.'

'And Kat tells me you live in London,' Mum said.

'That's right,' said Wren.

Mum raised an eyebrow. 'Not Italy?'

'Italy?' Wren frowned. 'No, why would you say that?'

Mum leaned in and lowered her voice. 'There's a rumour going round that you are a famous romance writer—'

'Krystalle Storm,' I put in.

'Come on,' Mum prompted. 'Tell us. We won't say a word.'

Wren leaned back in the wicker chair and grinned. Her eyes were glittering and it was obvious that the gin in the Pimm's was doing its job.

'You know I'd never— Oh!' Wren spluttered and started to choke. She clawed at her throat, trying to catch her breath.

Mum and I sprang to our feet in a panic as Wren pointed at her bag. She was gasping for breath. 'My . . . my inhaler.'

I went for it just as she did and the bag upended, spilling all the contents onto the flagstones. I grabbed the inhaler and she snatched it, taking in deep gulps.

'Breathe slowly!' Mum exclaimed. 'Oh God.'

As I ducked down to put Wren's things back into her bag, I saw her mobile phone case had flapped open. Inside the wallet was a photo of Wren with a rugged man dressed in a T-shirt with his arm around an adorable little girl of about four who was hugging a black Labrador. It was a family snap.

'I'm okay now,' said Wren. 'Sorry about that.'

I showed it to Wren. 'How sweet. Is this your niece?'

A flicker of alarm crossed her features. 'Yes. But I think I want to go now. I don't feel very well.'

'So soon? But you haven't had any cheese!' Mum cried.

Wren stood up but had to reach out to the chair to steady herself. I felt a stab of guilt – but it didn't last long. 'Are you sure you're okay?'

'I'm fine,' she whispered.

'Let me help you to your car.' I didn't wait for an answer. I just took her arm and gently led her away.

'Come right back, Kat,' Mum called out.

Wren weaved across the courtyard.

'Are you sure you can drive?' I was now getting worried. What if Wren had another attack on her way back to the shepherd's hut? I was also growing tired of her lies. 'Perhaps you should walk back – there's a shortcut through Honeywell Wood.'

'No, thanks,' said Wren. 'It gives me the creeps.'

She wrenched her car door open and half fell into the driver's seat. 'That was very kind of your mother to invite me.' She gave a heavy sigh. 'How lucky you are to have each other. Mother and daughter. I never had that kind of relationship with my mother. She didn't care about me. Not really.' Her eyes filled with tears. 'My mother ran off, you know. Ran off with my uncle Ben. She left . . . just like that— God, I feel so depressed. Are you sure you didn't put gin in the Pimm's?'

'Not a drop,' I lied. 'I doubt if you're going to do much writing now.'

She shook her head. 'No. I just have to check in with Dax. Lily had a play date today—' She went to close the door but I was faster and stopped her. 'Oh.'

'Who are you?' I demanded. 'Because you're definitely not a writer.'

Wren looked defeated.

'You're a reporter, aren't you?' I said.

'Please let me leave,' she whispered and tried in vain to close the door but I held on.

'Are you a friend of Ginny Riley's?'

'I'm sorry,' she said. 'Please . . .'

'Tell me why you're here!' I exclaimed but then I was distracted as Delia Evans appeared in the courtyard riding her bicycle.

Wren took her chance, pulled her car door shut, turned the ignition and floored it, narrowly missing Delia who only just managed to keep her balance.

Delia pedalled up to me. I saw a posy of sweet peas and a bottle of Sharpham bubbly in the pannier. She looked shocked. 'Wasn't that Krystalle Storm?'

'No, Delia,' I said irritated. 'She is not Krystalle Storm.'

'I know Iris is home,' Delia went on. 'Her car is here and you're here . . . I really need to talk to her but I don't want to talk to her alone.'

'She's in the suntrap,' I said with a sigh.

Chapter Twenty

Delia seemed nervous as she handed my mother the posy of sweet peas. She had even tied it with pink ribbon.

'And I know how much you love Sharpham babbly . . . I mean bubbly,' Delia stammered. 'Oh, you've been drinking Pimm's. How nice.'

I waited for the inevitable question of why hadn't Delia been invited but she just perched on the edge of a chair. Her body was stiff.

Delia's nerves were making me nervous.

'I think I'll leave you both to it,' I said.

'No!' they chorused.

'Kat, open the bubbly,' Mum commanded. 'We'll just use the same glasses we used for the Pimm's.'

I eyed the dirty tumblers that had the remnants of fruit in the bottom. 'Don't you think we should have fresh ones?'

'Nonsense.' Mum picked each glass up and tossed the fruit into one of the planters. 'Delia won't mind. She likes second-hand cast-offs. Let's give her Wren— I mean Krystalle Storm's glass. You'll love that, won't you, Delia?'

'Oh yes,' Delia said. 'Thank you.'

'No more for me,' I said.

'Then all the more for us,' Mum beamed. 'Right, Delia?'

I gave Mum a warning look. Wren may well have been plastered but my mother had been drinking steadily too.

I opened the bubbly with a loud pop and poured two glasses. The bubbles shot over the top of the tumblers.

'Oops,' said Mum. 'I don't think the bubbly liked riding in your pannier, Delia.'

Delia bristled. 'There are a lot of potholes in the service road.'

I handed them paper serviettes to wipe their fingers. Delia put her glass down on the table.

No one spoke.

My mother was sitting back in her chair watching Delia who started to work her mouth in a very peculiar way – it was as if she was chewing on a piece a toffee. Her hands were clasped together, knuckles white. Twice she cleared her throat but didn't speak.

Mum leaned in. 'Are you all right? Have you got something in your teeth?'

Delia took a deep breath. 'I don't want to ruin our friendship—'

'Ruin our *friendship*?' Mum exclaimed. 'How could you possibly ruin our friendship?'

'You can't choose who you fall in love with,' Delia

blurted out. 'And Monty and I are in love.' Delia reached for her glass and took a huge gulp.

Mum gave a little cry of dismay. 'Monty? *My* Monty?' She put her hand on her heart in exaggerated anguish. 'How could you? You are my best friend!'

'We never meant it to happen,' Delia rushed on. 'I mean . . . nothing has happened. I've wanted to tell you for ages.' Her expression changed to one of pity. 'I know it must hurt and I'm sorry. I can't live a lie. I'm just not that kind of woman.'

'You and Monty,' Mum whispered. 'I can't believe it.'

'Nothing physical has happened yet—'

Mum turned on her, suddenly furious. 'But that's not true, is it?'

Delia recoiled. 'Excuse me?'

'Really?' said Mum. 'Will you swear on your precious son Guy's life that you have not so much as had a cuddle with *my* boyfriend?'

Delia reddened. 'I don't know what you are talking about.'

'Tell her, Kat,' Mum said. 'Tell Delia what you saw!'

'No.' I threw up my hands in defeat. 'Don't get me involved in this. In fact, I am going to leave you both to it.' I stood up.

'Please don't go!' Delia begged.

'Sit down!' Mum shouted.

I sat down.

'If Kat won't tell you, I'll tell you what she told me!' Mum said. 'It so happens that Kat saw you in Monty's Rolls yesterday afternoon tucked down the bridleway near Bridge Cottage.'

'She's lying!' Delia whimpered.

'Kat said that the windows were steamed up and . . . without putting too fine a point on it . . . the vehicle was *bouncing* around.' Mum sounded outraged. 'Isn't that right, Kat?'

'Mum! Stop!'

Delia shot me a look of pure venom, her distress now forgotten. 'All right. So yes. I've been in Monty's bed for weeks now.'

'And he's been in mine,' Mum lied.

Delia blanched. 'He told me he'd not touched you. He told me that it was you who was always after him—'

Mum's eyes flashed with anger. 'He said *what*?'

Delia thrust out her jaw. 'And that he felt sorry for you.'

I stood up again. 'Okay, I'm off.'

'No!' They chorused again.

Mum brought out her mobile. 'Well, let's hear what he has to say, shall we?'

I sat down. Again.

With painstaking slowness she started tapping on the keypad. 'Wait. Wait. I know it's here somewhere. Recording . . . where is the recording feature?' She thrust the mobile at me. 'Kat? You have to help me find it.'

'I have no idea,' I lied. 'And it's not a good idea either.'

'I give up,' Mum declared. 'Let's call Monty right now! And we'll put him on speakerphone.'

Delia remained defiant. 'Go ahead.'

Mum scrolled down to find his number.

'Mum, please don't do this,' I said again.

'Iris, I want you to do this,' Delia declared. 'But don't blame me if you're upset about what you hear.'

Mum gave a snort of derision. 'I think it's the other way around— Oh, Monty darling!'

'Iris!' Sir Monty boomed on speakerphone. 'I hardly dare hope but . . . are you calling to say yes?'

Delia sat bolt upright.

Mum leaned over to Delia and whispered, 'He asked me to marry him,' then added brightly, 'I'm still thinking about it. But I heard some disturbing news today.'

'About what?' Sir Monty said sharply. 'If it's anything to do with Charlie Green I told you I never met him.'

'No, darling,' said Mum smoothly. 'Someone told me that you have been seeing my best friend Delia Evans in the biblical sense.'

'Didn't we have this conversation already?' said Sir Monty.

'Some new information has come to light so perhaps you would like to tell me again,' Mum said.

'Remind me who it is we are talking about,' said Sir Monty.

'Don't be silly. The housekeeper,' Mum prompted, barely able to hide her glee.

'What? Mrs E?' said Sir Monty.

'Not *your* housekeeper,' Mum said. 'The housekeeper at Honeychurch Hall!'

There was a silence. Delia sat rigid.

'Monty?' Mum said. 'Are you still there?'

'I've only got eyes for you,' said the odious man. 'Whoever said that is just trying to drive a wedge between us.'

Delia turned white.

'What if I told you it was Delia herself who told me?' Mum demanded.

'Oh – *her*,' he said. 'Wears a funny-coloured wig?'

Mum's lips tightened. 'Now don't be unkind,' she said. 'Delia is a dear friend. I'm sure there must be a misunderstanding. Why don't the three of us sort it out together?'

'No need, no need at all,' blustered Sir Monty. 'She's delusional. I'll handle it. Set her straight.'

I felt so bad for Delia and despised Sir Monty more than ever.

'No, darling,' Mum said quickly. 'Let's just forget it. I've forgotten about it already.'

'That's my girl.' Sir Monty gave a dirty laugh. 'When are we going to have a jolly good slap and tickle? You know you can't keep me at arm's length for ever.'

'You're right,' she said tightly. 'You really could do with a jolly good *slap*. Bye.'

Mum disconnected the line and exploded with rage. 'Horrible, disgusting man!'

Delia burst into tears. She got up to leave.

Mum flew to her side and pulled Delia into a hug. 'You're better off without him. Truly you are. I am so sorry you had to hear that.' And to my surprise, I saw that my mother really was contrite.

Moments later, a phone rang – a Rolling Stones ringtone – but it wasn't Mum's phone. It was coming from Delia's basket.

'Oh, good grief.' Mum pulled a face. 'Is that Mick Jagger singing "Start Me Up"?'

'It's Monty!' Delia was overwrought. 'What should I do?'

'Don't answer it,' Mum said. 'You're not going to cave in to that *cad* are you?'

'Never,' Delia whispered. 'I married a cheat and a liar and I'm not about to do it again.'

Mick Jagger kept on singing until he went to voicemail. Mum topped up their tumblers as Delia spilled her feelings.

I had to take my hat off to her. It took a lot of courage to come clean.

'Sneaking around all the time,' she went on miserably. 'Never in public, whilst he took you racing and you met Pearl Clayton in the members' enclosure at Newton Abbot racecourse!'

Mum laid her hand gently on Delia's bare arm and gave it a squeeze. 'I'm sorry that all you were to Monty was a bit of rough, dear.'

'Mum!' I groaned.

'Yes. You're right. I was his bit of rough,' Delia agreed. 'Sometimes he'd tell me he was taking me somewhere romantic where we could be alone and I thought – oh, a lovely hotel on the seafront in Torquay – but then we would drive out to this hut on Dartmoor with a bottle of Asti Spumante and a few cushions.'

'You're worth more than that,' Mum said, and I do believe she meant it. 'He's got no respect. No respect for you at all.'

'I'm such a fool,' Delia said.

Mum thought for a moment. A look of determination crossed her features. 'We're going to teach him a lesson, Delia. But it's critical that we all go on acting as normal – and that includes you, Katherine. I've got a really good idea.'

Leaving them to their good idea, I finally made my escape. I felt utterly exhausted from all the drama. But, at least for a while, it had distracted me from my own.

I had to track down this mysterious man called Leslie and that meant I would have to call Sir Monty-the-cad myself.

Chapter Twenty-One

Sir Monty answered on the first ring. I couldn't believe how cheerful he sounded. It was all I could do not to say something but I had to trust that whatever punishment Mum had in store for him would be worth my silence.

'Looks like we might be family soon,' he crowed. 'I knew I'd win her over in the end. Do you think she'll be happy living at Stubbs Place?'

'Ecstatic.' I forced myself to be civil. 'Speaking of family. Can I have Leslie's phone number, please?'

There was a deathly hush on the other end of the line.

'Leslie?' said Sir Monty. 'I don't know a Leslie.'

'According to Violet, someone called Leslie came to clear out the contents from Lavender's bedroom and she told me that it was you who had arranged it.' Violet hadn't said that, of course, but it was worth a try.

'I never did any such thing,' Sir Monty blustered. 'She's going senile.'

'No problem,' I said. 'I'll call Luxtons. I'm sure they will

know. There can't be that many house-clearance companies
in the area. I bet Ronnie knows him.'

'Ronnie?' Sir Monty said. 'What's he got to do with it?'
I could detect rising hysteria in his voice. 'What's so
important anyway? It was just a load of junk.'

'*Was* it?' I was growing suspicious. 'Edith wants her
doll's house back.' That wasn't true either but any mention
of the dowager countess usually put the fear of God in
anyone who knew her.

'Doll's house? What doll's house?' Sir Monty's panic was
tangible. 'I don't know anything about a doll's house.'

'Edith had it made especially for Charlotte – she was
Charlie Green's sister,' I said. 'You know, the man who
was discovered in Honeywell Wood?'

'I'm not involved in any way at all,' Sir Monty said
hastily. 'And since we'll soon be family, let me give you
some advice, Katherine. Stay out of this. Do you hear me?
Stay out of it!'

And he promptly disconnected the line.

I sat there trying to figure out what had just happened.
Was Sir Monty threatening me or warning me? What on
earth was going on? This was something I definitely
planned on talking about to Shawn.

At nine thirty on the dot Shawn rang in from his kitchen
wearing the same navy sweatshirt as yesterday. A woman in
her sixties appeared in the background. With her shoulder-
length highlighted blonde hair swept off her face, Shawn's
mother-in-law was a picture of elegance. I often wondered

what it must be like having lost both her husband and her daughter to cancer. One thing I did know was how devoted Lizzie was to her grandchildren. She leaned in over his shoulder and smiled into the camera.

'Hi Lizzie,' I said. 'How do you like London?'

'It's certainly different,' she said. 'Nice to see you, Kat. I'll leave you to chat. I know Shawn's only got a few minutes.'

Of course he has, I thought to myself.

'What's the news?' he said. 'How is Mallory handling everything?'

'How was your day, Kat?' I said to him. 'What did you do?'

Shawn rubbed his eyes. 'Sorry. Been a lot going on here.'

'Well, there's been a lot going on here too,' I said and went on to fill him in about the day's discoveries. 'Eric's been arrested for murder.'

'What?' Shawn seemed shocked.

'He's in police custody,' I said. 'They found Charlie Green's motorbike hidden in his scrapyard. Do you think he really killed him?'

'Kat,' said Shawn with a sigh. 'I can't interfere.'

'I'm just asking your opinion,' I said.

'Can we talk about something else?'

'Fine. Yes. If you like.' I did *not* like. 'Mum plied that Wren Fraser with Pimm's laced with a lot of gin and I can tell you right now that she is not a writer. I think she's an undercover reporter.'

'Did you ask her?' Shawn said.

'She refused to answer,' I said. 'But she gave herself away when she started talking about someone called Dax and a little girl called Lily—'

'Sorry,' he said suddenly. 'I have to go. I'm getting a text message from my boss. I'll see you on Thursday. I really am sorry – it's urgent.'

And, to my astonishment, he ended the call. I was frustrated. There had been so much I needed to talk to him about. Mum's close call as Krystalle Storm being just one, but what about my ride with Edith out to Moreleigh Mount which Charlie Green rented from the Honeychurch estate? And the weird conversation with Sir Monty which – the more I thought about it – I was certain hadn't been a warning: it had been a threat.

It was obvious that Shawn was no longer interested in life in Little Dipperton – or me.

It was then that I noticed I had missed a call from Violet. She had left a message saying that she had made a mistake about the lease on the farm building and that it had cost twenty-five pounds fifty pence a month. She also mentioned that she had remembered where she had seen Leslie before and to call her straight back. I tried, but there was no answer.

It would have to wait until the morning.

Chapter Twenty-Two

The moment I pulled into the alley next to Rose Cottage, I knew that something wasn't right. Although it was gone nine, the back door was locked and everywhere seemed eerily quiet.

I peered through the window but the kitchen was empty when usually, at this time of the morning, Violet would be preparing breakfast and listening to the sounds of BBC Radio Devon.

I got out my mobile and dialled her landline. I could hear her telephone ringing inside the kitchen but after a dozen rings, I gave up.

I walked to the front of the tearoom and, just as I feared, the 'Closed' sign was still hanging inside the partly glazed front door.

'Kat!' came a shout from across the road. Willow jumped off the low wall where she must have been waiting for Violet to open up. She took out her ear pods and popped her mobile into a canvas bag and hurried over.

Willow looked worried. 'Miss Green likes me here at eight thirty but she wasn't answering the door. I tried knocking and called her phone but – do you think she overslept?'

I thought that unlikely but I was concerned that perhaps Violet had had a fall. 'I'm going to see if I can get inside. Let's see what the back looks like.'

Willow trailed after me to the rear of the building where a narrow, cobbled passage ran along the back of the cottages for the recycling bins. Opposite stood a ragged hedge and a rusting gate that led to the village allotments beyond.

Behind Rose Cottage was a large sycamore tree that had been planted too close to the building. Its roots had broken through the cobbles and its branches were resting on the catslide roof.

I glanced up. The window at the back – Violet's bedroom – had the curtains closed. The little window on the landing was also closed but I hoped I could break the glass and get in that way. Luckily, there was a wooden water barrel with a broken lid and, although I didn't hold out much hope for the gutter being a safe handhold, at least it would get me onto the roof.

'If you give me a leg up onto the water barrel I can do it,' said Willow.

'No,' I said quickly. 'You stay here.' Of course I would have preferred Willow to climb up in my place but I had no idea what she might find inside. 'I'll just put my tote bag in my car first.'

When I returned Willow handed me her canvas bag and pointed to the lid of a recycling bin where she'd emptied the contents – her mobile, a make-up bag, keys and a journal.

'I found a bit of brick,' she said. 'You might need it to break that window.'

'Very enterprising,' I said with a smile and slipped the bag strap over my shoulder.

Willow proved to be surprisingly strong and hoisted me up onto the barrel as if she were tossing the caber. I made a wild grab for a low branch and only just stopped myself from sailing right over and joining the contents of her bag.

'Sorry!' she said with a nervous giggle.

The sycamore got me onto the catslide roof and I was able to scramble the short distance to the window ledge, making sure to avoid a number of cracked tiles.

Just as Willow had suspected, the window was jammed shut, but I swung the canvas bag and broke the glass. She gave me a thumbs-up.

Taking care to avoid the shards, I tucked my hand inside the frame and worked the latch until it came loose.

I clambered inside and dropped onto the carpet.

The three doors on the landing were all closed. I felt an overwhelming sense of dread. I called out Violet's name even though I knew she wouldn't answer me.

I looked into Violet's bedroom first. The room was in darkness. I flipped the light. Her bed was empty but it had been neatly turned down for the night. On the bedside table stood a carafe of water capped with a glass along with a copy of my mother's latest release, *Betrayed*. I crossed the landing and checked Lavender's bedroom. It was just as I'd found it yesterday – other than the furniture – empty.

Finally, with a pounding heart, I opened the bathroom door.

Violet had drawn a bath but had never got in. It was full of water and stone cold. A bathmat had been laid on the pink linoleum and a tumbler of amber liquid stood on a narrow freestanding table next to the bath. I picked up the glass and took a whiff. It was whisky. The book that she had told me about, *Swedish Death Cleaning* by Margareta Magnusson, sat on top of a folded pink bath towel on the closed loo seat.

Dread pooled in the pit of my stomach as I headed for the staircase and opened the latch door at the top. There, my worst fears were realised.

Violet was lying face down in her pink candlewick dressing gown at the bottom of the stairs. Her neck was at an unnatural angle and I knew straight away that she was dead.

I hurried down to Violet's side but when I checked her vitals, her body was cold to the touch.

I sank down on the step above her in shock. Violet must have drawn a bath and for some reason, gone back downstairs and missed her footing. Why on earth hadn't Violet put the light on? She'd warned me about how treacherous the stairs could be.

I climbed over her to open the latch door to the little passage and walked quickly to the kitchen to call the police and ambulance. Then I broke the news to Willow.

'Why don't you go home and I'll wait for the ambulance,' I said. 'Your aunt is going to need you. I know Doreen was Violet's closest friend. I'd come with you but I have to stay here.'

Willow nodded. 'There are customers waiting at the front for Miss Green to open,' she said. 'What should I tell them?'

'I'll handle it,' I said.

I walked with Willow to the alley and watched her turn left towards the pub before going back inside to write a note – 'Closed Until Further Notice' – that I put in the bay front window. There were a handful of customers but I ignored them and retreated to the kitchen.

As I sat and waited, I thought about Violet's drawn bath. What had made her come downstairs? What had she forgotten? It was then that I noticed three cups and saucers on the draining board. They'd been rinsed out with the saucers resting on each upturned cup. Violet was a stickler for a tidy kitchen. Had she had visitors after she'd closed up yesterday?

A tap on the back door broke into my thoughts. It was Mallory.

He stepped inside and promptly cracked his head on the low doorway. 'Christ!' he exclaimed.

'Are you okay?' I said.

'I'm getting used to it,' he said grimly, but when he turned to close and lock the door behind him, he struck his head again. This time the expletive was more colourful.

'Where is she?' he asked.

'This way,' I said. 'At the bottom of the stairs.' As we walked, I told him what I knew and how I had broken in and found her.

The moment he saw Violet's body Mallory held me back. 'Stay right there.' He brought out his disposable gloves and booties and put them on.

'Violet was going to take a bath and must have come downstairs for something and tripped,' I said.

Mallory nodded. 'Assume nothing, believe nothing and challenge everything, Kat.' He pointed to the light switch at the bottom of the stairs. 'Was this on or off?'

'It was off,' I said.

'I see,' said Mallory. 'Have you touched anything?'

'Well . . . yes,' I said. 'I'm sorry.'

'So long as I know,' said Mallory. 'Please return to the kitchen.'

I didn't. Instead, I stayed out of his line of sight and watched Mallory at work. First, he took out a pocket Dictaphone and switched it on. He then proceeded to record exactly what he was seeing, the staircase, the lighting and the unusual location of Violet's slippers at the bottom of the stairs. He bent down to turn Violet over, and must have ears like a bat because he swung around and caught me staring.

'Kat, please!' he protested. 'Return to the kitchen and wait for Banks to come— Ah. I can hear someone knocking at the kitchen door. Please let them in. I locked it.'

It was the paramedics, Tony and John Cruickshank, with their medical equipment and a stretcher.

'You all right, Kat?' said Tony – at least I thought it was

Tony. With their ruddy faces and curly brown hair, I found it hard to tell the identical twins apart.

'Yes. A bit shocked,' I said. 'Violet must have fallen down the stairs.'

'We won't be getting a cup of tea this morning then, will we, Tony?' quipped John with his usual gallows humour.

Mallory stepped into the kitchen. 'I'm afraid I need more time before you take Miss Green's body away. Someone will notify you when it is convenient.'

Tony and John's jaws dropped in unison.

Mallory's expression grew grave. 'I'm afraid this is a crime scene.'

My heart skipped a beat.

Tony whistled. 'Bloody hell.'

'Maybe someone didn't like her tea,' said John. No one laughed.

'We'd best get up to the pub,' said Tony. 'Tell Doreen what's going on. She'll be gutted.'

'No one tells anyone anything,' Mallory said coldly. 'I'm not having any more village gossip. When I know more I will issue an official statement.'

I raised my hand – Mallory made me feel as if I was in the classroom. 'Willow, that's Doreen's niece, will have already told her about the fall. But she won't know anything else at this point.'

'If Doreen knows,' said John. 'Then trust me, everyone knows.'

The twins left, slamming the door a little bit harder than necessary.

'Since you found Miss Green's body, I will have questions,' said Mallory. 'Will you be home later today?'

I nodded a yes.

'And I'll want to talk to Willow – you mentioned she was here, too?'

'She didn't find Violet's body,' I said. 'Willow just helped me get inside.'

Mallory took out his police notebook and scanned the tiny kitchen. Despite the clutter of teapots and every available shelf being taken up with cups, saucers and jugs, it was neat. His eyes rested on the draining board and the used cups and saucers.

'This may not be important,' I said. 'But Violet had a thing about a tidy kitchen and never leaving the washing-up for the next morning.'

Mallory wrote something down.

'There's a drawn bath upstairs,' I said and went on to describe the bathroom.

Mallory nodded. 'There are no signs of a forced entry,' he said. 'So you're suggesting she had a late-night cup of tea with people she knew?'

'Violet was in her dressing gown,' I said. 'It would have had to be a friend.' I thought of Doreen Mutters.

'Clearly not Eric Pugsley,' said Mallory. 'Since he is still in police custody. I thought you would like to know that he confessed to hiding the deceased's motorbike in his scrapyard.'

I was dismayed. 'But Eric was so distraught when he found Charlie's body.'

'Does Eric Pugsley own a gun?' he asked.

I hesitated. 'Surely you would know that?' I said carefully. 'Why?'

'I'm afraid I'm not at liberty to say,' said Mallory. 'Please answer the question.'

'I think he has a twelve-bore but – are you saying that Charlie was *shot*?' I was stunned. 'Eric didn't say anything about seeing a gunshot wound.'

'I don't suppose he would,' said Mallory.

'Surely you're not suggesting that *Eric* shot him?' I shook my head vehemently. 'No. I just don't believe it.'

Mallory gave a small smile. 'Your faith in human nature is truly inspiring. Everyone is capable of murder. Everyone. Even you.'

'I would never do anything like that!' I exclaimed.

'Probably not,' said Mallory. 'I'm just making a point. Personal grudges can last a lifetime. I have a degree in Criminal Justice and Psychology and find the human condition fascinating. People make their own truth to fit their narrative. Isn't that what's said these days? Your version of events is the only one you want to believe and so it becomes your truth and must be accepted by all.'

I shook my head. 'You're the expert.' But Mallory was an enigma to me. 'And here you are, swapping a city career for a quiet life in the country.'

'Hardly quiet,' said Mallory. 'And you're wrong. It's in small communities like this that jealousy, greed and anger fester. They tend to get lost in big cities – I am finding life in Little Dipperton very enlightening – ah, here is Banks now.'

Clive – and his fluorescent green visibility vest – loomed large behind the glass-paned back door.

I let him into the kitchen.

'Burglary gone wrong, eh?' said Clive cheerfully. 'I heard she was pushed down the stairs.'

The tick in Mallory's eye began to twitch. 'Is that your theory, Banks?'

'There's one way to find out. Oh. Gloves!' He pulled out a disposable pair of gloves and with a look at Mallory as if to say, *See, I remembered*, went to the kitchen drawer and withdrew a petty cash tin. I noticed that the key was in the lock.

Clive opened the lid and said, 'Oh. Now that's strange.' He took out a wad of money. 'Now you'd think they'd have taken that. Everyone knows where Violet keeps her cash.'

We watched Clive unroll the notes and flip through them with practised efficiency. 'Blimey, there's over a grand here. Maybe Violet's tea wasn't so bad after all.'

'A thousand pounds?' Mallory said sharply.

'The house-clearance people came yesterday,' I explained. 'They took away all the boxes of Lavender's car boot sale stock and gave her—'

'What?' Clive cut in, stunned. '*A thousand* quid? Never! The missus and I used to go car booting and Lavender's stuff was all mismatched plates and whatnot. Pure junk.' Clive regarded Mallory keenly. 'So . . . was it an accident or not?'

'That's what we're going to find out,' said Mallory. 'I want to keep a lid on this for the time being. The official line is that Miss Green fell.'

'That's not what's going around the village. But yeah, got it,' Clive said and caught my eye. 'I really have.'

Telling Mallory that I would be home later that afternoon, I left them to it.

Outside, Malcolm, the desk sergeant – also dressed in a high-visibility vest – was manning the alley, clearly enjoying another day out of the office. I could hear him fielding questions from the villagers – 'Not at liberty to say' and 'Move along now, there's nothing to see.'

I got into my car.

Malcolm – with sweeping hand gestures that would make an air traffic controller proud – directed me out of the alley and into the road. I headed for Dartmouth, but the moment I got out of the village and into the countryside again, I pulled over and called my mother.

'Violet Green's dead,' I blurted out and to my dismay, got all choked up.

I heard a tiny intake of breath. 'I'm so sorry, darling, I didn't know you were that close.'

'It was horrible. I found her,' I said. 'Someone pushed her down the stairs.'

'Then come back home,' she said briskly. 'I'm in my writing house. The mobile police unit has been moved elsewhere. No wonder it's called a mobile unit. How much more mobile can it get?'

I filled Mum in on why Mallory had declared Rose Cottage a crime scene. 'And it had to be someone she knew,' I pointed out. 'She would hardly make a stranger a cup of tea wearing her dressing gown.'

'And it can't be Eric,' said Mum. 'He's still in police custody. But . . . you say there was *whisky* by the bath? I always thought she preferred sherry.'

'It's obvious that Violet must have had something that someone wanted,' I said. 'Otherwise the cash would have been taken.' And then the thought struck me. 'Mum, you didn't mention the Drake Six to Sir Monty, did you?'

There was a pause on the other end of the line. 'You asked me to find out why he was helping Violet sell her antique furniture.'

'That's not what I said.'

There was another pause. 'I mentioned the doll's house, but he asked *me* if you'd found anything interesting among the car boot stuff. I may have mentioned the limnings – just to test his general knowledge – but I definitely didn't mention the word Drake.'

Despite Sir Monty's denials that he had anything to do with clearing the contents of Lavender's bedroom, it was too much of a coincidence.

'Do you know a man called Leslie by any chance?' I said. 'Apparently he's very small.'

And there was yet another pause.

'Mum!' I said sharply. 'Are you multi-tasking?'

'I'm listening,' Mum protested. 'And *yes*, I am multi-tasking. I remember being introduced to a Leslie at the racetrack. He was a jockey.'

'A *jockey*?' This made no sense. 'Do you know his surname? I need to contact him. It's really important and

I'm positive that your boyfriend knows who he is. He's involved in this. I know it!'

There wasn't a pause now. There was just silence. I waited for my mother to speak and after a long moment she said, 'I'll see what I can find out. But frankly, I think you are barking up the wrong tree, dear. Even though Monty has revealed himself to be a cad, I can't see him pushing Violet down the stairs for her teapot collection.'

'But someone did,' I said quietly. 'Does Violet have a next of kin?'

'Doreen Mutters would know,' Mum said. 'She's her best friend – and frankly, I can say from experience that best friends can turn out to be the most treacherous of all!'

I thought of Mallory's comment that everyone was capable of murder.

'Why don't you ask your detective what he thinks,' Mum went on.

Promising to stop by later that afternoon, I disconnected the line and immediately called Shawn. I knew that he wasn't the detective my mother had in mind, but as far as I was concerned, Shawn was still mine.

Chapter Twenty-Three

'I'm sorry,' said a male voice. 'But DI Cropper is in a meeting and is going to be tied up all day.'

I had already tried Shawn's mobile and had left a message on that and now I'd done something he had always asked me not to do – called him at work.

'Will you tell him it's urgent,' I said.

There was a slight hesitation and then, 'Please hold the line.'

I waited for what seemed like forever but was probably only a minute or two. The man came back on. 'He says he will call you this evening and sends his apologies.'

I felt miffed. 'I left a message on his mobile. Can you ask him to listen to that when he has the *time*?' And rang off.

Shawn sends his *apologies*? I was upset. Was this how life would be now he had this big job? And we weren't even living together yet. I'd told him it was urgent. Why didn't he care?

I set off once again for Dartmouth, determined to push Shawn and poor Violet out of my mind, but it was hard.

I kept seeing her sprawled at the bottom of the stairs and wondering who had stopped in to see her so late.

At least I could solve one mystery myself – that of the Drake Six.

I had wanted to visit the Dartmouth Naval Academy ever since I'd moved to the south-west and discovered the beautiful fishing port of Dartmouth.

I stopped at the security booth barrier for my pass and was addressed by a polished, polite and undeniably handsome officer in uniform. Delia's mother was right. There were plenty more fish in the sea and I was definitely at the right place to find one.

The Britannia Royal Naval College – to use its correct name – is the official naval academy of the United Kingdom. Designed by Sir Aston Webb and with the foundation stone laid by King Edward VII in 1902, the building is Wrennean in style and simply magnificent.

Perched on the bluff overlooking the harbour, the grounds slope steeply down to the River Dart, both to the south and to the east. The three-storeyed building with two tiers of attics is finished in Portland stone, red brick and Cornish slate. The walls of the many terraces and steps are made of Torquay limestone topped with parapets of Cornish granite.

The parade ground stands in front of the central block and has an imperial stair rising to the entrance flanked by curving drives. A tympanum displays the Royal Arms above, a cupola incorporates a clock and many Royal Naval motifs – letterings, crowns and carvings of historic ship prows – and, under the parapet, is the heart-stirring inscription: '*It is on the navy under the good providence of God that our wealth, prosperity and peace depend.*' It made me feel proud to be British.

Below the outer windows, panels were carved with the names of Hawke, Howe, Nelson – and Drake – the reason for my visit.

Another handsome naval officer – or maybe it was just the uniform that did it – was waiting at the main entrance to escort me along glazed bricked corridors painted in a delicate shade of green. In between the tall sash windows, with views of the harbour far below, ranged stunning maritime oil paintings.

I was taken to a large outer office filled with mahogany and walnut furniture where a woman in her forties, also dressed in uniform, stood up to greet me. I presumed this must be Jennifer.

At twelve hundred hours exactly, she gestured for me to follow her through two double doors that led into the Commodore's opulent office.

A clean-shaven, distinguished man in his early fifties with salt-and-pepper hair stood up to shake my hand.

'It's a pleasure to meet you, Miss Stanford. My wife is a great fan of yours,' he said. 'She was very disappointed when you retired. Coffee?'

He'd hit the intercom button before I had a chance to reply but coffee was the last thing on my mind.

I saw them straight away.

The Drake Six were displayed on the wall to the left of

the vast marble fireplace. On the right stood a full-length portrait of Sir Francis Drake. One hand rested on a globe that represented his astonishing feat circumnavigating the world. He wore the famous Drake jewel – a pendant made of gold and enamel, rubies and a drop pearl, hanging at waist level on a ribbon from his neck. It had been a gift from Queen Elizabeth I.

Following my gaze the Commodore said, 'Yes. There they are. Pansy has told me everything. But first, let's have coffee.'

Jennifer returned with a cafetière on a tray with porcelain cups and saucers.

'I've been a long-time admirer of Sir Francis Drake,' he began as Jennifer poured our coffees.

'Just black for me, please,' I said.

'He was an explorer, sea captain, slave trader, privateer and, as many believed, a cold-hearted pirate. King Philip II of Spain offered a reward of twenty thousand ducats for his capture or death – about six million pounds today,' the Commodore continued. 'Poor chap died of dysentery, hardly a dignified death. He was buried at sea in full armour in a sealed lead-lined coffin. His body has never been found although it's rumoured to be near the wrecks of two British ships that were scuttled in Portobello Bay.'

I told the Commodore that my mother and I had visited Buckland Abbey and enjoyed it very much.

'You saw the snare drum, of course,' the Commodore continued. 'Rumour has it that Drake said that should England ever be in danger, someone was to beat the drum and he would come back to defend his country. I wonder what he would make of our world today.'

The Commodore gestured to the miniatures on the wall. 'Those are his favourite ships – the *Pelican* – which became the *Golden Hind* as I am sure you know – the *Judith*, *Pasha*, *Swan* and *Marigold*. Naturally he commanded other vessels but those were the ones that Drake chose for Svetlana Winkler.'

I listened politely as the Commodore banged on about Drake and his ships and the gifted Winkler until at last, he said, 'Well! I've done all the talking. Let's take a look at these fakes of yours.'

He cleared a space on his desk.

I produced the two velvet pouches and handed my miniatures over. The Commodore switched on his angled desk lamp. First he looked at the *Pelican* and then the *Golden Hind*.

For some moments he didn't speak and then, 'These are magnificent copies. Extraordinary. Where did you find them?'

'A client,' I said carefully. 'And they wouldn't be copies since Winkler never painted copies, as I'm sure *you* know.'

He nodded agreement and frowned. 'So forgeries,' he said. 'And you have all six?'

'No,' I said. 'Just these two.'

The Commodore looked surprised. 'That is very strange. Their value comes as a collection. What would be the point of forging just two?'

'Can I compare mine to yours?'

The Commodore needed no encouragement. He leapt

to his feet and strode to the fireplace, removing the *Pelican* and *Golden Hind.*

Side by side, the oval portraits looked identical. I brought out my steel ruler and noted the measurements. The Commodore's frames had exact dimensions but mine were off by a fraction of a millimetre.

At first glance, the portraits of Drake looked the same. I handed the Commodore my OptiVisor and offered him the *Pelican* miniature. 'Look at Drake's nose.'

The Commodore raised an eyebrow but did as I asked. It took him a few moments but then he said, 'There's a mark on it. A speck. Mine are flawless.'

'It's not a speck,' I said. 'Drake had a small wart on the tip of his nose.'

'Good grief!' he exclaimed. 'Are you certain.'

'A few years ago a painting of Sir Francis Drake led an Old Masters sale at Bonhams. No one knew the artist but the presence of the wart clinched its authenticity.'

The Commodore was not looking so cheerful now.

I'd already come prepared with assorted tools to give the miniatures a thorough inspection. 'Let's take them out of the frames.'

Carefully, I unclipped the back of my *Pelican* and removed it from its frame. I did the same for the Commodore's.

'More light, I think,' he muttered and swung the angled desk lamp closer to me.

I examined the card back of my *Pelican* and the Commodore's and my stomach turned over.

'I need to look at the others too, please,' I said.

The Commodore brought the four over. I repeated the process.

It was exactly as I suspected. I sat back, trying to quell the excitement mixed with anxiety that was racing through me. 'Do you want the bad news?'

The Commodore blinked. 'No.'

'In the sixteenth century, miniature portraits were painted on vellum. Forgers can buy sixteenth-century vellum. It's not difficult,' I said. 'The portrait was then mounted on the back of a sixteenth-century playing card – again, not impossible to get hold of – with starch paste. This was smoothed down with a burnisher – usually a dog-tooth with a wooden handle.'

'Yes, yes, I know all that.' The Commodore was getting impatient. 'Mine *are* on the back of playing cards. Look! There!' He jabbed a finger at his *Pelican*. 'It's the Ace of Diamonds.'

'I see that,' I said. 'And that is where the forger made his second mistake. Yes, a variety of playing cards were used but the choice of suit was significant. Diamonds were chosen for royalty.' I pushed my *Pelican* towards him. 'Spades were used for the military class. The *Pelican* and *Golden Hind* are painted on the King of Spades.'

The Commodore was flabbergasted. I told him more about the fascinating use of playing cards at that time. 'The French suits represented their class system differently – Spades for the nobility, Hearts, the clergy, Clubs for peasants and Diamonds for merchants. Even using a French playing card would have been incorrect.'

The Commodore scratched his head. 'I . . . I just don't know what to say! How can I have missed this?'

'You wouldn't have known what to look for,' I said. 'Yours are excellent forgeries.'

The Commodore didn't speak for some moments. 'So you're saying that my chum, Admiral Forbes-Mathers, didn't know they were forgeries either? They've been in his family for generations.'

'I'm not saying that at all,' I said. 'Pansy told me that you bought them at auction.'

'That's right, Luxtons,' said the Commodore. 'I would have purchased them privately had I known they were going to be sold.' He hit the intercom button again and told Jennifer to bring in the Luxtons sale catalogue with the Drake Six.

As we waited, I put the miniatures back together. Jennifer returned with the catalogue holding open the exact page.

The Commodore gave it to me. 'Here. Look.'

The Drake Six was headlining the marine sale. The description was very detailed, right down to the history behind the artist and Winkler's fondness for opium. I looked at the date of the sale. It was seven years ago. A coincidence? The timing seemed to be yet another connection to Charlie Green, however far-fetched.

It was becoming obvious now that the missing four miniatures had to have been hidden in Lavender's bedroom and I'd missed them.

'Drake is an enormous part of our maritime history and

this academy.' The Commodore was anxious. 'The academy was determined to acquire them and not lose them overseas.'

'Do you know who valued them?' I asked.

'Michael Luxton valued these himself.'

I knew Michael well. Surely he couldn't be involved in anything underhand.

'So what do we do?' the Commodore declared. 'Call in the fraud squad?'

I smiled at that. 'Not yet.'

I needed more information. I needed to talk to Michael Luxton first to be absolutely sure I had not made a mistake. If there was fraud going on and Luxtons was involved, this was much bigger than I could handle alone. I would have to involve David. It was what he did best.

'What we do,' I said finally, 'is put your miniatures back on the wall. Do not tell Jennifer. Do not tell Pansy. It's critical that we keep this under wraps for the time being.'

The Commodore gave a nod. 'You have my word.'

I put my tools and my *Pelican* and *Golden Hind* back into their velvet pouches and into my tote bag.

The Commodore hit the intercom again. 'Miss Stanford is leaving.'

Jennifer reappeared to escort me out.

I paused at the door. 'Just one more thing,' I said. 'Did you attend the sale yourself?'

'Yes, of course,' said the Commodore.

'And after the sale, did you take the miniatures with you?'

'Yes,' he said. 'Why?'

'I just wondered.' If the Commodore had taken them directly from the saleroom the switch would have been made at the saleroom itself, which would imply that Michael Luxton would have known.

As I walked back to my car my head was spinning. Was Luxtons involved in fraud? I couldn't believe it and yet what other answer could there be?

It looked like I was about to find out.

Chapter Twenty-Four

The traffic grew heavier as I drew closer to Newton Abbot. Located on the River Teign and halfway between the south Devon coast and Dartmoor, the market town is steeped in history.

Referred to as the New Town of the Abbots, of nearby Torre Abbey, it was renamed Newton Abbot by 1300 and spent the next few centuries enjoying the prosperities brought in by the wool, leather, granite and clay industries. With the Industrial Revolution, the town grew rapidly in the Victorian era as the home of the South Devon Railway locomotive works. Even in the 1930s and 1940s the Great Western Railway was thriving and employed over a thousand locals. It is also home to one of the top racecourses in England.

A news bulletin came on with, thankfully, no mention of the body found near 'Kat Stanford's Devon hideaway' nor was there mention of Violet Green's death. It would seem that Clive was doing what he was told.

I passed Heathfield Business Park where Luxtons had their storage facility. The land had once belonged to a stately home called Heathfield Place. The eighteenth-century house had been pulled down thirty years ago to make way for the town's bypass – yet another casualty to progress. All that was left were the two stone pillars that used to flank the main entrance but were now covered in graffiti. It was here that items were stored for upcoming auctions before being moved to the actual saleroom in the High Street. It would be here that Violet's oak benches would have been taken to on Sunday evening.

I pulled into the car park at the rear of the old bank that housed Luxtons auction house. It was packed but I managed to find a space to park in a residential side street.

I always loved coming to this saleroom although I often found it sad, especially with estate sales. Today was focused on the contents of Stone Park, an Elizabethan manor house in north Devon. I had visited Stone Park years ago when I took *Fakes & Treasures* on the road. Just like Honeychurch Hall, Stone Park had been in the same family for generations, but with the elderly Lady Caroline Manners' recent death, the younger members of the family had decided to sell the estate to a property developer who was going to convert it into a luxury retirement village.

Perhaps Pansy was right. These big houses had to find a way to pay their way otherwise there was no alternative other than to take them to pieces.

I entered the saleroom and, as always, saw many familiar faces. There was something about the smell of furniture polish overlaid with oil paint and dust that I just absolutely loved. I was immediately struck by the high-quality pieces on offer – especially the seventeenth-century oak furniture. Sir Monty had picked a good venue in which to sell Violet's oak benches.

I made my way through a maze of tables, coffers, old glass cabinets and sets of chairs; armoires, tallboys and huge gilt-framed mirrors. Oil paintings lined the walls but with no sense of order. A Flemish tapestry lay draped over a Knole sofa. I knew that the last time I'd seen the tapestry was when it was hanging in the long gallery at Stone Park. Somehow, furniture and furnishings had dignity and life when set in their rightful place, but here in the saleroom, they just looked shabby and neglected.

I viewed all five salerooms but couldn't see Violet's oak benches anywhere. They were listed in my catalogue – with no photograph. They must have been withdrawn from the sale after all.

I had yet to see Michael Luxton. However, I did find my friend Johnny, the auction house manager. Johnny oversaw the running of the saleroom and managed the saleroom porters. He had started work as a saleroom porter when he left school at sixteen but had never wanted to be an auctioneer, preferring the drama of backstage.

Johnny was easy to spot. Stocky and in his sixties, he wore the Luxtons' hunter-green overall. He was standing in front of a pretty George III oak longcase clock answering questions from a well-dressed couple. I hovered in the background and waited for him to finish his conversation.

I didn't need to wait for long. Johnny soon caught my eye and broke away to join me. After exchanging a few pleasantries about the weather, the upcoming sale and asking after his wife who'd recently had surgery, I cut straight to the chase.

'That would be lots 213 and 214,' said Johnny. 'A late entry, so no photograph. They were picked up this morning from Stubbs Place. They should be here any minute.'

'Stubbs Place?' I said sharply. 'Not the warehouse?'

Johnny shook his head. 'No. They came straight from the seller.'

But I had seen Ronnie – dressed in the Luxtons' hunter-green overall – and Gavin of the day-of-the-week polo shirt pick them up from Rose Cottage on Sunday, and said so.

'Ronnie Lubbock?' Johnny shook his head again. 'He wasn't working Sunday. Why?'

'Maybe I got it wrong.' Maybe Ronnie was doing a bit of moonlighting for Sir Monty. But why wear the overall if he was off-duty?

'Does a man called Leslie work here?' I said.

'No Leslie works here,' said Johnny. 'Ah, here's Ronnie now.' He pointed over my shoulder. I turned to see Ronnie carrying one end of Violet's bench and Tim, an older porter who had worked at Luxtons for ever, taking the other.

Johnny spotted someone and touched my shoulder. 'Excuse me. It's Mrs Clayton,' he said and left to speak to a tall thin woman in her sixties with a honey-coloured bob. Immaculately turned out in tailored trousers and a red blazer, she used a cane that had a mother-of-pearl handle.

So this was the famous Pearl Clayton. There was something familiar about her. With a jolt, I realised exactly where I had seen her before.

I'd met her at the wheel of her white BMW on her way to Okehampton when Edith and I were out riding.

'Kat?' came a familiar voice. I turned to find Michael Luxton.

In his early seventies, Michael was slightly built and wore his hallmark black-rimmed glasses that were very Austin Powers, a dapper suit and a red bow tie. Michael was hugely knowledgeable about his trade and even though Sotheby's was permanently on a quest to buy Luxtons out, he held firm. Michael was fiercely proud of Luxtons' legacy. I just couldn't believe he was involved in fraud.

As well as being the main auctioneer for the auction house, Michael took on the job as commentator for Newton Abbot Racecourse. His racing commentaries there were legendary and always amusing.

He took my hand and shook it warmly. Michael sent a lot of work my way. It was thanks to him that my mobile valuation service was doing so well.

'We pipped Sotheby's to the post with Stone Park,' Michael beamed. 'There's a lot of international interest especially from Hong Kong. The phone lines are going to be hot!'

I knew I had to talk to him about the Drake Six but I dreaded it. If Luxtons were involved in some way, it would destroy his reputation at best and his livelihood at worst.

'I heard about Violet Green's death,' said Michael.

He must have seen my surprise because he added, 'Doreen Mutters – her close friend – called to let me know that she wants the oak benches to stay in the sale with a reserve of five thousand apiece. They should fetch that at least.'

'Doreen Mutters is the beneficiary?' I thought of the three cups and saucers on the draining board in Violet's kitchen. Violet wouldn't have thought twice about letting Doreen and her husband Stan into the house late at night. Mallory believed that everyone was capable of murder and Mum's comment about treacherous best friends hit me afresh.

Michael smiled. 'I'm probably not allowed to confirm it, but yes. We must have sold most of the Green family fortune over the years,' he went on. 'I'm surprised that there is any furniture left. You live on the Honeychurch estate, don't you, Kat? Awful business.'

'Yes, awful,' I agreed. 'Did you know Charlie at all?'

'Oh yes.' Michael nodded. 'Quite a character. He was a good storyteller. He was a regular at the racetrack until he moved to Ireland. He must have come back under the radar.'

'It certainly seems so,' I said. 'I wonder why?'

'Charlie owed a fortune at Ladbrokes,' said Michael. 'And a few other places besides. I offered to help him sell his motorbike collection but he refused. Now, I don't want to hold you up—'

'I always like talking to you,' I said. 'In fact, I have a question about the Drake Six. Do you remember them? It was quite a few years ago.'

I tried to keep my voice casual but I was watching closely for the slightest flicker of guilt but Michael's eyes lit up.

'Oh yes,' he said eagerly. 'I remember them well. Extremely rare. The artist was Svetlana Winkler who was the Annie Leibovitz of the sixteenth century. She painted her subjects with – literally, in Drake's case – warts and all!'

'And the backing for each portrait?' I asked.

'Why, the King of Spades of course,' said Michael. 'Nothing could be better for Drake – that renegade!'

Relief flooded through me. Without knowing it, Michael had confirmed that he'd valued my miniatures, not the Commodore's. But the question remained – how did the switch take place?

Michael raised an eyebrow. 'Why are you asking? Surely the Commodore isn't selling his collection. He fought tooth and nail with a buyer from Hong Kong for those. It was a very exciting day.'

'Winkler never painted copies, did she?' I knew she didn't but I wanted confirmation from Michael on that fact, too.

'Never,' Michael agreed. 'All Winkler's work was one-off and she was a stickler for detail hence why she painted the *Pelican* a second time when the ship was renamed the *Golden Hind*.'

'She sounds like me,' came a voice. 'I'm a stickler for detail, too.'

We turned to find Pearl Clayton. 'I'm sorry to interrupt, Michael.' She extended her hand in greeting. 'I am one of your biggest fans, Ms Stanford. I never missed an episode of *Fakes & Treasures*.'

Michael smiled. 'Mrs Clayton has bought The Priory.'

'And I need to furnish it,' she said. 'So I'm doing the saleroom rounds in the hope of finding rare and unusual pieces.'

Michael rested a hand on her arm and gave a nod to where Johnny was beckoning him over. 'Will you excuse me, my presence is needed – oh, I meant to congratulate you on Oyster Girl's win last Saturday.'

Pearl Clayton beamed. 'Thank you. We've got high hopes for Lingfield Park next weekend.'

I remembered seeing a photograph of Oyster Girl on the front page of the *Dipperton Deal* and added my congratulations too.

'My late husband bought her as a yearling,' she said. 'Unfortunately he passed away. I like to think he's watching over her. Are you a horse lover?'

'I am,' I said. 'And in fact, we met yesterday. You were lost and our mare had cast a shoe.'

Pearl Clayton seemed embarrassed. 'Good heavens. Was that *you*?' she said. 'How did you get all that hair under your riding hat?'

'With difficulty,' I grinned.

'And your horse?' she said. 'I hope your horse was all right.'

'Tinkerbell – yes, we got home eventually,' I said. 'I hope you found your way to Okehampton.'

'Yes, *eventually*,' she echoed. 'I will never attempt to take a shortcut again! What do you think of the sale?'

'There are some beautiful pieces here,' I said. 'Is there anything that's caught your eye?'

'Everything!' she said firmly. 'Furnishing The Priory is going to be a very big job. Perhaps you would like to help me do it? I would pay you a commission for every piece as well as for your time. It would be fun. And please, call me Pearl.'

I was a bit taken aback. 'I'm really flattered,' I said. 'But interior design is not my area of expertise. I am sure there are many who would jump at the chance.'

She gave a dismissive wave. 'I already have someone but it needs a woman's touch – ah, here he is now. Monty darling!'

I couldn't hide my surprise and nor could Sir Monty at seeing me standing with Pearl Clayton. He looked decidedly hot and bothered. Pearl Clayton waved him over, 'The antique circuit is such a small world. You must know each other.'

'I believe you've met my mother too,' I said. 'Iris Stanford?'

Pearl Clayton frowned. 'The name does ring a bell.'

'You met her at the summer ball last Saturday, I believe,' I said. 'She was with Sir Monty.'

Pearl Clayton turned to Sir Monty who seemed unusually agitated. 'Another of your lady friends, Monty?'

'Just a friend,' he blustered. 'A friend. Nothing more.'

Just a friend? Could Sir Monty sink any lower in my estimation?

'I was trying to persuade Kat to help furnish The Priory,' she went on. 'We both agree that it needs a woman's touch. You just might be out of a job, Monty.' She laughed and with a 'Please think about it, Kat. Monty has my number' to me, wandered off with Sir Monty trailing after her.

It sounded like Pearl Clayton had a lot of money. It also sounded like Sir Monty was pursuing her too.

When I got back in my car I noticed I'd missed a call from the Commodore. I'd put my phone to silent when I was viewing the sale. He'd left a message for me to call him back straight away.

Jennifer put me through immediately.

'I made a mistake,' said the Commodore. 'Jennifer handles my diary and she reminded me that I didn't take the Drake Six home after the sale because I had an engagement that evening.'

My stomach turned over. 'You're positive?'

'Luxtons delivered them to me the following Monday,' the Commodore went on. 'It was very annoying because I had arranged an unveiling and reception for the donors on the Saturday night.'

'And you are certain that it was Luxtons who delivered the miniatures,' I asked.

'Absolutely,' he replied.

It confirmed my suspicion that the switch was done during the delivery process. I had thought it a huge feat to forge six miniatures in such a short space of time, but with a delay, it was possible.

I was certain that Michael Luxton didn't have a clue. I was equally certain that Ronnie Lubbock was involved since Sir Monty would have to have someone on the inside to make the delivery look official.

'Do you remember who delivered them? The name of the driver perhaps?' I asked. 'Wouldn't he have had to have a pass to get onto the base?'

'Yes, he would,' said the Commodore. 'Do you want to hold so I can check?'

'I'll hold.' Finally, real progress!

I sat in my car waiting for what seemed like ages until the Commodore came back on the line. 'The driver was called Leslie O'Sullivan from Luxtons.'

My stomach turned over again. 'Are you certain?'

'Of course I am. He had to produce his ID.'

The mysterious Leslie, the Leslie who had cleared out Lavender's bedroom and the Leslie that did not work at Luxtons at all. My mother had mentioned a Leslie, too – a jockey she had met at Newton Abbot – and Willow's description sounded as if it were the same man.

'Would you have a contact number?' I said suddenly.

'Jennifer will have it,' he said. 'I'll ask her.'

Moments later he came back on the line again. 'Do you have a pen?'

'Yes!' He dictated the phone number. The moment we ended the call I dialled Leslie's number.

But just seconds later my hopes were dashed. An automated message told me that the number I had dialled was no longer in service and to please check the number and dial again.

I'd reached a dead end – or had I?

I thought of Violet's oak benches being picked up from Luxtons on Sunday but instead of being taken to the warehouse, they'd gone straight to Stubbs Place where they had stayed for two nights. Was that where the forgeries were done?

It was time to recruit my mother to do a bit of sleuthing.

Chapter Twenty-Five

I found Mum hovering over the kitchen counter leafing through the *Dipperton Deal*. She was dressed in something I never in a million years thought she'd wear – a black polo neck, a pair of black jeggings and trainers, and – to my shock – a black bumbag!

Mum looked up. 'Oh, it's you.' She seemed surprised.

'Who else were you expecting?'

'Well, she's gone,' said Mum, neatly avoiding my question.

'Who has gone?' I asked.

'Wren Fraser,' she said. 'I suppose we must have frightened her off.'

'How do you know she's gone?'

'Delia told me,' said Mum. 'Our Wren flew the coop without any explanation. Delia saw her drive away and when she went to stock up her hospitality basket, she noticed Wren had stripped the bed, folded the towels and left her a five-pound tip.'

'So she *was* a reporter,' I declared. 'I knew it!'

I pulled out a chair and sat down, utterly exhausted. 'Do you want to come up for supper tonight? I have a lot to tell you and something I need you to do for me.'

Mum hesitated. 'I can't this evening. I have plans.'

I regarded my mother with suspicion. 'You're going out dressed like that?' It wasn't that she didn't look smart – my mother always looked smart. 'You look like a mature version of Catwoman.'

Mum smirked. 'That wasn't my intention but what's wrong with being Catwoman?'

'I don't think I've ever seen your legs before,' I said. 'They're not bad.'

'Thank you,' said Mum. 'What was it you wanted me to do?'

I told her that I was convinced that Sir Monty was a key player in a forgery business. 'He picked up Violet's oak benches on Sunday and took them back to his house – not to the warehouse, his *house*,' I said. 'Why do you think he did that?'

'Perhaps he wanted to sit on them?' Mum suggested.

'Be serious!' I went on to tell her about my visit to the Commodore, the wart on Sir Francis Drake's nose and the significance of the King of Spades playing card.

'Really, darling? How fascinating,' she said, not sounding fascinated at all. 'You're saying the miniatures you have are the originals and the ones in the Commodore's office are fakes?'

'Exactly!' I cried. 'But the originals are copied after they're picked up from the seller and the forgery is done before being put into the sale. The originals are *in* the actual sale but then – voilà – they are switched during the delivery process.'

'Gosh,' said Mum. 'And why do you think Monty is involved?'

'I don't like him. I don't trust him and he is the common denominator!' I was disappointed at my mother's apparent lack of interest.

'Can you prove it?' she said.

'*You* might be able to,' I said. 'I think the forgeries are done at Stubbs Place.'

'He does have a lot of outbuildings,' Mum mused.

'And perhaps you can get hold of his mobile,' I said.

'Why?' Mum said.

'Check his contact list,' I said. 'I need a number for Leslie O'Sullivan.'

'The jockey?' Mum asked.

'Yes!' I exclaimed. 'I'm pretty sure that he's the man who picked up the stuff from Lavender's bedroom and he was the driver who delivered the forged Drake Six to the Commodore!'

'All right, dear,' Mum said. 'No need to shout. Why would he have done that?'

I was getting exasperated. 'I think the other four original Drake miniatures were hidden in Lavender's bedroom and your boyfriend got Leslie to go and get them!'

'You're raising your voice and it's really unnecessary,' said Mum. 'I'm standing right here.'

I was getting a headache. 'Tell me what you know about Leslie O'Sullivan.'

'Just that he's Pearl Clayton's jockey and rides her racehorse.'

'I met Pearl Clayton this afternoon at Luxtons,' I said. 'Did you know that Sir Monty is helping her furnish The Priory?'

Mum scowled. 'No, I didn't.'

'And that's not all,' I said. 'I'm afraid – I don't know how to tell you this – but when your name came up in conversation, Sir Monty just said you were good friends.'

Mum's expression darkened. 'Did he now.'

'If he's cheating on you with Delia, why wouldn't he cheat on Delia too?' I said.

Mum's jaw hardened. 'So what exactly do you want me to find out?'

'Are you seeing him tonight?'

'You could say that,' said Mum.

'Ask for a tour of Stubbs Place,' I said. 'What we're looking for is a workshop – somewhere he can restore or repair furniture.'

'All right, we'll do it – I mean, I'll do it,' Mum said hastily.

'Great,' I said. 'Take your phone and take photographs. Although . . .' I hesitated as I thought of the exquisite details of the Drake Six. 'Monty would need a professional artist to copy those paintings.'

'Like Alfred?' Mum suggested.

'Yes, like Alfred,' I agreed.

'And don't forget to go through Sir Monty's contact list.'

'What am I looking for – other than Leslie O'Sullivan?'

'I don't know!' I was getting excited. 'An artist!'

'Perhaps I'll look under F for Forger,' Mum said.

'Very funny,' I said. 'But please be careful, Mum. Don't do anything stupid.'

'Cooeee,' came a familiar cry. 'Are you ready?'

Delia walked into the kitchen and my jaw dropped. There was no other word for it. She looked as if she was about to stand on a street corner in a red-light district – scarlet lipstick, fishnet tights, a very short pleather skirt that showed off firm thighs and thick ankles, and a low-cut black satin blouse that exposed a tiny ribbon of red lace.

I looked to my mother in her Catwoman attire and back at Delia.

'What's going on?' I demanded. 'You two are up to something. I know you are.'

'Nothing,' Delia said innocently. 'Come on, Iris. I'm raring to go.'

My suspicion deepened. 'I thought you were going to see Sir Monty, Mum?' A horrible thought flashed across my mind about a threesome but fortunately Delia stopped it by saying, 'I hear your Shawn is back.'

'Excuse me?' I said sharply. 'How do you know?'

Delia clapped her hand over her mouth in mock horror. 'Oops. Oh dear. Have I put my foot in it?'

'No. Why would you think that?' I said. 'I just didn't expect him back until Thursday . . .'

'Shawn's back because he couldn't wait a day longer to see Kat,' Mum said firmly, which shut Delia up. 'He's come back to surprise her. Just you see. Come along. We don't want to be late for our rendezvous.'

The three of us left the Carriage House.

Delia only just managed to slide into the front passenger seat of Mum's Mini. Her skirt was far too tight and I got an eyeful of red underwear.

I marched over to the car window and knocked. Mum hit the button. 'Yes, dear?'

'Whatever you two have planned tonight,' I said. 'Just *don't.*'

'We promise to behave ourselves,' said Mum with a mischievous grin. Delia began to titter. They were like naughty schoolgirls off on some jape. 'And don't worry, I'll do what you asked.'

Mum gave two cheerful beeps of the horn and roared out of the courtyard leaving me anxious about what they were up to. But there were two of them and only one of him.

I was happy that Shawn had come back early. I would race home, freshen up, and then go around to see him. But no sooner had I reached Jane's Cottage than there was a ping from an incoming text.

It was from Shawn and full of typos. *Looking forward to Thurs. Will spk then. Lob yo.*

Delia was wrong. He wasn't home after all.

I was desperate for Shawn's advice. I rang his mobile – it went straight to voicemail – then I called his London house. Lizzie answered.

She was unusually chatty as we talked about the twins and how they'd discovered Tae Kwon Do and loved it. And then, to my astonishment, after asking after my mother,

Lizzie said, 'So lovely to have a chance to talk to you without Shawn here.'

'He's not there?' I said sharply.

For the first time ever, Lizzie seemed uncomfortable. 'He's . . . he's out. Can I give him a message?'

'No, it's okay,' I said quickly. 'I'll catch up with him when he comes down this week.'

'Yes. You should do that.' She sounded relieved and we ended the call.

I was thoroughly confused. Was Shawn in Devon or wasn't he? And if he was, why was he avoiding me?

There was only one thing to do.

I grabbed my car keys.

Chapter Twenty-Six

Shawn lived in a small hamlet on the outskirts of Little Dipperton in a semi-detached Edwardian house with a wood-framed front porch. I pulled up behind his car that was parked close to the picket fence on the narrow lane.

Delia was right. He was home and Lizzie had lied to me.

My heart began to race and I felt inexplicably nervous. At the same time, I was angry but I was determined to have it out with him, once and for all.

It was no longer just about our relationship. Charlie Green had been murdered. Violet had been murdered. I'd discovered forged paintings and I was positive that Sir Monty was the ringleader.

I marched up to the front door and rang the bell, but as I waited, I began to have doubts about just turning up. In the past, I wouldn't have thought twice about surprising him with a visit, but things between us had deteriorated so much that I didn't think he'd be pleased to see me.

I was just about to turn away when Shawn opened the door and his face fell. I was right.

'Outside,' he said quickly and ushered me backwards, closing the door behind him. He took my arm and propelled me along the brick path to a bench that was tucked in the corner of the tiny front garden.

I sat down. 'I've been trying to talk to you for days.'

'I know,' he said in a low voice. 'And I said we would talk on Thursday. I've got a lot going on at the moment.'

I'd lost count of the number of times he had said just that.

Shawn turned to face me. I saw sorrow in his eyes and felt this horrible sinking feeling that it must be over between us.

'But today is Tuesday!' I whispered. 'So much has been happening and I just don't know what to do.'

'Okay. Go ahead,' he said. 'I'm listening.'

'You want me to tell you outside?' I was incredulous. 'Can't we at least go indoors?'

'I'm in the middle of something important,' he said.

I stifled the urge to walk away but only because I was desperate. I told him all about Charlie Green and Violet and her oak benches and then about the two Drake miniatures that I had found in Lavender's bedroom. 'The Commodore has six on his wall at Dartmouth Naval Academy and they are all fake!' I knew I was gabbling. 'Sir Monty is the mastermind behind it all. He switches the originals and delivers the forgeries to the buyer and then' – I shrugged – 'must sell the originals on the black market.'

'Go on,' said Shawn quietly.

'I think Charlie Green was caught up in it,' I said. 'I found postcards from Ireland in Lavender's bedroom – one was dated just six weeks ago!'

'Postcards!' he exclaimed. 'What do you mean, *postcards*?'

'As if to imply that Charlie was still alive,' I said. 'Which I suppose he could have been. Maybe he just came back under the radar. That's what Michael Luxton suggested.'

'You've been discussing this with Michael *Luxton*?' Shawn's voice was hard.

'No,' I protested. 'It just came up in the conversation when I viewed the sale this afternoon. He said Charlie owed money everywhere.'

'Where are the postcards?' said Shawn.

'I have photographs of them on my phone but the postcards have gone,' I said. 'Sir Monty sent someone called Leslie O'Sullivan to clear out Lavender's bedroom. By the way, that awful man asked my mother to marry him but he's cheating on her with Delia Evans and I'm positive that his next mark is Pearl Clayton – have you heard of her? She's a widow and loaded, with a racehorse and—'

'Kat!' Shawn interrupted. 'Okay. I can see you're upset.'

'*Upset?*' I was stunned. 'Doesn't any of this mean anything to you?'

'Stop talking,' he said. 'I have to think.'

I sat there with my hands clasped together staring out into the lane. And then, I saw the Honda CR-V.

I jumped up. 'I don't believe it!'

'Where are you going?' Shawn said suddenly.

But I wasn't listening. I hurried down the path and over to the car in question.

It was Wren's. I recognised the child car seat in the back and the dog guard.

Shawn was behind me. He took my shoulders but I angrily stepped away from his touch. 'Why is Wren Fraser's car parked outside your house?'

Shawn gave a heavy sigh. 'I think you'd better come in.'

Wren was hovering by the kitchen counter with a glass of red wine in her hand. She looked nervous. She gave a small smile but I ignored it.

Shawn pointed to a chair. 'Sit down, Kat.'

A laptop computer was open on the pine table along with a stack of manila folders stuffed with documents. Although there was an open bottle of wine, a tumbler of sparkling water was next to Shawn's laptop. It looked like he was drinking Perrier.

Under the glare of the fluorescent lighting, Shawn looked terrible. Dark rings bloomed under his eyes. He looked as if he hadn't slept for weeks.

'I promise that there is nothing untoward going on here,' said Wren. 'I am happily married with—'

'A husband called Dax, a daughter called Lily and a black Labrador,' I said coldly.

'I'm just useless,' she moaned.

'Well?' I demanded. 'Is someone going to tell me what's going on?'

'I'm sorry,' said Wren. 'I can't.'

'Either you tell me exactly what's happening here, Shawn, or it's over between us.' *If it isn't over already*, I wanted to add.

Wren stood up with her wine glass. 'I'll leave you two to talk,' she said hastily. 'Upstairs? Yes.'

'The boys' room,' said Shawn. 'You'll need to make up a bed.'

I was shocked. 'She's staying *here*?' I was utterly confused. 'You know each other from where? London? But why—?'

Wren shot a look at me that was full of remorse. 'It's not what you think,' she said and left the kitchen.

Shawn didn't speak until we heard the sound of her footsteps going up the stairs.

He took a deep breath. 'Wren is an undercover police officer,' he said. 'Unfortunately, she's not a very good one. She's the Commissioner's niece. When Charlie's body was discovered, we had to move quickly. The woman we had earmarked for this operation was ill and Wren stepped in.'

'You could have told me,' I said. 'And what operation?'

'It was also her first assignment.' Shawn ignored my question. 'Wren was purely there on surveillance. Her orders were just to observe.'

'Explain the shepherd's hut,' I demanded. 'It only arrived hours before she turned up.'

'That was a stroke of luck,' he said. 'I was looking for somewhere for her to stay and asked Gran.'

'But what on earth made Wren pick Krystalle Storm as a cover?'

'We'd agreed on her being a writer, but it was her idea to pick Krystalle Storm,' said Shawn. 'She admitted she got the idea when she saw all your mother's books in the community shop.'

'My mother's own cover was nearly blown,' I said and told him about Mallory insisting on looking at the below stairs family tree in Mum's writing house. 'Clive saw Mum's stuff but I managed to convince him that she's Dear Amanda.'

Shawn didn't smile. 'I'll handle Mallory. I don't want you discussing any of this with him.'

'That's hardly fair,' I exclaimed. 'I found Violet's body!'

'Different department, different investigation,' he said curtly.

'But surely they overlap?' I said.

'Stay out of it, Kat,' said Shawn. 'I'm serious.'

'At least pour me a glass of wine.'

Shawn got up and returned with two wine glasses and poured out a glass each.

'Why couldn't you tell me all this?' I said. 'Why all the secrecy? Don't you trust me?'

He hesitated and then responded, 'All right. But you cannot repeat this to anyone – especially your mother.' He took another deep breath. 'I'm not in counter terrorism, I'm in the NCA – the National Crime Agency. It's rather like the FBI because it deals with cross-border cases.'

'I don't understand.' I struggled to process this new lie.

'Every part of the UK is split into regions,' he went on. 'There are three levels of crime force.' He ticked his fingers, 'Within border, cross border and triangular. OCGs – the acronym for Organised Crime Groups – fall under national and international jurisdiction, hence the NCA.'

'I didn't mean about not understanding *that*,' I said irritably. 'I just don't understand why you suddenly decided to move to London.'

Shawn took a sip of wine. 'It's a case that is very personal to me. You see, Charlie asked for my help the night he went missing. I wanted to believe he'd gone to Ireland but deep down I suspected that he hadn't. He was scared and said that someone was following him. But you have to understand, he'd said that many times before. He turned up at bath time. The twins were babies. Helen was having a meltdown.'

Oh. My. God. He mentioned his wretched dead wife Helen again! Shawn must have seen by my expression that he'd put his foot in it. 'For heaven's sake, Kat!' he exclaimed. 'I had a life before you!'

'I'm sorry . . . I just . . . you always mention her,' I protested. 'You can't help yourself!'

'I'm mentioning her because it's important to the story,' Shawn snapped. 'Charlie wanted me to look after something for him but I told him I didn't want to handle dodgy goods.'

Suddenly, my ego was no longer important. 'What was it?'

'I don't know,' said Shawn. 'It was in a small knapsack. He didn't show me. I told him to go and see his aunt. I'm afraid I wasn't very kind.'

I felt a surge of excitement. 'He must have had the Drake miniatures inside that knapsack,' I said. 'And he *did* go and see his aunt—'

'And hid the miniatures among her car boot sale junk,' said Shawn.

'Two in the doll's house and the others . . . wait' – I shook my head. 'If he had, why did he then go and see Eric and ask him to do the same thing? I think Charlie split the miniatures up.'

'Maybe he saw Eric first before he came to see me?' Shawn said.

I shook my head again. 'You just told me that Charlie turned up at the twins' bath time. And anyway, Peggy Cropper said she saw Charlie in the walled garden with Vera much later when she was going to bed. Charlie must have hidden the other miniatures, and whoever killed him wanted to know where. Someone followed him to Honeychurch Hall. But why did Charlie have them in the first place?'

Shawn scratched his chin. 'People get killed for four reasons. They saw something, they heard something, they have something or they know something. Charlie ticked all those boxes. He was always in trouble . . .'

'Michael Luxton told me Charlie owed money at Ladbrokes—' I snapped my fingers. 'He could have been blackmailing the gang to pay off a debt?'

Shawn raised an eyebrow. 'Have you ever thought of a career in the police force?'

Our eyes met and we smiled. Perhaps it was going to be all right between us after all.

He reached for my hand. 'I'm sorry, Kat,' he said. 'It won't always be like this.'

'And I'm sorry for behaving like a deranged teenager,' I said. 'Will you promise that even if you can't tell me the details, you will at least tell me you can't tell me – if that makes sense?'

Shawn sat back in his chair, still keeping hold of my hand. 'What I can tell you is that Charlie had got caught up in a very violent and dangerous national gang that are based in the south-west. Apart from the usual money laundering, they are loan sharks – particularly at the racetrack, which is where Charlie must have first got into trouble – and over the last few years this gang has branched out into art forgery and fraud.'

'And that's where Sir Monty comes in,' I said. 'So, are you saying that he's not the head guy at all?'

'Yes,' said Shawn. 'But it wouldn't surprise me if he takes the fall. That's what this gang does. Nothing is ever traced back to them. Ever. That's why Operation Oyster is so critical. For the first time in years, we got a tip – from a museum in Brussels in fact. David Wynne sends his regards – no, sorry, wrong message. He sends his *love*.'

'Excuse me?' I said.

'David?' said Shawn. 'Your ex-fiancé, or had you forgotten you had a life before we met? I'm surprised you hadn't contacted him yourself.' Shawn's tone had an edge to it. I knew he and David couldn't stand each other but I hadn't expected Shawn to reach out to him, even in a professional capacity. I was beginning to understand how serious this case must be.

'I have tried to talk to you many times,' I said. 'But if you remember, you weren't interested.'

'It wasn't that and besides, it's irrelevant now,' said Shawn. 'David told me they would need a workshop to do the forgeries—'

'Yes, I thought so too and I'm certain that it's at Sir Monty's place because that's where Luxtons went to pick up Violet's oak benches.' But then my heart turned over. 'Oh no.'

'What's wrong?' said Shawn.

'My mother . . . she and Delia were going there tonight and I told her to look around.'

Shawn gasped. 'You did *what!* What were you thinking?' He was angry.

'How was I to know what was going on!' I retorted hotly.

Shawn reached for his mobile and was about to dial, but then hit 'end'. 'No. That won't work. Damn!' He struggled to keep his temper. 'They'll tip him off. They may not mean to but it will happen—'

'They won't!' I protested. 'I told Mum to be discreet—'

'*Discreet?* Ha! Iris *discreet!*' Shawn ran his fingers through his hair. 'I need to think about this. You'd better leave. I have to make some calls.'

'But . . . but what about my mother?' I said. 'Is she in danger?'

'Let's hope not,' said Shawn. 'Can you see yourself out? Oh, and not a word to Mallory about any of this. I will handle Mallory.'

And with that, he picked up his phone and left the kitchen.

I walked back to my car feeling wretched. I was horrified. If anything happened to Mum it would be my fault. I could understand the need for confidentiality, but this was a side of Shawn that I had never seen before and wasn't sure if I actually liked it. If it was dangerous work, how could my mother not be in danger? I had to warn her.

I tried Mum's mobile but it went straight to voicemail, which meant she was probably home, but when I drove via the Carriage House, her Mini wasn't there and as I passed Honeychurch Cottages, it wasn't there either.

When I got home my heart sank.

Mallory's Peugeot was parked on the hardstanding.

Chapter Twenty-Seven

Mallory got out of his car and stretched. I wondered just how long he had been waiting for me.

'Not too late I hope,' he said as he locked his car door.

The air was heavy with rain and had that quietness that heralds a big storm.

I was worried. It was all very well for Shawn to say don't talk to Mallory but now he was here, I couldn't avoid it.

Large drops of rain began to fall and suddenly, there was an ear-splitting crack and boom of thunder. The rain just hammered down. Even in the short distance to the front porch Mallory and I got drenched.

I fumbled with my keys, dropping them twice. The second time, Mallory bent down to pick them up and we clashed heads.

'Are you all right?' he said above the thundering rain. 'I'm rather used to it.'

Finally, we burst inside. My hair was plastered to my face. Mallory's suit was ruined.

'I'll get you a towel,' I said.

When I returned from the bathroom, he'd taken off his jacket and tie and was standing in his shirtsleeves. He was very buff, something I hadn't noticed before since he was always wearing a suit.

'Why don't you change and I'll put the kettle on,' he said in a tone that implied I was not to argue with him. 'Coffee, I assume, since I think you've been drinking?'

He must have smelled the wine on my breath.

'A little,' I said. 'Just with a . . . friend.' How horribly awkward this was going to be!

I had to let Shawn know that Mallory was here, but to my dismay, I realised that I had left my mobile in my Golf.

When I returned to the sitting room in my sweats and a hoodie, two mugs of black coffee were on the coffee table, along with a half-full cafetière.

He waited for me to sit down before settling on the sofa opposite with notebook in hand.

'I thought you would like to know that we went to Charlie Green's cottage in Staverton,' Mallory began. 'A neighbour told us that his post was being forwarded to an address in Ireland, which she gave us. We are getting that verified.'

I was curious. 'What state was the cottage in?'

'The same neighbour told us that she saw someone pop in once a month. She didn't have a name. She just said it was a man.' He glanced down at his notebook. 'A thorough search of Violet's kitchen revealed dozens of cashbooks. We were able to confirm that a rent of twenty-five pounds fifty pence is still being paid to Lord Rupert Honeychurch for a farm building which was being used to restore motorbikes on Moreleigh Mount . . .' He paused to take a sip of coffee. I took a sip too, remembering all too late that drinking coffee at night was never a good idea for me. I was already wired. I'd never sleep now.

'I spoke to the dowager countess who told me that you had ridden out to inspect the farm building yesterday,' said Mallory. 'I'm rather disappointed that you didn't tell me about it.'

I felt like a deer in headlights and could only mumble a pathetic, 'Sorry.' I should have told Shawn about the building on Moreleigh Mount, too, but I hadn't had a chance.

'Would you like to tell me what you observed at this farm building?' Mallory said.

'Nothing,' I said. 'It was all very clean and tidy. The windows were blacked out and both doors – there was a double door at the rear – were padlocked. I saw a security camera as well. It looked like it was still working since there was a red light flashing.'

'Yes.' Mallory nodded. 'His lordship remembered Charlie asking if he could install an alarm system.'

'That makes sense if he kept his motorbikes there,' I said.

'We'll be sending up a team tomorrow to take a look. Back to Miss Green for a moment,' Mallory continued. 'We're quite certain she knew her attacker. The three cups and saucers on the draining board and her penchant for tidiness – as confirmed by Willow – indicate that the perpetrator was hoping to get rid of any DNA.' He flipped back a few pages. 'Which reminds me of a curious thing that Doreen Mutters told me when I spoke to her.'

I waited for this revelation.

'She mentioned that when Charlie came to see Violet and Lavender Green on the night before the beating of the bounds, Charlie had asked Violet if he could— No, in fact, she caught him emptying out the cash from her petty cash box.'

Violet had told me the same thing but when I agreed, Mallory was annoyed again. 'Why didn't you tell me this before?'

'I didn't think it was important,' I said.

'The devil is in the details, Kat,' he scolded. 'Because my theory is that whoever killed Violet Green was looking for something. The theft of an empty petty cash box implies that he would be using it for something other than money. Don't you agree?' Mallory cocked his head and his eyes practically bored into my skull. 'The deceased had a small knapsack with him. Why? I suggest that he used it to transport this petty cash box. What do you think was inside?'

My tote bag with the Drake miniatures was practically smoking with evidence.

As the sound of the rain continued to hammer on the roof and at the windows, I struggled with my conscience, torn between being told by my boyfriend to keep quiet and facing a grilling by a police officer who would soon guess I was hiding something.

Mallory poured himself another cup. 'Banks tells me that Wren Fraser has vanished. Would you happen to know why she left so suddenly?'

'Um. No,' I lied.

'There was a rumour that she was that internationally bestselling author, Krystalle Storm,' he said. 'Do you know anything about that?'

'I heard the rumour,' I said. 'But of course she's far too young to be Krystalle Storm.'

'That's what I thought, too. My mother is a fan.' Mallory nodded. 'Don't you think it strange that Miss Fraser had only been here for forty-eight hours and when Lady Lavinia attempted to phone her to ask her why, Miss Fraser's phone was no longer in service?'

'Gosh,' I said. 'That is strange.'

'You see . . . when we did the grid search in Honeywell Wood, we found this.' Mallory brought out an evidence bag. It looked like one of Wren Fraser's inhalers. 'Delia Evans told me that Miss Fraser suffered from allergies so I presume this belonged to her.'

'Perhaps that's why she left early?' I said quickly. 'When my mother and I were having drinks with her, Wren had an attack. There's a lot of ragwort in the walled garden. I bet that's the reason why she had to leave. She couldn't handle the pollen.' This seemed perfectly plausible to me.

Mallory hesitated. 'But that doesn't explain why her phone is out of service or that she didn't ask for a refund – which she would have been entitled to. Three thousand pounds is a lot of money.'

I shrugged. 'No, it doesn't explain why.'

'I see,' said Mallory tightly. 'So you don't know anything about this Wren Fraser.'

There was a knocking at the door followed by a loud crack of thunder.

'That could be my mother,' I said and darted to open up just as a bolt of lightning crackled across the sky.

But it wasn't my mother.

It was Shawn.

Chapter Twenty-Eight

'I haven't told the inspector anything at all!' I said quickly. 'He was waiting for me when I got home.'

'Cropper, I presume,' said Mallory with a nod.

'Mallory.' Shawn nodded back.

There was an ugly silence. The two men eyed each other like gladiators. Shawn began to shiver.

'Shawn,' I said. 'Can I get you a towel?'

'Yes, please,' said Shawn tightly.

I darted to the bathroom to bring back a towel and grabbed one of my own baggy sweaters. Too late I saw it was in a feminine shade of periwinkle blue.

Shawn removed his wet sweatshirt and revealed his pale, naked torso. Physically, the two men couldn't be more different. Mallory – with a mat of chest hairs now visible through his damp shirt – had the solid physique of a rugby player, whereas Shawn – thin and toned – was more of a whippet.

Shawn donned the sweater.

Mallory tried to keep a straight face. 'Good colour.'

'I can take things from here now, Mallory, thank you,' Shawn said stiffly.

Mallory smirked. 'That's very kind of you but not necessary,' he said. 'I have two murders on my hands that fall under my jurisdiction.'

'I'm afraid it is very necessary,' said Shawn. 'I have reason to believe that the deaths of Charlie Green and his aunt, Violet Green, are part of a larger national investigation. I must ask you to turn over any evidence or information to the NCA.'

A flicker of annoyance crossed Mallory's features. 'And I'm afraid that I can't do that without a written authorisation from your superior officer.'

'Shall we sit down?' I said with forced gaiety but was promptly ignored.

'You can have your written authorisation in the morning,' Shawn declared. 'But time is of the essence. I must insist you hand over all your preliminary findings and reports *now*.'

'And I must insist on the written authorisation,' Mallory persisted. 'Surely a few hours won't make a difference.'

Shawn's jaw had hardened and the little tick in Mallory's eye had started to twitch again.

'For heaven's sake, you two,' I said. 'Can't we all work together?'

Neither man spoke.

'Fine,' I said. 'In that case, I'll just tell you everything I know. And Mallory, Shawn is right. Time *is* of the essence. My mother is at Stubbs Place as we speak.'

'Your *mother*?' Mallory said sharply. 'What has she got to do with any of it and where is Stubbs Place?'

I hadn't intended to throw my mother into the mix but if she *were* in danger – and Delia too – then I would never forgive myself, or these men and their egos, if something happened to them.

'Why don't I go and make another pot of coffee whilst you two can make nice.' I picked up the empty cafetière and returned to the kitchen where I waited, dreading the sound of raised voices or the slam of the front door.

The rain continued to pound on the roof.

I rejoined them in the sitting room just as Mallory said, 'All right, Pugsley will be released first thing tomorrow morning. But as you may or may not know, we found a gun on the premises.'

'Yes,' said Shawn. 'And as you may or may not know, the gunshot wound was not caused by a twelve-bore shotgun.'

'Execution style,' said Mallory grimly.

I looked at Mallory. 'I told you that Eric would never have done that.'

'Unfortunately, the damage done by Mr Pugsley's shovel to the deceased's skull initially threw us off the scent.'

'But a *gun*.' I was appalled. I hadn't dwelled on how Charlie had been killed but – a *gun*? *Execution* style. I'd assumed Charlie must have been hit on the head. Shawn had said this gang were dangerous but I hadn't realised to what extent.

'I want it noted that Pugsley admitted to deliberately hiding the motorbike which inadvertently led to Charlie Green's death,' Mallory declared.

'That's taking it a bit too far, Mallory,' Shawn retorted, clearly not happy.

'Is it?' Mallory offered me his mug so I could pour him a fresh cup. Shawn gave a nod, so I poured one for him, too.

'We know that Charlie Green was in fear for his life,' Mallory continued. 'The motorbike would have allowed him to get away, but instead he was forced to seek shelter in Honeywell Wood where he was apprehended and shot.'

Hearing it put that way made me feel sick. I glanced at Shawn who seemed distressed. It sounded like it wasn't just Shawn who had let Charlie down that night. Eric had let him down, too.

'Our grid search turned up some critical forensic evidence that I am confident will confirm my findings,' said Mallory. 'I'm also willing to share the results of my interviews with the residents of Honeychurch Hall and those of my house-to-house enquiries in the village.'

Shawn gave an almost imperceptible nod. I thought Mallory was being a team player and said so. 'You see!' I added. 'You may have the big picture details, Shawn, but Mallory has the devil-in-the-detail . . . details.' Out of the corner of my eye I saw Mallory smile. Encouraged I added, 'And both of you need my professional advice on the forgeries.'

'*Forgeries?*' said Mallory sharply. 'What forgeries?'

Shawn shot me a furious glare. 'It doesn't exactly affect this case—'

'But of course it does!' I exclaimed. 'They're connected to the Frozen Charlottes.'

'The Frozen *Charlottes*?' said Shawn just as sharply. 'What are you talking about?'

Mallory smirked again. 'The deceased sister – Charlotte Green—'

'I knew Charlotte Green,' said Shawn. 'And I know what Frozen Charlottes are. My grandmother used to put them in the Christmas pudding, but I don't see what this has to do with two murders.'

So I told Shawn about Charlotte's Frozen Charlottes in the cigar box that I had found in Lavender's bedroom. 'There were seven and there should have been eight.'

'We have reason to believe that the eighth doll was in the deceased's pocket,' said Mallory, adding, 'With a noose around its neck.'

Shawn couldn't hide his horror. 'Of course!' he exclaimed. 'Charlie was sending a message. It must have been one of his stupid clues. If only I'd known . . . if only . . .' He trailed off miserably.

To my surprise, Mallory regarded Shawn with compassion. 'Whatever he was up to would have been beyond your control. We can't save everyone.'

Shawn nodded bleakly. 'And what about Violet Green?'

'The manner of death – a violent push down the stairs – suggests frustration at something she may not have known anything about.'

'They must have been looking for the miniatures,' I said.

Shawn took a deep breath and finally began to talk. 'Codename, Operation Oyster,' he said. 'The NCA have been pursuing this family for decades but up until now, we've had no leads. They never use their own name. They are adept at hiding behind others and if someone gets in their way or threatens to expose their activities – as I believe Charlie was doing – those threats are eliminated.'

'So you don't think Charlie Green was working for this crime family?' I said.

'I don't,' Shawn agreed. 'It wasn't Charlie's style. He was a gambler and got into debt. He lived the high life and enjoyed his toys—'

'Restoring his motorbikes,' I put in.

'And Operation Oyster was launched when exactly?' Mallory said.

'It's been in the pipeline for months,' said Shawn. 'We got a tip from a museum in Brussels that a Greek statue that had been bought at auction for half a million pounds was in fact a fake. It was traced back to Luxtons in Newton Abbot.'

'And this is where the forgeries come in?' Mallory asked.

'Kat, over to you,' said Shawn.

'Dartmouth Naval Academy bought the Drake Six – six miniatures of Sir Francis Drake – for a huge sum believing they were authentic, but which turned out to be forgeries. I visited the Commodore today with the two I have and—'

'Excuse me? Why am I only hearing this now?' The tell-tale tick in Mallory's eye began to twitch again.

'I didn't tell you because I wasn't sure,' I protested. 'I had to compare mine with the Commodore's, and even so, I only have two of the six. I found those two in Lavender Green's bedroom stuck on the wall of a doll's house.'

Mallory nodded slowly. 'It sounds like the deceased had found all six and perhaps was planning on double-crossing this gang?'

'I think it's possible,' I said. 'I also wonder if the light I saw in Honeywell Wood in the early hours of Monday morning was someone looking for those miniatures.'

Shawn frowned. 'Movement in the woods?'

'Kat also saw another figure approach from Honeychurch Cottages,' Mallory chimed in. 'I have reason to believe it was the woman who was renting the shepherd's hut and who subsequently disappeared. We found her inhaler, which was identified by the housekeeper, Delia Evans.'

Shawn took another deep breath. 'I think I can explain.' And so he did but added that Wren Fraser was not her real name and that, for purposes of keeping her identity a secret, he wasn't about to disclose it.

Yet again, I felt disappointed. How many more secrets was Shawn going to keep from me?

'And whoever entered that wood used the old drive entrance,' I said. 'Meaning—'

'That it was someone who had not been to the Hall for years,' said Shawn. 'Unlike Charlie, I'm not a gambling man, but I would put money on the fact that whoever came back that night was the person who put Charlie in the ground all those years ago.'

We fell silent for a moment.

'We should be able to identify the make and year of the vehicle,' said Mallory. 'I was able to collect shards of glass from a broken mirror.'

I was beginning to see how difficult it was going to be to collar this OCG and I could also sense that Shawn was growing discouraged.

'Kat, can you explain how the forgeries work?' said Mallory.

So I did. I told him that I believed the item was picked up from the seller by a Luxtons employee but not taken to the Luxtons warehouse. Instead it was taken to Stubbs Place where it would be photographed, measurements taken and, if it was an easy job, copied there and then.

'The original still goes into the sale,' I said. 'So the buyer believes he has the real thing. But then it's switched during the delivery process. The collector receives an excellent forgery and the original is sold overseas on the black market.'

'And you have proof of this?' Mallory said.

'Only the fact that Violet Green's Charles II oak benches were picked up from her tearoom on Sunday and were not taken to Luxtons warehouse as they were supposed to be. Instead, they went to Sir Monty's house and were picked up from there to be delivered to the saleroom in time for the preview.'

'So Luxtons must be in on it, too,' mused Mallory.

'I don't think so,' I said. 'At least, not Michael Luxton, but I believe Ronnie Lubbock, a floor porter, is. He was sent by Sir Monty to pick up the benches using a white Transit van. It wasn't a regular Luxtons van, which is hunter green, but it did have the Luxtons logo.'

Mallory seemed surprised. 'Then why not arrest Sir Monty now?'

Shawn shook his head. 'He's just a cog in the wheel. Even if he's arrested, we can't touch the top people. We have to catch them red-handed, find their workshop and even then, pinning it on Pearl Clayton will be a miracle.'

'Clayton?' I gasped. 'Surely not . . . *the* Pearl Clayton?'

'The very same,' said Shawn with a tinge of bitterness. 'A pillar of respectable society.'

'No,' I said forcefully. 'I don't believe it. Everyone likes her!'

'Of course they do,' said Shawn. 'It's all a front. Her so-called dead husband is very much alive. His real name is Gavin.'

Gavin of the day-of-the-week polo shirt! I would never have put him and Pearl together, let alone married.

'I saw Pearl this afternoon at Luxtons,' I said. 'Actually, she offered me a job.'

Shawn's eyes widened. 'She did *what*?'

'A calculated strategy to befriend you and get you on her side,' said Mallory. 'I've heard of the Claytons. I'm afraid Shawn is right. She's untouchable.'

'I'm sorry,' I said, as if something was my fault.

Mallory thought for a moment. 'Has Pearl Clayton ever met Violet Green before?'

'Yes,' I said with a nod. 'She went to the tearoom only last week. Violet is – was – easily impressed by anyone in a position of authority. Do you think it was Pearl Clayton and Gavin who made that late-night visit?'

There was a ping of an incoming text. It was Shawn's mobile. He glanced down and instantly was on high alert. 'Excuse me.'

Mallory and I watched Shawn hurry into the kitchen out of earshot. Neither of us spoke while we waited for him to return.

When he did, he seemed excited. 'My Super wants us to raid Stubbs Place.' He looked at Mallory. 'Are you in?'

'You bet.' Mallory nodded and jumped to his feet.

I jumped to my feet, too. 'But what about my mother? And Delia! What if they're still there?'

'We'll make sure they won't come to any harm,' said Shawn. 'Don't worry.'

I wasn't happy about it but I knew there was nothing I could do. 'Can't I at least warn her that you are coming?'

'I'm sorry, but no,' said Shawn. 'Trust me. All will be well.' He turned to Mallory again. 'We'll go back to my place.'

'Or we can use the mobile police unit in the church car park,' Mallory said.

I could sense the alpha-male power struggle, but then it was gone. 'Fine,' said Shawn. 'I'll be right with you. I'll meet you there. I need to talk to Kat.'

Mallory opened the door and disappeared into the rainy night but Shawn turned back to me. 'I came here tonight to speak to you,' he said. 'I'm sorry for what happened at my house. You took me by surprise.'

I felt guarded. 'That's a bit of an understatement, isn't it?'

He took both my hands and looked deeply into my eyes. 'All I seem to do is apologise to you,' he said. 'I hope you understand everything now.'

I didn't answer because I didn't understand. His lack of trust in our relationship really bothered me.

'I promise it won't be like this for ever,' Shawn said for the umpteenth time. 'I'm sorry I didn't tell you about Wren – actually, her name is Julia Lark.'

'*Lark?* Wren? Funny,' I said, not thinking it funny at all.

'You have to believe me,' Shawn went on. 'For this whole operation to have worked, I had to play the part . . .'

I wasn't sure if I believed that. 'Even uprooting your children to London?'

'Why else do you think I haven't sold my house? Or rented it out?' Shawn searched my eyes. 'Believe me, Kat. You are very special to me. You do know that, don't you?'

I didn't answer.

'When this is over, I'll—'

Mallory's car horn – two insistent beeps – cut whatever Shawn was about to say short.

Shawn look annoyed. 'I told him I'd meet him there,' he said. 'We'll talk more tomorrow. Now, sit tight. Don't worry.'

He left. I waited until both cars had driven away. Shawn was delusional if he thought I wasn't going to warn my mother, especially if there was a gun involved. I called her mobile. She didn't answer. It was almost ten thirty. I should have asked Shawn more questions such as, when exactly were they planning this raid? Were they going in batons blazing?

It was hard to settle to anything. I kept replaying the conversation with both men. I brought out the miniatures and looked at them again. I took another look at the Frozen

Charlottes and thought of Shawn's belief that Charlie was trying to tell us something.

And then I was struck by a bizarre notion. Pansy had chirped about thinking *inside* the box instead of outside the box. She'd joked about the icehouse. Edith had mentioned the icehouse and so had Eric. It seemed so simple a possibility, but what if the icehouse held a clue?

There was only one way to find out. I grabbed my raincoat, my mobile and my car keys.

Chapter Twenty-Nine

I parked outside Honeychurch Cottages. Thankfully, the rain had eased off a little. The only lights came from Peggy Cropper's cottage. Delia's and Eric's were still in darkness.

As I waded through the weeds in the walled garden I cursed my stupidity for not donning Wellington boots. The legs of my sweatpants were soon soaked through.

The beehive-shaped icehouse stood in the opposite corner to the shepherd's hut. Half a dozen steps led down to the wooden door. Made of brick, it was partially below ground. The concept of an icehouse in which to store ice had been around since the mid-seventeenth century. Only richer households could afford to build them. This one was quite small and certainly not big enough for the so-called romantic tryst that Eric had believed Charlie and Vera were having.

I had to do everything by torch but, after finding a broom and dustpan and brush in the shepherd's hut, I managed to move all the detritus that had accumulated at the bottom of the steps and get the door open.

Inside, it was damp and cold. The floor rounded at the bottom where, at one time, it would have held melted ice. As I shone my torch around the brick-lined interior I tried to think what Charlie would do with a cash box. Had he buried it in the floor or the walls?

I thought of Mallory's grid search of Honeywell Wood and dropped to my hands and knees and began to methodically work my way across the floor. It wasn't pleasant. My nails were ruined but I didn't care. And then, I saw that one of the crevices between two bricks seemed wider, but I couldn't get any leverage. Quickly, I darted back to the shepherd's hut and grabbed a sharp knife.

It did the trick. I removed the brick and my heart skipped a beat as my torch caught a glint of metal.

It was a cash box.

My hands were trembling with excitement. There was no key in the lock – something I had dreaded. Inside wrapped in striped deckchair fabric from Lavender's bedroom were Drake's miniatures of the *Judith* and the *Pasha*.

I was euphoric until it struck me that the cash box had been large enough to store all four miniatures. Had Charlie hidden the remaining two elsewhere?

I trooped back to my car, muddy, wet and excited. I was desperate to tell Shawn but knew it would have to wait until the morning.

I felt agitated. What was happening? Had they raided Stubbs Place yet? I kept checking my phone in the hope

that Shawn, at the very least, would send me a text, but he
didn't – and nor did my mother.

It was now eleven thirty. I called Mum's landline but she
didn't answer. I tried her mobile, and it went straight to
voicemail again. At eleven forty-five I called both *again*
with no luck – and yet *again*, at midnight.

I sent Shawn a text. He didn't reply, so I texted Mallory,
who rang me.

'Shawn asked me to call you,' he said. 'We're going in at
O-one hundred hours.'

I was surprised. 'Are you there now?'

'Yes. To use a cliché, the place is surrounded,' said
Mallory. 'I'm parked in my car in the undergrowth.'

'Tell Shawn I found two of the miniatures,' I said. 'They
were in the icehouse.'

'The icehouse?' Mallory gave a short laugh. 'A clever
clue from beyond the grave. Well done.'

'The frozen in the Frozen Charlottes,' I said. 'But there
are still two missing.'

'Perhaps we'll be lucky and find them here,' said
Mallory. 'How were your mother and Delia Evans?'

My stomach turned right over. 'She's not home yet.'

There was a long silence and then, 'We've been here for
the last couple of hours and there has been no activity,'
he said.

'Did you see a red Mini?' I asked.

'No. Let me make some enquiries,' he said. 'I'll call you
back when I can. I've got to go.'

I stared at my phone and struggled to quell the sense

that something wasn't right. I'd assumed Mum had gone to Stubbs Place with Delia. What if they'd gone elsewhere?

And then I had an idea.

Grabbing my iPad I jumped on the Find My app and logged in using my mother's email address and her password, 'Exposed'.

I stared at the screen with increasing dismay. The blue dot was far away, out towards Dartmoor. It was around Moreleigh Mount.

Suddenly, it all fell into place.

Edith and I had seen Pearl Clayton driving in the area. Like a fool, I had believed that she was lost. Perhaps Charlie had been letting the Clayton's use the farm building for their forgeries? They wouldn't have known that the building did not belong to Charlie but was owned by Lord Rupert Honeychurch. Shawn had been right when he said that nothing was ever traced back to the Claytons.

But what was my mother doing there?

Desperate, I tried both Shawn and Mallory's mobiles again but got no response. I left a message to say what I was going to do. I had to find my mother.

Chapter Thirty

The rain had finally stopped but flash floods pooled along the narrow lanes. Several times I feared for the suspension on my car as it struck hidden holes and sent up torrents of water. I kept checking the blue dot on the Find My app. It didn't move.

I seemed to be driving forever when at last I saw the turning to Moreleigh Mount. Taking the grassy track I was suddenly blinded by a single headlamp coming towards me at speed. Panicked, I slammed on my brakes and reversed a few yards to get out of his way, but my car struck a boulder with a horrible crunch.

It was a motorbike. It swerved around me and tore away. A glance in my rear-view mirror showed it slowing down. My heart was hammering in my chest but then the bike made a turn and accelerated away into the night leaving me scared and shaken.

Was it one of Charlie's motorbikes? I glanced down at the Find My app again. The blue dot still hadn't moved.

I was nervous now, more aware than ever of just how isolated I was up here. I felt vulnerable. In the car I kept a torch for emergencies. I was an idiot. I should have waited until what . . . the morning? I couldn't possibly do that. What if Mum and Delia were in danger? But I didn't know what to expect ahead, especially if the figure on the motorbike had not been Sir Monty.

On a whim, I tried Mum's mobile again, but again – as I expected – it went straight to voicemail. I realised that since it hadn't actually given me a ring tone, the phone could be switched off.

I reversed back the way I'd come as far as the first five-bar gate. It opened into a stubble field and was a good place to hide my car. I left it there, took the torch and small pepper spray that I always kept in my glove box, and continued on foot.

Being under cover of darkness made me feel less exposed. Every few moments I stopped to listen for the sound of a returning motorbike, but heard nothing but silence.

When I reached the farm building my hopes soared.

Mum's Mini was parked behind Sir Monty's Rolls-Royce. She was here!

Cautiously, I approached the Rolls-Royce. I noticed that the two tyres on the driver's side were flat.

I retraced my steps and looked on the passenger side of the car. Those tyres were also flat. I thought of Mum's black attire and Delia's trampy outfit and it suddenly became clear what their plan must have been.

Delia had mentioned how disappointed she was with Sir Monty's choices of unromantic rendezvous. Was it possible that Delia had lured Sir Monty up here with the promise of a night of passion, but in fact, the plan had been for both women to get their revenge?

To be abandoned on Dartmoor with four flat tyres and a long walk home would be punishment enough, but if so, where was everyone? What if it had all gone horribly wrong and Sir Monty had turned the tables and then escaped on one of Charlie's old motorbikes?

I thought again. Wouldn't Sir Monty have taken Mum's car instead – unless she'd tossed the keys into the undergrowth? Mum and Delia were here somewhere and I had to find them.

I desperately wanted to call out but until I knew what lay ahead, I had to keep quiet. There was no moon and the sky felt oppressive, heavy again with rain.

I looked up to the CCTV camera but there was no red light. The door was padlocked. I skirted the building and came to the rear where my mouth went dry. I quickly drew back.

A white Transit van with a broken side mirror and a piece of fence sticking out of the bumper was backed up to the rear loading doors that stood wide open.

It was the same Transit van that had been used to pick up Violet's oak benches and it also fitted the description that Willow had given of the van that came to clear out Lavender's bedroom – without the Luxtons logo, which must have been a decal.

I brought the pepper spray out of my pocket and readied the button.

Heart in mouth, I slipped around the back of the Transit van and into the dark building, listening for the slightest noise.

All was quiet. Whoever had been here, had gone – and that included my mother and Delia.

Using my torch, I skimmed the walls until I found a switch and flipped it on.

A series of fluorescent lights flickered and lit up the empty building. Empty, that is, apart from four vintage motorbikes partially covered by an old green tarpaulin.

I strode to the back of the Transit van and found it was fully loaded with two workbenches, boxes of drills and equipment and Violet's oak benches, which I guessed had to be the copies. The switch would happen later on in the week.

Tucked towards the back I saw the neatly labelled boxes from Lavender's bedroom and, to my joy, spied the distinctive roof of Charlotte's doll's house. I couldn't help wondering what the Claytons had planned on doing with Lavender's things had Sir Monty's tyres not been let down. Take them to the fly-tip? Burn them? Now Charlotte's doll's house of Honeychurch Hall could join Edith's much larger version on display at my space in Dartmouth Antique Emporium. They would never be for sale. Nor would Starlight the old rocking horse.

And then it hit me.

Shawn and Mallory were raiding the wrong location! It was here that the Claytons did their forgeries. Pearl

Clayton must have raised the alarm when we'd seen her out riding.

They had been clearing out the building but their plan had been derailed when Sir Monty turned up unexpectedly to meet Delia and caught them in the act. My mother's idea to let down his tyres so he couldn't get away had almost stopped the gang from getting away, too. I thought of the motorbike and didn't think for one minute that it had been Sir Monty.

So where were they?

I checked the Find My app again.

The blue dot still hadn't moved but when I enlarged the image, I saw that the blue dot wasn't where I was standing at all. It was some distance away.

I may have been confident that the building had been abandoned but what about the exterior? Was someone lurking in the undergrowth waiting for me? Was I going to be one of those stupid women in movies that Mum called 'too dumb to live'?

I sent off a flurry of texts to Shawn and to Mallory. Next, I looked in the Transit van and hunted through the box of tools used for forgeries for anything I could use as a weapon. Most needed electricity but I spied a battery-operated paint spray gun that would have been used to spray lacquer on furniture. I took it and a couple of screwdrivers, not sure exactly what I planned on doing with them if I was attacked.

I kept hearing Shawn's warning that the gang were armed and dangerous. They were killers and had murdered Charlie and Violet Green.

But as fear for my mother's safety grew, so did my courage.

I stepped out from the light of the farm building and set off in the direction of Dartmoor with just the solitary blue dot to show me the way.

Chapter Thirty-One

As I made ever-widening circles shining my torch left and right, I gave up on trying to be quiet. I was convinced now more than ever that the Claytons had abandoned ship and Sir Monty had too. All I could think of was finding my mother and Delia.

Rain began to fall again but I hardly noticed.

I left the farm building behind and entered the uncertain and treacherous terrain of the moors with its deadly bogs and the infamous mist. It was said that very few prisoners who escaped from the notorious Dartmoor Prison ever reached safety.

And then, the light of my torch caught a strip of red fabric draped on a gorse bush.

It was a red thong decorated with black feathers. I remember catching a glimpse of Delia's underwear as she slid into the front seat of Mum's Mini. It had to be hers.

'Mum!' I shrieked. 'Mum! Delia! Where are you?'

But there was no answer to my increasingly frantic cries.

I followed the narrow track using my torch. The path fell away and high banks of gorse seemed to close in. I came to a bank of gnarled old trees and there, dangling from a low branch, was Delia's aubergine-coloured wig.

Delia had left a trail and if she left a trail, that meant they had either been on the run, or been forced to come this way.

It was dark. All I had was my torch. Everywhere was so quiet and still. I was in the middle of nowhere and even the lights that I had left on at Moreleigh Mount were no longer in sight.

I was terrified.

And then, one moment I was walking on the grass and the next, my foot sank up to my calf in cloying mud. It was a bog. I hurled myself sideways and landed hard on a flat sheet of slate.

And saw Mum's mobile.

They were here! They had to be!

I started screaming into the night over and over again, breaking for a few moments to listen, until . . . I heard a faint cry coming from very close by.

Frantic, I swung the torch around but couldn't see anything. I was mad with anxiety and fear. 'Where are you?' I yelled. 'Mum! Delia!'

'Help, help!' The cries became more hysterical.

'We're drowning!' Delia screamed. 'Help!'

And then I stumbled into a clearing and saw the skull and crossbones sign displayed on a barrier that covered the entrance to a disused mineshaft. Their voices were coming from underground.

I hurled the metal barrier aside and was about to race in but stopped. I had no idea where the mineshaft actually fell away.

'Mum!' I cried out. 'Thank God!'

'The cavalry has arrived, Delia,' I heard Mum say. 'We're going to be all right.'

But the cavalry hadn't arrived. It was only me.

'We're down here.' Mum sounded calm now that I was there. 'Delia! Delia! Listen to me. It's all right,' she said again. 'Kat is here.'

Delia was sobbing. 'The water . . . it's rising.'

I took a tentative step.

'Careful!' Mum shrieked.

I stopped. I had been literally standing on the edge of a pit. Dropping to my hands and knees I shone the light down below. Three faces looked up. Mum and Delia – minus her wig – were propping up a very pale Sir Monty between them. The water had already reached their knees. The long-awaited rains had come and were flooding the old mine.

'We thought you'd never come,' Mum went on.

'How did she know?' Sir Monty whispered.

'I used the Find My app,' I said.

'Let me tell you, we got sick of Monty winning I-spy,' Mum attempted to joke.

'Please, Kat, hurry.' Delia's teeth were chattering. 'I'm so cold. So very cold.'

'I'll find a rope or a ladder,' I said. 'I'll be right back.'

'Right back?' Mum exclaimed. 'But . . . where are you going? Didn't you bring the police?'

I couldn't answer her. 'I'll be right back,' I said again and scrambled out of the mine trying to control my horror.

Desperate, I brought out my phone. But then I heard a hum in the distance. My stomach roiled in fear. The motorbike was coming back. The hum grew louder. And louder. But it was coming from the sky.

Flashing lights came into view overhead and the hum became a low thwump thwump thwump.

It was a helicopter!

Quickly, I turned my torch up to the sky and flashed an S-O-S. The helicopter circled and came in low, then lifted up and flew away. It was trying to land.

I scrambled up a slope, tripping into gullies and over stones, oblivious to my grazed elbows and bruised knees.

The helicopter had to land. It *had* to! There was no time to lose.

I crested the brow and tumbled onto a mud-packed road just as the clouds parted and there was the upright beam of Gibbet Cross silhouetted against the distant tors.

The helicopter landed. The rotors stopped and Shawn and Mallory leapt out, followed by four officers carrying firearms – a rare sight in Devon.

The cavalry had finally arrived.

Shawn grabbed me with a mixture of love and fear on his face, but whatever he had been about to say, I cut short. 'They're drowning.'

The water had reached Mum's waist by the time they were rescued, pulled up one by one. Sir Monty had fainted from pain and Delia was close to collapse. Only my mother seemed cheerful until she said, 'Take good care of Delia. She's not wearing any knickers.' And burst into tears.

It wasn't until the next afternoon that Shawn and Mallory turned up at the Carriage House to check on my mother. I'd forced her to stay on the sofa under a duvet but she seemed eager to tell Shawn and Mallory what had happened and they were anxious to hear it.

The raid hadn't been a complete waste of time. They discovered that Stubbs Place was a holding area for the furniture to be transported to and from Luxtons. Shawn had woken up Sir Monty's housekeeper who lived at the back of the property but always went to bed early. Mrs E confirmed that Sir Monty had not required an evening meal because he had an engagement and had left home at six thirty. She had not known where he had gone.

It was my frantic texts that enabled Shawn and Mallory to track my location at Moreleigh Mount via mobile-phone triangulation and, ironically, Pearl Clayton's map that showed exactly where I had ended up.

'We seized the white Transit van which – by the way – was registered in Sir Monty's name,' said Shawn. 'His leg is shattered in several places but once he is able to answer our questions he'll be facing charges of fraud. We will be working with David Wynne on the black-market angle, but frankly, we don't hold out much hope for a Clayton conviction.'

'What about Eric?' I said.

'I admit I was doubtful as to his innocence,' said

Mallory, 'but now I am getting to know everyone in the village, I like to believe his story.'

'Which is?' Mum prompted.

'Eric Pugsley admitted that he had deliberately hidden Charlie Green's motorbike out of spite,' said Shawn. 'After seeing Charlie with Vera, he flew into a jealous rage. He wanted nothing more than for Charlie to have a long walk home.'

Which was exactly what my mother and Delia had planned for Sir Monty.

'What about the icehouse?' I asked.

'Eric told us that Charlie had begged Vera to hide something for him,' said Shawn. 'She refused because she knew it would upset Eric but Charlie had already decided to bury the cash box there.'

'And if it hadn't been for Iris letting down Sir Monty's tyres, we wouldn't have been able to collect evidence from the farm building and confirm that it had been used as the Claytons' workshop,' said Mallory. 'I'm curious, Iris. What made you do that?'

So Mum told them and didn't spare the details. 'Delia said Monty liked a bit of rough,' she said. 'It was her idea to lure him to Moreleigh Mount because *apparently*, that's where they often had trysts in a hut – which, as it turned out, was actually that farm building. She was the decoy whilst I let down his tyres.'

'But . . .' I had a thought. 'Surely Sir Monty knew that Delia couldn't drive? How did he think she would get there?'

'You're right. She can't drive.' Mum shook her head with disgust. 'I suppose he thought she'd ride her bicycle.'

'It's miles!' I exclaimed.

'Go on with the story, please,' said Shawn.

Mum thought for a moment. 'It was when we got to the building that I heard raised voices. A man was shouting at Monty, using a lot of bad language.'

'Who was this man?' Shawn demanded.

'He was wearing a polo shirt with the day of the week on it,' Mum said. 'It said Tuesday.'

'Gavin Clayton,' Shawn said to Mallory, unable to hide his bitterness. 'And he's gone in the wind, too.'

'It was quite horrible,' Mum went on. 'When Gavin realised he couldn't drive away because Monty's Rolls blocked his escape, he took one of the motorbikes. I was surprised that it actually started.'

'So it *was* Gavin that passed me on the road,' I said.

'I felt awful that we couldn't stop him, but you see, he had a gun,' said Mum. 'I immediately guessed what was going on. I asked him if he'd killed Charlie Green and Violet Green and he said that he had! He even admitted that he and Pearl Clayton – and to think that I would have voted for her – visited Violet that night and had pushed poor Violet down the stairs! Gavin was quite smug about it and made a joke that for once Pearl did the washing-up.' She frowned. 'Monty just stood there looking pathetic. I thought at least he would try to overpower him—'

'That's very difficult to do with a gun,' Mallory said grimly.

'I asked him about the Drake Six,' Mum went on. 'He was shocked that I knew what they were and admitted that Charlie had been trying to blackmail them by stealing the originals. Apparently someone in Hong Kong was very cross when the deal fell through. I told him that whoever had forged the paintings was rubbish because they'd missed out Drake's wart and painted the portrait on the wrong playing card.'

'Oh, Mum,' I whispered.

'I threw him a bone by saying that the forged stamps from Ireland were very good – that was just a wild guess, but he fell for it and admitted to forging those too. I should have known that he was the forger with his long fingers but I'm afraid it made him very angry.'

I felt tears sting my eyes. 'You could have been killed.'

'Anyway, it all ended when Gavin said we had two choices.' Mum swallowed and for a moment, I caught a glimpse of the terror she must have felt last night. 'He said we could either opt for a bullet or starve to death.'

'Mum,' I whispered again. The thought of how close I came to losing her hit me again. I brushed away a tear.

'I said that I needed to lose some weight so I'd rather starve.' Mum bit her lip and looked down at her hands.

'We understand he walked the three of you to the mineshaft,' Mallory said gently.

'"After you",' Mum said. 'Such a gentleman. That's when I threw my mobile into the bushes. Even if we were never found, I hoped that one day someone would find out what really happened.'

'But you *were* found,' I said.

'And then Gavin pushed us over the ledge,' Mum said simply. 'Monty first. Which wasn't so gallant but lucky for us. Delia and I both landed on him which does have a funny side.'

Shawn frowned. 'I don't see how.'

Mum gave a mischievous smile. 'According to Delia, it was one of his favourite positions.'

'Mum!' I groaned. '*Please.*'

'And that's how Monty broke his leg,' Mum finished.

'It was very innovative of Mrs Evans to leave a *paper* trail,' Mallory said trying to keep a straight face. I tried not to look at him as I thought of Delia's feathered thong and wig.

'She was very brave,' Mum declared. 'And I'll tell you one thing, men come and go but friendships are for ever.' She gave a happy sigh. 'Thank heavens it's all over and those awful people will go to prison.'

Shawn's face was a picture of misery. 'Unfortunately, we can't pin a thing on Pearl Clayton, and Gavin cleared his place out in Torquay.'

'But what about the CCTV footage at Moreleigh Mount?' I exclaimed.

'It was wiped clean,' said Shawn. 'Nothing.'

'And Leslie O'Sullivan?' I asked.

Shawn shook his head. 'It turns out that Leslie O'Sullivan was just doing a favour for Pearl Clayton and has no ties whatsoever to her business. The same goes for Ronnie Lubbock. He was just the hired help and did nothing illegal. And, as you know, the white Transit van was licensed to Sir Monty Stubbs-Thomas. I'm afraid we're back to square one.'

'I'm really sorry, Shawn,' I said.

'But . . . that's where you're wrong,' Mum said gleefully. 'Fetch my mobile, will you, darling.'

I grabbed it from the coffee table and handed it over.

We watched in silence as she slowly tapped and scrolled, sighing with exasperation here and there until finally, 'Ah. Here is the recording.'

Shawn gasped. 'You recorded it?'

'Of course I did.' Mum gave me a knowing look. 'I had the phone in my bumbag. I think you'll find you have everything you need on there, Shawn.'

'Iris Stanford,' Shawn gushed. 'I think I love you.' And in three strides he engulfed my mother and kissed her. Mum turned pink.

'Don't get too excited,' I said quickly. 'My mother doesn't know *how* to record.'

'If you're talking about recording that conversation I had with Monty about Delia,' said Mum smugly, 'I pretended I couldn't find it. Monty had been far more cruel about Delia when we spoke in person than he was on speakerphone.'

'You are amazing,' I said and gave her a hug too. 'So what happens next?'

'There's a lot to do,' said Shawn. 'I'll have to go back to London now but Greg has promised to keep an eye on you two.'

Mallory smiled.

'And the other two Drake miniatures?' I said. 'Do you think you will find them?'

Shawn shrugged. 'Let's hope so.'

I wanted to ask Shawn if it meant he was coming back to Little Dipperton but I could tell that his mind was already consumed with catching the Claytons now that he had the evidence to do so.

'You won't be staying on until Saturday for the beating of the bounds?' I tried to keep the disappointment out of my voice.

Shawn gave an apologetic smile. 'Not this time,' he said. 'But let's talk later. There is something I want to ask you.'

Chapter Thirty-Two

Although Gibbet Cross would not have been my first choice for a picnic location, now we had stopped for the much-anticipated lunch, I could see why. The view was spectacular. As Mum would say, it was very *Titanic*.

So many people had turned out to beat the bounds – even Ginny Riley had donned her trainers to enjoy the fame of local-girl-made-good after having had the exclusive scoop of the century. The success of Operation Oyster, the downfall of the Clayton crime gang and the fascinating story of the Drake Six miniatures graced every front page in the country.

'Would you like another cucumber sandwich?' said Willow breaking into my thoughts. She was carrying a large platter. Refreshments that had been promised by Pearl Clayton had naturally fallen by the wayside following her arrest, but the villagers had rallied and the resulting potluck had been terrific.

'No, thanks,' I said. 'I've already eaten three. How is Doreen holding up?'

I had noticed Willow's aunt talking to Clive and Malcolm – who held two slices of cake, one in each hand. Doreen wore a smile but I could see by the tension in her face that it must have been a huge effort.

'She misses Miss Green so much,' Willow said. 'It's funny really because I always thought they didn't like each other that much. Friendships can be such funny things.'

I thought of my mother's friendship with Delia and looked over to where the two of them were sitting on a tartan blanket laughing at some private joke. Mum poured a clear liquid from a thermos flask into a paper cup and handed it to Delia. I was quite certain it was gin.

There had been something bothering me these past few days. I'd wanted to talk to Shawn and Mallory about it, but they were too caught up in the aftermath of writing reports and tying up the loose ends.

'Willow,' I began. 'This is an odd question but I wanted to ask you about some postcards that I saw in Lavender's bedroom.'

'The ones on the mantelpiece?' she said.

'Yes!' I was surprised. 'The postcards kept arriving from Ireland but it seemed that Violet never wrote to tell Charlie that Lavender had died. Why would she put them in Lavender's bedroom?'

'Miss Green had bought a book with an awful title called' – she shuddered – '*Swedish Death Cleaning.*'

'Oh yes, I know it,' I said.

'Miss Green was tidying the drawers in her sideboard and gave me the postcards to throw away but I didn't like to,' said Willow. 'So I just took them upstairs and put them on the mantelpiece.'

Mystery solved. 'And there was something else,' I went on. 'Violet had mentioned that Leslie – the man who you helped to move the doll's house – had seemed familiar. Do you know anything about that?'

'Oh yes,' said Willow. 'His photograph was on the front page of the *Dipperton Deal* when he won on Oyster Girl. Actually, there is something that I want to ask you.' Willow glanced at Doreen who gave her an encouraging nod. She lowered her voice. 'Everyone always thought that Miss Green was Dear Amanda – even my aunt,' she said. 'But it can't be true because her column still ran in today's newspaper.'

I nodded. 'Ah yes. I noticed that, too.'

In fact, when Mum and I had read it as we always did on Saturday mornings, she was convinced that Shawn had written in. It wouldn't be the first time that he had sought Dear Amanda's counsel.

I remembered the letter off by heart:

> Dear Amanda, I have to go away for a few months and I asked a colleague to keep an eye on my girl-friend. Do you think it's a mistake?
>
> Signed: Worried.
>
> Amanda says: To coin Julia Roberts, yes, BIG mistake.

Willow licked her lips and moved in closer. 'My aunt

heard a rumour that Dear Amanda . . . it could be . . . might be . . . your mother.'

'Really?' I exclaimed with mock surprise. 'But how can that be? The Dear Amanda column has been going on for decades. Well before my mother arrived in the village.'

'That's what I told her.' Willow began to relax. 'Auntie was just worried that your mother knew about her secret credit cards in the freezer—' She clapped her hand over her mouth, mortified.

I grinned. 'I didn't hear that.'

Willow looked to her aunt again who mouthed something unintelligible. 'And what about Krystalle Storm? Do you know why she left so suddenly?'

'I suspect she met her deadline,' I said.

Willow nodded. 'That's what I thought, too— Oh look!'

We turned to see Harry – home from his Sea Scout trip – riding Thunder, Edith and Lavinia on Tinkerbell and Jupiter, and Mr Chips prancing alongside, barking happily. Rupert's Range Rover crested the hill with Eric riding shotgun with Peggy Cropper and Alfred sitting in the back seat.

I felt as if I had stepped back in time as the villagers en masse scrambled to their feet to line up out of respect for the Honeychurch dynasty that still – even in this day and age – was such a large part of their life.

I walked over to greet Edith and Tinkerbell.

'A lovely day for a picnic,' Edith said. 'I think everyone from the village is here. I'm glad to see that Iris and Delia survived their ordeal. I can't think of anything worse than being in a mineshaft with Monty. What on earth did they do to pass the time?'

'They played I-spy,' I said.

'Not hangman?' she said. 'That was always a favourite game of ours, for obvious reasons.' She pointed to the upright beam of the gibbet.

Hangman.

My jaw dropped.

I thought of the Frozen Charlotte with the noose around her neck. Had Charlie stolen the miniatures from the farm building and buried the first two here?

'What's the matter, dear?' Edith said. 'Catching flies?'

'I need to borrow Mr Chips.'

And there, surrounded by Edith's subjects, Mr Chips started to dig at the bottom of the upright beam. Harry leapt off Thunder and darted in to help the little dog, using his hands to move away the earth, as Ginny stood by with her camera.

Everyone had read about the missing miniatures and despite Sir Francis Drake's controversial reputation, he was after all a local man. No one spoke and all that could be heard was the sound of birds singing and the scrabbling of Mr Chips' front paws as he did what he did best.

The hole grew larger until Harry reached down and pulled up a small package wrapped in oilcloth. Solemnly, he handed it to me.

There were cries of excitement that turned to whoops of joy and laughter as the last two miniatures of the Drake Six were revealed – the *Swan* and the *Marigold*.

I was anxious to get home. I needed to confirm that the miniatures were indeed the originals. I couldn't wait to tell the Commodore the happy news. After all, they belonged to the academy.

'Kat?'

I turned to find Mallory towering over me, grinning from ear to ear. I was surprised. I couldn't see his car and he hadn't been walking with the group. He'd also given up his smart suit and was wearing jeans and a white polo shirt.

'Congratulations. What an exciting discovery!' He gestured to all the people who made up the Honeychurch estate and the village of Little Dipperton. 'You know, I didn't think I'd ever say it but this beats living in a big city.'

'I know,' I agreed. 'What are you doing here?'

'I cheated and came by car – I'm kidding. Full disclosure—' Mallory pointed down the hill to Moreleigh Mount. 'We're going over that building with a fine-tooth comb. I heard all the shouting and came to see what was going on.'

'It's been a happy day,' I said and showed him the two miniatures that Mr Chips had recovered at Gibbet Cross.

'Ah, of course. The noose on the Frozen Charlotte,' he said. 'Charlie Green knew how to plant a good clue.' He hesitated before adding, 'I'm finishing up in a few minutes and I can give you a lift back to Little Dipperton – that is unless you want to carry on walking.'

It was my turn to hesitate. Why did I feel conflicted about Mallory's offer? It was just a lift home, wasn't it?

Shawn had asked me to wait for him and I'd told him I would but I wouldn't wait for ever. I'd done that with David and wouldn't make the same mistake again.

'Chocolate brownie?' Mum pushed the plate under Mallory's nose. I saw Delia gloat as if to say, *I knew it.* 'Oh— Was I interrupting an important conversation?'

I felt my face redden. Mallory sprang back but then we both lunged for the chocolate brownies at the same time. I popped one into my mouth, confused as to why my mother's question made me feel guilty and remembering, all too late, Mallory's comment about eating so you 'don't have to answer any questions'.

Mallory popped the brownie into his mouth and, as his grey-green eyes met mine, we both grinned.

'Thank you,' I said more stiffly than I intended. 'But I promised myself I'd walk the entire boundary.'

Mallory nodded and took another chocolate brownie. 'One for the road.'

And he left.

'When the cat's away the mice will play,' Delia said with a tinge of malice.

'You're too cynical, Delia,' Mum scolded. 'Not this Kat.'

Mum and Delia walked away. Mallory had reached the edge of the mud-packed trail. He paused at the top of the path that led down the slope to Moreleigh Mount and turned around and saw me watching him. For a long moment, he just stood there.

And then he raised his hand and waved.

I smiled and waved back.

Acknowledgements

When my friend Stefanija Winkler joked that she'd like to appear in one of my books, I decided to take her up on it.

Our friendship began more than three decades ago when we met working as freelance flight attendants on an ancient Boeing 707 flying a head of state around the world. The plane's interior was decked out in gold and marble and had a deep shag-pile carpet that made it impossible to push a drinks trolley up and down the aisle – but we did our best. I don't think I have ever laughed so much. I knew I could never make her the villain or a victim, so the question was, how could I put her into a murder mystery? And then I had an idea.

Stefanija – who is part Czech, part British and lives in Amsterdam with her husband – is a gifted artist. And so, the Elizabethan court painter Svetlana Winkler was created, a woman ahead of her time and one who enjoyed adventure – just like my good friend. Although I must point out that Stefanija has never painted any portraits of Sir Francis Drake!

The Drake Six are pure invention, but the use of playing cards as backing in sixteenth-century miniature portraits is true. A big thank you to Prof. Dr Karin Leonhard for her fascinating article 'Game of Thrones: Early Modern Playing Cards and Portrait Miniature Painting'. Another little-known fact is the recent discovery that Drake did indeed have a wart on the end of his nose which rarely appears in any of his thousands of portraits. Who knew?

The ghoulish Frozen Charlotte dolls, which were inspired by the 1840 poem 'A Corpse Going to a Ball' by Seba Smith, can still be found quite easily on eBay. Diana Swayne gave me a Frozen Charlotte shortly before she passed away at the astonishing age of 104. Diana was a keen collector of antique dolls and bears, several of which have appeared in other Honeychurch Hall mysteries.

My heartfelt thanks go to:
Debra Mumford for showing me her charming shepherd's hut deep in the Devonshire countryside, which I'm desperate to rent myself when I am facing my next deadline. That is, if I'm not taking advantage of a writing house in the Yorkshire Dales! Thanks to Ali and Ant Bagshawe for making this gem available to me – and for the constant supply of snacks.

Detective Inspector Steve Davies for sharing his knowledge of the NCA among other things over countless cyberspace lunches. Any inaccuracies in police procedure within these pages are entirely my own.

My long-suffering boss Mark Davis, Chairman and CEO of Davis Elen Advertising in Los Angeles, who has been championing my writing endeavours from the very beginning.

My wonderful agents Dominick Abel and David Grossman. Thank you for taking such good care of me on both sides of the Atlantic.

My incredible publishing team at Constable with a special thank you to Krystyna Green, my dream editor, along with copyeditor Nicky Gyopari, whose sharp eye and attention to detail makes me look good.

I am so grateful to my talented writer friends – Rhys Bowen, Elizabeth Duncan, Mark Durel, Carolyn Hart, Clare Langley-Hawthorne, Jenn McKinlay, Andra St. Ivanyi, Alan Rose, Julian Unthank, Marty Wingate and Daryl Wood Gerber – for their love and support. I'm forever indebted to Claire Carmichael, my writing instructor at the UCLA Extension Writers' Program, who gave me the confidence to send my stories into the world.

And of course, I speak for all my kindred spirits when I thank YOU, the reader. Without you, none of our stories would be given life.

And finally, to all my family who have always encouraged me to follow my dreams, with special thanks to my much-missed dad for passing on his sense of humour, my daughter Sarah who keeps me organised, and to the canine gods for sending me my muses, the Hungarian Vizslas, Draco and Athena.